'Complex and compelling in all the right
JANE HARPER

'An utterly gripping portrayal of guilt and blame in the modern age.
I couldn't put it down.'
MARK BRANDI

'Written with heart and aplomb, *Three Boys Gone* is a consuming,
taut mystery that explores the cascading effects of tragedy. Mark
Smith has perfectly captured the maddening and claustrophobic
atmosphere of media obsession, and the endless speculation that
comes when the unthinkable happens. An absolute cracker of a
novel from a strong new voice in crime fiction.'
J.P. POMARE

'The thrilling twists kept me guessing right to the last page.'
MICHAEL BRISSENDEN

'Very authentic and also very Aussie without being cliched in any
way.'
SARAH BAILEY

'Could not put it down.'
KATE MILDENHALL

'Utterly gripping, harrowing and unputdownable.'
DINUKA McKENZIE

'Smith taps into a primal fear in all of us and doesn't let go – *Three
Boys Gone* drags you under like a rip and keeps you there, twisting
through impossible choices until the very last page.'
R.W.R. McDONALD

'*Three Boys Gone* is a masterful novel of tension, menace and grief.
It's a rollercoaster.'
ROBERT GOTT

Mark Smith has written four young adult novels including the highly acclaimed Winter Trilogy. The first book in the series, *The Road to Winter*, was a finalist for multiple awards and has become a popular teaching text in schools throughout Australia. The sequel, *Wilder Country*, won the 2018 Australian Indie Book Award for Young Adults.

Beyond his novels, Mark is an award-winning writer of short fiction, with his work featured in prominent publications both in Australia and overseas. He has also co-curated two short story anthologies: *Minds Went Walking: Paul Kelly's Songs Reimagined* and *Into Your Arms: Nick Cave's Songs Reimagined*.

Also by Mark Smith

The Road to Winter
Wilder Country
Land of Fences
If Not Us

THREE
BOYS
GONE

MARK SMITH

MACMILLAN
Pan Macmillan Australia

Pan Macmillan acknowledges the Traditional Custodians of Country throughout Australia and their connections to lands, waters and communities. We pay our respect to Elders past and present and extend that respect to all Aboriginal and Torres Strait Islander peoples today. We honour more than sixty thousand years of storytelling, art and culture.

First published 2025 in Macmillan by Pan Macmillan Australia Pty Ltd
1 Market Street, Sydney, New South Wales, Australia, 2000

Reprinted 2024

Copyright © Mark Smith 2025

A catalogue record for this book is available from the National Library of Australia

Typeset in 12.5/18 pt Bembo MT Pro by Post Pre-press Group, Brisbane
Printed by IVE

Cover images: Sean Gladwell / Getty; Brian Flaherty / Shutterstock; encierro / Shutterstock; Olezzo / Shutterstock; EllenM / iStock

For all the outdoor educators who take their students into wild places and bring them back forever changed.

To those devoid of imagination, a blank place on the map
is a useless waste; to others, the most valuable part.
— Aldo Leopold

THREE
BOYS
GONE

BUREAU OF METEOROLOGY
TOP PRIORITY FOR IMMEDIATE BROADCAST
ISSUED MONDAY 6.00PM AEST

Severe Weather Warning

A strong cold front and associated low pressure system are forecast to cross western and central waters during Tuesday, with the low expected to be located over the eastern Bass Strait by evening.

A cold and unstable south-westerly airstream will follow in the wake of the front. Strong to gale force winds are expected to impact coastal areas in the western forecast district. This is a fast-moving system and conditions are predicted to moderate by Wednesday morning.

Damaging surf conditions are expected within the forecast period, with waves in excess of five metres along exposed beaches to the west of Cape Nelson.

Further Warnings

The Victoria State Emergency Service and Life Saving Victoria advise that people should be aware of potential impacts, including strong ocean currents, dangerous waves, instability to cliff areas and potential flooding in low-lying coastal areas.

Damaging surf conditions are dangerous to swimmers, surfers and rock fishers. Boats in harbours, estuaries and shallow coastal areas should return to shore.

1

Grace locked the bus and checked the trailer. She lifted her backpack and shrugged it into position, sitting it comfortably on her hips. There was rain on the way, so she kept her waterproof jacket handy, looping it through the harness on one side. Then she followed the track through the dunes towards the viewing platform above the beach. Cresting a small rise, the full sweep of Juliet Bay came into view, a wide mustard-yellow ribbon unfurling all the way to Moonlight Head.

At the platform, Grace took stock of the conditions. The wind had picked up and swung earlier than forecast. She would have it at her back as she made her way towards the rendezvous point with her outdoor ed students, who were on their second day of the Great Western Walk. She'd wait for them where the track reached the beach before guiding them back to the bus and their overnight camp.

Grace pressed herself against the rail of the platform and pulled her phone from her pocket. She took a photo and uploaded it to Instagram while she still had a signal.

#bestjobintheworld #dreamjob #Juliet #loveyoumum

Juliet was a special place. Not long after her mum, Sophie, was diagnosed with cancer, the two of them had come here to camp for a weekend. Grace had returned every year on the anniversary of her mum's passing, barring the last two, when she'd been working in Perth.

Juliet was remote, wild and windswept. Today, hectored by the strengthening westerly and fed by a huge Southern Ocean swell, the bay was a maelstrom of whitecaps. Waves rose in massive grey walls and broke in a confusion of whitewater as they hit hidden reefs and sandbars. Grace's attention was drawn to the gash of the Juliet River sweeping across the beach and emptying into the sea. She'd scheduled the walk so her students would reach Juliet on the dropping tide. By the time they got to the river mouth later in the afternoon, it would be an easy crossing. Now, though, the tide was only a third of the way out. She'd have to be careful crossing, but she had time on her side. It would take the boys and the accompanying staff – Gerard Kruger and Tom Winter – at least another two hours to get to the beach from their overnight camp at Crayfish Bay, while she was only an hour and a half away from their rendezvous.

She descended the rough pine-log steps to the open beach and headed for the river mouth, a couple of hundred metres away.

When she reached the high bank, she moved a little way upstream. The water was dark with tannin washed down from the forest, but it was less affected by the waves pushing into the mouth. She took off her socks and boots, unbuttoned her shorts and dropped them to the sand. Tying the laces together, she hung her boots around her neck, picked up her shorts and socks and slid down the bank into the knee-deep water. She was halfway across when a wave surged towards her, the water rising above her waist. Bracing against the current, she waited for the wave to pass and pressed on, making the opposite bank before the next one hit.

The wind was stronger now, and the rain hit her legs like cold darts. She'd managed to keep her shorts clear of the water, but her underwear was soaked. She slipped them off and pulled a dry pair from the side pocket of her pack. Bare arse to the wind, she smiled at the thought of the sight she'd present, dancing around on the sand and struggling to dress herself.

She added the extra layer of her waterproof jacket, put her boots back on and resumed the walk towards Moonlight Head. Despite the wind, despite the rain now lashing her, she was at home here. She felt her mum's presence. Her ponytail whipped around her shoulders, and she rubbed her cheeks with her hands, feeling the salt crusted in her eyebrows and the sand in her hairline.

The beach thinned, widened and thinned again, shaped by the constant battle between land and sea. Grace strode out, seeking the hard-packed sand where her boots didn't sink too deeply. It was tough going, but she loved the beautiful, unthinking rhythm of walking with a pack on her back. To her left, the dunes rose abruptly, their tops crowned with pigface and the snaking tendrils of grasses seeking moisture in the air. In the folded hills beyond the dunes, scrabbly gums leaned away from the barrage of the wind.

To Grace's right, the ocean growled and heaved.

Eventually, the trailhead came into view. It was marked by a large post — a lump of driftwood topped with an orange fishing buoy that walkers had pushed into the sand. She checked her watch. The river crossing had slowed her progress, but she'd still be well ahead of the boys.

When she looked again, she thought she saw movement in the little creek mouth adjacent to the track. The rain was heavier now, sheeting across the beach, but she could see the outline of backpacks sitting on the sand. Though they hadn't seen any other walkers on the track on Monday, it was a popular route, and this was most likely another group, ahead of hers.

As she drew nearer, three figures broke from the creek mouth and sprinted across the beach towards the water.

Jesus, Grace thought, *who's in charge of them?*

She stopped and leaned forwards, as though the lack of movement might allow her to see more clearly. The wind dropped momentarily, and her heart leapt into her mouth.

They were teenage boys. Her boys. Three of them, racing each other into the sea.

2

They had arrived at Crayfish Bay on Monday afternoon. It was a small, secluded campsite, sheltered from the prevailing south-westerlies by the rocky buttress of Moonlight Head. The beach was fronted by a flat, grassy terrace that accommodated a dozen tents. There was a drop toilet with a tank that caught rain off its roof and a wide stretch of sand leading to the water. An offshore reef protected the beach, allowing only ripples to make their way into the lagoon. The water was cold, but Grace allowed the boys to wade in up to their waists.

The sun had shone brightly all day, tempered by a zephyr off the ocean. Crayfish Bay was ten kilometres into the Great Western Walk, an easy first day along a track that hugged the coast and offered views of the ocean to the south and tree-lined ridges to the north. The boys had been slow to start after the torpor of the long bus ride, but they found their energy once they got moving. Grace had walked most of the way with them before doubling back to pick up the bus and drive it to the nearest car park, three kilometres from the campsite.

This was Grace's second term at St Finbar's. After two years in Perth, she'd been desperate to find a job back in Victoria, both to be closer to her dad and to leave the mess of her previous school behind. It had taken her a while to find her feet, but by the end of first term she had settled into her role teaching Outdoor and Environmental Education. She had been welcomed by the other St Finbar's teachers, becoming a regular at Friday night drinks at the Tiler's Arms and a reliable goal attack on the staff netball team. And she'd met Lou. After everything that had happened in Perth, her life was finally back on track.

Of the two staff on the trip, Grace knew Gerard Kruger best. He was a phys ed teacher in his mid-forties who she liked for reasons she couldn't quite explain. Maybe it was his boyishness or his slightly awkward manner when he spoke to her, never quite knowing where to let his eyes settle. He was popular with the students and a regular in the gym, where he ran before-school classes. Throughout the first day of the walk, he'd been his cheerful self, checking how each of the boys was faring, helping them adjust their packs and encouraging them to keep a steady pace.

Grace hardly knew the other teacher, Tom Winter, but she was grateful he had volunteered when the senior outdoor ed teacher,

Eve Slater, had pulled out at the last minute. Eve was meant to be running the trip, but that responsibility had now fallen to Grace. It would be her first excursion as teacher-in-charge. Tom was on the IT team, and he taught data processing, whatever that was. He was something of a celebrity at school because he'd represented Victoria in pistol shooting. He was softly spoken and always accommodating when Grace had a problem with her computer or needed upgrades installed. He was an experienced bushwalker, turning up with all his own gear, and he worked well with the boys on the walk through to Crayfish Bay.

Resting against her pack while the students set up their tents, Grace observed the dynamics of the group. In her mind she split the class into the leaders, the quasi-leaders and the followers. The followers, a dozen assorted Liams, Justins, Joneseys and Aarons, were the easiest to manage, trudging along wherever the others led them. To Grace, they morphed into a homogenous group of harmless, acne-faced, hair-gelled boys who rarely ventured an opinion or made a decision for themselves.

The quasi-leaders were the footballers who thought leadership was as simple as being at the front, looking confident and telling jokes to keep the other boys amused. Jake Bolton and Tim Simpson fell into this category; both were brash, loud and certain of themselves.

At the information night in February, Grace had met Jake's father, Rick, a bull of a man with a grin that bordered on a leer. A car salesman in designer polo shirt and slacks, he'd stood with his arm around his son's shoulder and told Grace that Jake was more of friend than a son to him.

'He'll be happy to help out the other boys on your trips, I can guarantee it,' he'd said, his eyes sliding over her breasts. 'Probably even teach you a couple of things.'

Tim Simpson played in the same football team as Jake on weekends, and their conversations were consumed with deconstructing games and speculating about the rest of the season. As far as Grace could see, Tim lived in Jake's shadow, laughing at his jokes and looking to him for clues on how to navigate adolescence.

Then there were the Lombardi twins – Roberto loud and funny, friends with Jake and Tim – and Daniel quiet and withdrawn, more of a follower. Grace liked them both. There were a lot of southern European boys at the school and most had a strong sense of family. If they swore once too often, Grace would joke that she'd ring their nonna and get them to repeat the words to her.

There was only one real leader in the group – Harry Edwards, an unassuming, intelligent kid who spoke with adults as easily as he did with his peers. All day, Harry had ambled in the middle of the pack, quietly noting the track junctions and creeks along the route as he ticked off the markers on his map. He spoke to the quasi-leaders only when he needed to, doing so subtly by playing to their egos and appearing to be onside.

Harry's closest mate was Noah, a softly spoken scholarship student in his first year at St Finbar's. Grace saw a kindred spirit in Noah, both of them finding their way in a new school. Noah seemed determined to make a good impression on the walk, treading the fine line between showing enthusiasm and not being labelled a suck by the rest of the boys.

Looking at the group now, their streetwise bravado stripped away by exhaustion after a long day, Grace knew she'd do anything for them. Adolescent behaviours and questionable parents aside, they were good kids who bonded on trips like this, creating memories they would hold onto for years. Her job, a job she loved, was to help form those memories.

After they had cooked a meal of pasta on their Trangias, Grace gathered the group together on the coarse grass just above the beach to debrief Monday's walk and give instructions for the following day. The sun was westering, and the clouds hovering above the horizon were orange and red at the edges. The boys formed a rough circle, swatting at mosquitoes. Tom and Gerard sat among them. Grace knew the students hated this part – her attempting to get them to talk about their day. It was what her lecturers at uni had called *soft skills* – the coaxing of responses that put trips like this into some sort of educational perspective. But, for all their talents and potential as young men, reflection didn't come easily to sixteen-year-old boys. In their minds, there was no point looking back at what had passed because it was gone. They lived entirely in the present. Unless Grace carefully framed the questions, they would either say nothing at all or tell her just what she wanted to hear so they could get the debrief over as quickly as possible.

'So,' Grace began, 'how did we go today? What were the challenges?'

She knew not to throw the questions out to die in the silence, so she told them she'd work her way around the circle, with everyone contributing.

'Jake, let's start with you.'

The others stifled laughs and Tim Simpson nudged Jake with his elbow. 'Yeah, Jakey,' he said. 'How was your day?'

'Well, Miss,' Jake began, pausing to ensure he had the attention of the whole group. 'The bus trip was a real highlight for me.'

Laughter rippled around the circle.

Grace was ready. She had learned how to cut through Jake's smart-arse comments without acknowledging them. 'And once you got off the bus and we were on the trail, what then, Jake?'

'Yeah, I thought it was good, Miss.'

'What was good, specifically?'

'Ah, y'know, the scenery and that. The ocean and the bush.'

'Thank you, Jake. As erudite as ever.' The words had left her lips before she realised. Tom and Gerard smiled knowingly, but Jake was up for the challenge.

'Is that like Araldite, Miss? We use that in woodwork, don't we guys?' he said, his eyes darting left and right. 'It's creamy and sticky. You know all about that, don't you Simmo?' The boys erupted. Jake was on a roll. 'It's hard to get off your hands afterwards,' he added, leaning back and grabbing Tim's arm.

Grace could see her mistake in starting with Jake. 'Okay, okay,' she said. 'Let's move on.'

Tim shoved Jake. 'You're the wanker,' he said, keen to keep the joke going.

'Alright, you two. That's enough,' Gerard said.

Grace hated the way the boys responded differently to a male voice, the timbre striking them in a way hers couldn't.

She turned to Harry. The light was falling away, but she was sure she could detect a quiet understanding in his gaze.

'Who's next? Harry?'

This is where status mattered, in the space between confrontation and getting the session back on an even keel. The boys demurred to Harry in a way they were barely aware of.

'I reckon we did okay today, Miss,' Harry began. 'We stuck together pretty well, took breaks when we needed to and still made good time. And I really liked the variation in terrain, especially coming out onto the beach at Parker River.'

'What was special about that for you, Harry?' Grace felt the balance tilting back in her favour. She wished she could bottle the quiet gravitas Harry brought to the group.

'Just the way we came down out of the bush on that winding track, and then the beach opened out in front of us,' he said.

'It is a beautiful place, isn't it?'

'Yeah. I'd like to come back sometime, maybe on a weekend with some mates.'

Grace saw the opening Harry had provided. She addressed the whole group. 'What Harry said – that's what these trips are all about, giving you the skills to access environments like this on your own.'

Jake slumped back on his elbows and whispered something to Tim, who stifled a laugh. Grace chose to ignore it.

The rest of the session passed in a series of reflex responses and mumbles from the boys. It was left to Noah to help Grace bring the debrief to a close with an astute observation about how the faster boys needed to be careful of getting too far ahead of the main group tomorrow. The slower boys weren't getting enough time to rest during the breaks.

Grace wanted to reinforce this, as she wouldn't be with them for most of the following day. She had kept an eye on the forecast and, while it wasn't dire enough to consider pulling out, Tuesday would be cold and wet. 'Staying together and taking breaks where everyone gets a rest will be essential. There's rain coming, but we are well equipped to deal with it. Just make sure you have your jackets near the tops of your packs. I'll be driving the bus around to the Juliet campground, then walking back to meet you where the track comes out onto the beach.' She leaned forward then and slowed her words for emphasis. 'I want to make this crystal clear: no one – I repeat, *no one* – is to go near the water. It's protected here at Crayfish, but the beach is much more exposed once we get around Moonlight Head.'

The boys' attention had waned, fatigue pulling them towards sleep. Grace reminded them about litter and using the drop toilet properly, but by then she doubted any were listening. When she dismissed them, most wandered towards their tents without a word. Only Harry, Noah and Daniel lingered.

'Anything you need done, Miss?' Harry asked.

She smiled. 'No. Thanks for asking though.'

There was an awkward silence that fell into the gap between teacher and students.

'Did you enjoy the day, Noah?' Grace asked.

'Loved it,' he said, a little too eagerly. 'I go camping with my brother all the time. You know, fishing and that.'

'What about you, Daniel? You didn't say much in the debrief.'

Daniel shrugged. 'Yeah, it was good, Miss.'

She didn't press him. She was happy he was willing to be seen talking to the staff rather than skiving off with the others.

'Okay, good night, then,' Harry said, getting to his feet.

'Night, Miss. Night, Sirs,' Noah and Daniel said in unison.

The boys melted into the gloom, heading for their tents.

'Cuppa?' Gerard asked.

'Love one,' Grace replied.

'Me too,' Tom said.

Gerard struck a match and shielded it with his cupped hands. It briefly illuminated his smiling face. 'They're not a bad bunch,' he said, igniting the metho in the burner.

'Yeah, I know,' Grace said, finding a comfortable position against her pack.

'And they like you,' Gerard said.

Grace wobbled her head. 'I wish they'd speak up more,' she said. 'That debrief was like pulling teeth.'

'No use beating yourself up over it,' Gerard said. 'Sometimes I think ninety per cent of what I say in my classes goes straight through to the keeper.'

'You should try teaching them data processing,' Tom said. 'They reckon they know it all before the term even gets started.'

'They're sixteen,' Gerard said. 'There's only so much we can do. The rest is up to them.'

'God help us!' Grace replied, laughing. She enjoyed this camaraderie, the shared understanding of the frustrations and joys of teaching teenagers.

They sat with the silence for a minute, ears cocked for any boys fooling around. A thin rim of crimson light lined the horizon, while above them the first stars showed themselves. It would be a cold, clear night, ensuring the boys stayed in their tents, snug in their sleeping bags.

'What time are you off in the morning, Grace?' Tom asked.

'No rush. I'll get you lot on the track then head back out to the bus. I've got to go up to Lavers Hill to refuel, but I'll be at Juliet well ahead of you. Just remember to keep them in sight tomorrow. If I get delayed for some reason, I don't want any of them arriving at the beach without a staff member there to supervise.'

'No worries,' Gerard replied, pouring the tea.

3

Three boys were gone. Swallowed by the sea. The horror of those words folded over and over in Grace's mind on the long, slow march back towards the bus. As the afternoon descended into evening, the boys walked in small clusters, staying close, shocked into silence. They were weighed down by their own packs, but three pairs carried additional packs between them. When someone tired, another boy moved up to take his place, touching his shoulder and nodding before lifting the harness and continuing along the beach: like soldiers returning from battle, honouring their fallen comrades.

Grace was at the back with the slowest boys, while Gerard moved up and down the ragged line ahead of her, checking, reassuring, shepherding, occasionally holding the arms of those who stopped and wanted to go back to keep searching.

The rain had passed, but the wind was icy. Grace hugged her arms to her chest as she walked. If she wrapped them tightly enough, she might be able to stop the shuddering that racked her body. Somehow, she had held herself together back where it happened. Maybe it was the proximity to other bodies when the remaining boys arrived, maybe the need to appear in control when she felt entirely lost.

She'd scrambled to make sense of how quickly the day had turned from a routine hike into this nightmare. Through it all, she felt she was moving inside a body that wasn't hers, trying to get her arms and legs to respond to the most basic commands. There was nothing to focus on other than what needed to be done in the next couple of minutes.

In the immediate aftermath, the boys had been in varying states of shock, lost behind glazed eyes. Noah shook violently and wrung his hands, while Daniel had to be restrained from trying to run into the water. He hurled himself time and again at Gerard's huge frame, battering his chest with closed fists and sobbing. Some of the others formed a huddle high up the beach, as though the sea might somehow rise up and claim them, too. Eventually, they turned their backs on it and crawled in under the cover of the tea trees.

Five boys had stood in a line on top of the dune, straining to see beyond the breakers. One would suddenly lift an arm and point, only to drop it again after a few seconds.

Grace moved between the groups of boys, pushing her

own grief to one side to check in on them, murmuring words she hardly believed herself. She hugged them, rubbed their arms, asked if they were warm enough, tried to reassure them they would be away from there soon. Some of them welcomed her touch, while others, rigid and cold, barely acknowledged her presence.

Tom did little to help. He wandered in circles, his hands raking his hair, stopping occasionally to look at her with wide eyes. 'No, no, no . . .' he repeated, over and over. She had to drag him down towards the water and hold him by the shirt to get him to listen to her.

'Tom. Tom!' she shouted above the roar of the ocean. 'Get a grip. You have to help us here.'

He grabbed her by the arms. 'Get a grip?' he repeated, his voice breaking. She could feel the bruising strength in his hands as she tried to shake free of him. He pulled her in close, as though he had more to say, but then pushed her away and walked off.

Grace had sucked in half a dozen deep breaths to regain her composure. She thumped her fists into her thighs to get her legs moving and walked towards Gerard, who was kneeling in the sand with Daniel pressed to his chest. Gerard climbed slowly to his feet, lifted the boy and carried him in his arms. Even in the tumult that engulfed her mind, Grace saw how tender the movement was, how small Daniel looked in Gerard's arms.

Ignoring Tom, who was standing on his own again, Grace had gathered the boys together behind a large rock that blocked their view of the sea. She saw the way they leaned into each other, seeking the comfort of human contact. She organised them into a circle and looked into each boy's eyes. Most returned blank stares. Any semblance of the order they had taken for granted in their short lives had been shattered. The wind buffeted them, finding its way to cold skin under wet clothes. Grace knew the signs of hypothermia – the shivering and vagueness – and how similar the symptoms were to shock. Without any idea of what she was going to say, she began to speak.

'I want you to buddy up in pairs and work together. Help each other get your packs sorted, put on the warmest clothes you've got and be ready to move in twenty minutes.'

She knew she had to get them away from the site of the accident. Somewhere in her memory, this rang true. Was it the remote area first aid course she'd done at college? Or the trauma response training she did when she was freelancing? Regardless, action was needed, and explanations could come later. And there was another thing she had remembered: give people a job, something to do that distracts them from the enormity of what had happened.

While the boys readied themselves, Grace walked back up the track to find a private spot to change. She pulled clothes from her pack with shaking hands and wobbled on unsteady legs as she stepped into a dry pair of leggings. She buckled over and retched, wrapping her arms around her stomach. Finally, she put her boots back on and stood up.

Returning to the beach, she'd asked Gerard to follow her out onto the sand. They walked to where Tom was standing and she drew them in tight, close enough for their voices to be heard above the wind. Not for the first time, Grace felt small in the presence of the two men. She was uncertain of her seniority, but she was the only outdoor ed teacher on an outdoor ed trip, and someone had to make the decisions.

'Here's what we're going to do,' Grace began, before either of them could say anything. 'We need to get the boys back to the car park, to the bus. Keep them together. Reassure them. They're in shock, so we can't rush.'

Gerard nodded, but Tom looked past her towards the water.

'We can get reception on the lookout platform near the car park,' she continued. 'We'll call the police and the school from there.'

'I don't know how the boys will go with the walk,' Gerard said. 'They're exhausted. I doubt we'll be able to keep them together, so whoever gets to the car park first should make the calls.'

'Just the police,' Grace said. 'I'll talk to Jim Sheridan. He'll know what to do from the school's end, who needs to be told.'

'Who'd be a fucking principal, eh?' Gerard said.

Grace hadn't had time to check in on Gerard, to judge how he was coping. His comment seemed out of place, but she let it go.

'We'll wait at the car park for the police or the SES or whoever they send.' Just saying those words felt like a hammer hitting Grace in the chest. They'd have to deal with the authorities. Answer their questions. Account for every minute.

When they returned to the boys, they were standing in a circle with their arms around each other's shoulders. Noah was speaking, but Grace couldn't pick up the words. There was something rhythmic to them, though. Other boys joined in, and the mumble of words swelled into the Lord's Prayer. Tears streamed down their faces. They made room for the teachers in the circle.

On the walk back to the car park, Juliet seemed an entirely different beach to the one Grace had arrived at just hours before. All the precious memories attached to this place had been swept away in the bitter wind, replaced by guilt and hurt and grief. She tried again to remember what had happened after she had seen the boys run into the water, but somehow, everything had faded into a fog of uncertainty. She had yelled at them, she knew that much, and run towards them. But the wind was so strong, the rain falling in sheets, the ocean so loud. She tried to push through the fog, to find herself back in that moment, those critical few minutes – but the harder she tried, the more the memory evaporated.

When she attempted to separate herself from what had happened – to view the events of the afternoon more clearly – the waves of guilt returned. Those three boys, so young, so full of themselves and their golden futures. She could hardly bear to think of their families, blithely going about their evenings, picking up kids from netball training or music lessons, sitting down to dinner, watching TV, doing homework, unaware of the gaping hole that had been torn in their lives. She wondered if any of the parents had felt something, a fleeting jag at the heart, in an otherwise normal afternoon – a thought dismissed as they went about their day.

Gerard was right; it was impossible to keep the group together on the walk. He had gone ahead with the faster boys. Tom had gathered himself and taken over Gerard's role moving up and down the line, encouraging and supporting, while Grace brought up the rear with the slowest walkers. By the time she got to the river crossing with her group, there was no sign of the rest of the class. She guessed they'd be at the car park by now, and Gerard would have called the police. The tide was low, but the river was still ankle-deep. Before she could stop them, the boys she was with walked though without taking off their boots. They were either too traumatised to notice or beyond caring about wet feet and socks. The car park and the warmth of the bus were only minutes away.

Grace slid her pack off, sat down and began to remove her boots. The action triggered a short, sharp memory of sitting on the sand, frantically pulling at her laces, looking out at the roiling sea, and seeing one of the boys, his arm in the air, hair plastered across his face, disappearing and reappearing as he was swamped again and again. The laces were so wet and tight and her fingers so cold. When she had looked up again, he was gone.

As she climbed the track through the dunes to the car park, Grace realised she still had the keys. The boys were huddled around the bus, backs against the side panels or slumped to the ground. Some had trailed off to the toilet block that sat on a high bank above the car park. No one spoke. Gerard was still on his feet, talking to the boys – hand on their shoulders, squatting in front of others to see their faces. Tom was doing the same, but the boys didn't respond to him in the same way they did to Gerard.

Once Grace had unlocked the bus and the boys were inside, she started the engine to get the heaters going. Then she nodded to Tom and Gerard to meet outside.

'You made the call?' Grace asked Gerard when they had gathered in front of the bus.

'Yeah. It wasn't a great signal. Took ages to get them to understand where we are. The cops will come from Wheelers Bay. They'll bring the SES.'

Grace was distracted by the bobbing of a headtorch as a student made his way up the path to the toilet block. 'Okay,' she said, gathering herself. 'We can't leave until the police get here. You're both doing great with the boys,' she said, hoping Tom would believe her. 'Can you stay with them? Encourage them to eat if they've got anything handy in their packs. If they're still cold, get them into their sleeping bags. I'm worried about hypothermia.'

Tom nodded.

'What about you?' Gerard asked Grace.

She exhaled heavily, caught a shiver before it escaped. 'I have to call Jim,' she said. 'I'll go a bit further up the track above the platform.'

'I could call him,' Gerard said. 'I know him pretty well.'

Grace thought for a few seconds. 'No,' she said. 'It's my trip. I'll do it.'

'We should get our stories straight before we make any more calls,' Tom said abruptly.

Grace was shocked into momentary silence. 'What do you mean?' she asked after a few seconds.

'I mean, what are we going to tell them? The cops. Jim.' Tom had his arms folded across his chest. He stood to his full height, looming over Grace.

She hesitated. 'We'll tell them the truth. Exactly what happened,' she said.

'Which was?' Tom said.

Grace wasn't sure where this was going. 'That the boys ran ahead of the group. They got to the beach early, and for some reason they ran into the sea.'

'So, it was our fault, then?' Tom said.

'No. No, Tom. It wasn't your fault.' Grace looked to Gerard for support, but she could barely make out his features in the gloom.

'What about you?' Tom asked Grace. 'Where were you? Why weren't you there to stop them?'

'Fuck, Tom! We don't have time for this. The boys are in there freezing, potentially hypothermic. We need to get them somewhere warm and safe.'

'You didn't answer my question.' Tom persisted.

'Ease up, mate,' Gerard said, finally. 'Grace is right. We need to look after the boys.'

Tom shook his head and blew air from his cheeks. He turned his back on them and walked off.

'Where did that come from?' Grace asked.

'He's struggling,' Gerard said.

'We're all struggling!' Grace replied. 'But he's looking for someone to blame. Thinking about his own arse.'

'It's just the shock of what's happened.' He paused. 'And he's right. We need to be careful about what we say.'

Grace's brain was rushing ahead to the call she had yet to make to Jim. 'I know. But right now, we've got other priorities.' She took her phone out of her pocket and gripped it tightly.

'Go on, then,' Gerard said, his voice warmer, softer. 'Make the call. We've wasted enough time.'

She took a step closer to him and touched his arm. 'Thanks,' she said.

'Stay strong, kid,' he said, placing his hand over hers.

4

Jim Sheridan sank into the leather seats of the BMW and pinched the top of his nose where his glasses had sat all day. He hoped the pulsing in his temples wasn't the beginning of a migraine. Rifling through the console, he found the heavy-duty Panadol and swallowed two.

He was in his third year as principal of St Finbar's, but finance committee meetings were still a mystery to him. They were like being locked in a room for two hours with people who spoke a different language. He nodded a lot, asked for simple explanations of charts and spreadsheets that seemed to predict dire financial outcomes. He signed off on documents he didn't fully understand and hoped to hell the auditors didn't ask questions.

At least today he could get home at a reasonable hour. The kids would still be up. They would throw him a 'Hi, Dad. How was your day?' then return to their screens without waiting for an answer. After they'd gone to bed, he'd share a glass of red with Marion in the beautiful stillness that descended on the house at the end of a long day.

He pushed his phone into its cradle on the dash and started the engine. Cutting across the empty car park to the gate, he slowed to a stop to activate the boom. He was barely out onto the road when the phone vibrated with an incoming call.

Unknown Number

It was his work phone. He knew he should answer. But he declined the call, turned the radio on and hoped for a song he recognised. He swung out onto Ridge Road and found his place in the steady stream of evening commuters using it as a rabbit run to avoid tolls on the freeway. The rain started up again, spatters on the windscreen that quickly turned to a downpour.

The traffic slowed, and he came to a standstill in the middle of a little shopping strip – just a newsagent, a café, a chemist, a fish and chip shop and a Bakers Delight. Up ahead, he could see the flashing lights of the rail crossing. He rolled his shoulders and settled back into his seat, knowing he'd be there a while.

The phone rang again. Jim sighed and pressed the button on the steering wheel.

'Jim Sheridan.' He tried to sound cheery, the ever-diligent principal ready to help.

'Hello, Jim. It's Grace. Grace Disher.'

He didn't know Grace very well. An outdoor ed teacher, a late appointment just before Christmas, when Pete Snowdon quit unexpectedly. Jim hadn't been part of the interview, but his deputies, Fiona Knowles and Luke Thomas, had assured him she presented well over Zoom.

The line was full of static, a poor connection.

'Where are you calling from?' Jim asked. 'It's a shocking line, Grace.'

'Sorry,' she said, her voice distant. 'It's howling a gale down here.'

Down here? Jim thought. *Where's down here?*

'I've got some bad news,' Grace continued, her voice rising above the wind.

Jim's mind raced to remember if anyone had mentioned anything about Grace recently – a sick family member, maybe. There were a hundred and thirty staff at the school. It was hard to keep track of all their personal details.

'Where are you calling from?' Jim asked again.

'Juliet Beach. I'm on the outdoor ed trip with Gerard and Tom.'

Jim's heart jumped. There were always excursions heading off somewhere, but he didn't know about this one.

'Can you hear me, Jim?' Grace was yelling now.

'Yeah, yeah, I can hear you. What's happened?' The rain beat harder on the roof of the car, and Jim leaned closer to the phone to hear.

'We've –' Grace's voice hitched up an octave. 'We've lost three boys. They're gone.'

'Tell me what's happened, Grace. This was a bushwalking trip, was it? Have you done a search?'

'Sorry. Sorry, they're not lost. They've drowned.'

The words scythed through Jim. It took him a few seconds to find his voice again. 'Three students have drowned. Is that what you're telling me? How? What –?'

He flicked the indicator on and pulled to the side of the road. The chemist was just closing for the night, and a woman in a white dress and green cardigan slid the door closed. Jim unbuckled his seat belt, grabbed a pen and his diary from the passenger seat and squeezed his temples between a thumb and index finger.

The windscreen wipers continued their steady beat.

'Are you there, Jim?' Grace sounded as though she was crying now.

'Yeah, I'm here. Take a few deep breaths, Grace, and tell me what's happened.' Jim was conscious of trying to sound calm, but his heart was racing. *Where's Juliet Beach? Who do I have to contact? What are the protocols?* And then: *three boys! Fuck!*

The wind howled down the line.

'They ran ahead of the group,' Grace began, panting between sentences. 'Got to the beach before any staff were there. For some unknown reason, they ran into the surf. By the time any of us got there, they were gone.'

Jim jotted down the details as Grace spoke. 'So, who's there? Did you say Gerard and Tom?'

'Yes, Gerard Kruger and Tom Winter. We're with my year ten class.'

Jim wondered why Grace, a junior member of staff, was making the call. 'Are Gerard or Tom there now? Can I speak to one of them?'

'They're looking after the boys.'

'So, you've got three staff – and you're all okay?' Jim continued.

There was a long pause.

'How many boys are with you now?' he asked.

'We've got fifteen. They're in pretty bad shape. It's wet and cold down here.'

'And whereabouts are you exactly?'

Jim knew Grace was taking a moment to realise her principal didn't know the details of the trip.

'We're at Juliet Beach, down past Cape Nelson.'

Juliet. Something jogged in Jim's memory. He'd surfed down that way when he was young. 'And you're still at the site of the . . .' He paused. 'Accident?'

'No. We've all walked back to the car park.'

'You've moved the boys? That's good.' Jim felt an internal switch flick, pushing the shock of the news to one side so he could focus on the ramifications of what Grace had told him. 'Have you called the police? Emergency services?'

'Yes. They're coming from Wheelers Bay.'

His mind was galloping now, trying to prioritise. 'Right. Stay with the boys. Keep them warm. Have they eaten?'

'Just muesli bars and stuff. None of them want to eat much.'

'Fair enough. Keep this line open and only answer if it's me.

No one is to talk to the parents, you understand. And not the media either.'

'Got it.'

'Have any of the boys got phones?'

'No. I took them off them before we left school.'

'Thank Christ for that.'

Jim drummed his pen on the open page of his diary. *What else do I need to know right now?* 'Grace?'

'Yes.'

'I just want to confirm the details.' He drew breath, steadied himself. 'Three boys have drowned.'

'Yes.'

'And where are the bodies?'

'There are no bodies, Jim. They're gone.'

Jim froze, the pen paused above the page. 'What?'

'They're gone. They're still in the water. Somewhere.'

'Did no one –?'

'We couldn't get to them. They were swept away. The waves were huge. They didn't have a chance.'

Jim's mind threw back to his experiences surfing down that way. It was a wild stretch of coastline – rips and currents that tested the strongest surfer. Still, he couldn't understand how three boys could completely disappear.

'Did you . . .?'

'We waited there as long as we could, Jim. It got dark. There was nothing more we could do.'

Jim still didn't understand, but there'd be time to rake over the details later. For now, there was one more thing he needed to know, one more detail that would change the lives of three families. 'Okay Grace, you need to give me the boys' names. The ones we've lost.'

Static took over the line again, and Jim tried to picture Grace standing at some high point above the beach, the wind howling and moaning around her, her mind dark with loss and failure.

'Jake Bolton.'

Bells rang somewhere for Jim. A footballer, if he remembered rightly. Bit of a lad. A few weekend detentions. Otherwise, harmless.

'Roberto Lombardi.'

Shit! One of the twins. He could never tell them apart. Their father, Bruno, was on the school council.

'And Harry Edwards.'

Jim felt a great weight land in the middle of his chest, a stone that pressed on his lungs and stopped his breath. He slumped forwards and pressed his forehead against the steering wheel.

'Jesus Christ,' he said.

'Jim?'

'Yeah, I'm here. I'm here.' Fat tears dropped onto the open page of his diary, blurring the scribbled notes.

'He's your nephew, isn't he?' Grace's voice sounded even more distant.

Jim swiped the tears from his face, hoping against hope to gather himself.

'I've got to go,' Grace said.

5

Grace ended the call and pushed her palms hard against her eyes. It was the first time she had cried since the accident, the tears coming not in the midst of the experience but in the retelling. She wondered how many times she would have to relive it in the weeks, months and years to come – and how long it would be before she could do it without crying.

When she stood, she couldn't help looking back along the beach, thinking the three boys might magically reappear, running towards the platform, laughing and pushing each other, knowing they were in trouble but willing to cop the consequences for the stories they'd have for their mates.

Her thoughts were interrupted by a throbbing noise. On the walk back along the beach, she'd had the feeling of moths beating their wings against her ear drums, a steady thrum filtering every other sound. But this was external, increasing in volume until it took on the sound of something familiar.

A helicopter.

It was coming towards her from Moonlight Head, a search-light arcing along the water's edge and strafing the sand. On top of the dune, Grace raised both arms above her head and stood still, uncertain. She had been expecting the police or SES to come by road. When the chopper finally spotted her, it hovered low enough for sand to lift in gritty clouds, blinding her with its spotlight. She shielded herself from the glare and turned away to protect her face from the sandstorm. She waited for a sign, some acknowledgement that they were there to help. Realising they hadn't seen the bus, she started to walk downhill towards the car park. Maybe it was the noise, the thumping of the blades and the scream of the motor, or the fact that the chopper was just hovering there, observing her. Maybe she thought they might leave before knowing where to go. Whatever the reason, she broke into a run.

The beam followed her as she raced downhill. She stumbled on a grass tussock and fell, finding her feet quickly and continuing towards the platform. By the time she got there, she couldn't breathe. Her body was shaking. Sweat trickled down her face, and she wiped it away with trembling hands. Her heart raced. She buckled over and tried to get air into her lungs.

Suddenly, the spotlight was extinguished, and Grace was catapulted back into the dark. She grabbed the rail to pull herself upright and peer skywards, the roaring beast taking

shape as her eyes adjusted. There were lights along the side
and on top. She looked for the distinctive blue POLICE sign.
It was only when the chopper tilted, heading out to sea, that
Grace saw the red Channel Seven logo on its side.

She was still tracking the fading lights when Gerard and Tom
arrived at the platform.

'Where have they gone?' Gerard asked. 'Why didn't they
land in the campground?'

Grace shook her head. 'It wasn't the police,' she said. 'It was
Channel Seven.'

'What the fuck?' Tom said. 'How did . . .?'

'No idea,' Grace said. 'But they could have helped us.'
She was breathing more evenly now, though her heart still
pounded in her chest. 'We need to get back to the boys. You
shouldn't have left them.' It sounded harsher than she intended,
a rebuke, but neither of them responded. They turned with
her and walked towards the bus.

Inside, the windows were fogged, and the air was heavy.
The motor was still running, the heaters working overtime.
The boys hadn't washed in two days, and the bus smelled of
teenage sweat and Lynx. Grace moved slowly down the aisle,
checking in on each boy, murmuring reassurances. Gerard
followed her, talking gently to individuals, telling them they'd
be home soon. He took extra time to speak with Daniel.

Meanwhile, Tom sat in the driver's seat and plugged his
phone into the charger.

Grace found Noah sitting on his own at the back. His knees were drawn to his chest, and he rested his chin on them. She squatted in front of him, her hand on his foot.

'Hey, Noah,' she said. 'How are you doing?'

He stared vacantly at Grace, as though he didn't recognise her. He shook his head.

'We'll be on our way soon, I promise,' she said, unsure whether it was true or not. It had been an hour and a half since Gerard had called the police, and they were all still here in this shitty, crowded bus, waiting. How was it that a media chopper could reach them, but the help they really needed hadn't arrived?

'It doesn't make sense,' Noah said, in a low, lost voice. 'Why would they do it? Why would they be so stupid? They've messed up everything.'

Grace didn't know how to respond, but she knew Noah was right: they had messed up everything. She was about to try to explain the unexplainable when headlights pierced the trees and two vehicles drove into the car park. They slowed at the entrance, before the first car pulled ahead and stopped next to the bus. Grace wiped fog from the window and immediately saw the POLICE signage. She exhaled deeply and made her way down the aisle to the front. It was about to begin.

Grace pulled the door open and stepped down onto the gravel. Gerard was behind her, and Tom had come around from the driver's side. A police officer stood in the beam of a four-wheel drive's headlights, casting an enormous shadow on the screen of tea trees that lined the car park. The second vehicle, an SES ute with the familiar orange-and-white decal, had turned into a bay behind the police car. Grace waited for more vehicles to arrive, but none followed.

'Gerard?' the copper asked.

'That's me,' Gerard replied. 'And this is Grace and Tom.'

'I'm Senior Sergeant Peter Heaney, Wheelers Bay police. You're the group from St Finbar's? I understand there's been an accident.'

As he spoke, four people appeared behind him, three men and a woman, all dressed in orange SES coveralls. The fluorescent strips on their uniforms reflected brightly in the headlights.

'This afternoon,' Grace said, stepping forwards. 'Three boys. We think they've drowned.'

'They *have* drowned,' Tom said abruptly. 'We waited. We searched. They're gone.'

'Let's just . . .' Heaney began, slowly lifting his hand, palm out. 'How many students do you have on the bus? Are there any injuries? Do they need assistance?'

'No injuries,' Grace said. 'We've kept them warm, and they've eaten a little bit, but they're in shock.' The words spilled out of her. She was grateful to be on familiar territory, her attention directed to the living rather than the lost.

'And what about you three?' Heaney asked.

The SES crew had moved closer, forming a protective half circle around them.

'We're okay,' Gerard said, 'but we need to get the boys away from here.'

'Your group is all boys?' Heaney asked. 'No girls?'

'We're a boys' school,' Grace said, wondering why it mattered. She had taken off her jacket on the bus and now the cold hit her. She shivered.

'Let's get you warm.' A woman placed a silver space blanket over Grace's shoulders. 'Sarah Valence, SES,' she said.

Grace shrugged the blanket away. 'Please,' she said. 'You need to check on the boys.'

Sarah nodded and directed two of her crew to step into the bus. Tom followed them.

'We formulated a quick plan on the way here,' Heaney said. Silhouetted in the headlights, Grace couldn't tell who he was talking to, but she stepped closer to indicate she was the teacher in charge.

'Our priority is the boys on the bus. It's too far to drive back to Melbourne tonight, and by the sound of it they'll need to be checked by a doctor. We've called the hospital in Wheelers Bay, and we think you should go straight there. I've also got one of my officers chasing up accommodation in town, probably the Happy Wanderer. It's a motel on the main street.'

'What about a search party?' Grace asked.

Heaney crossed his arms. 'As you can see,' he said, nodding towards the cars, 'we're short on personnel. There are police units on their way from Colac . . .'

'And we've called on all SES crews in the region,' Sarah said. 'We'll be able to coordinate a search once we have more boots on the ground.'

'But . . .' Grace began.

'What time did the accident happen?' Heaney asked.

39

She was stopped in her tracks by the question. In the shock of everything that had occurred, she hadn't noted down times. Tom was right, they should have agreed on some of the facts before the police arrived.

'Mid, late afternoon,' she said, knowing how vague that sounded.

'We were all split up,' Gerard said, moving forwards to stand next to her. 'It's hard to say exactly what time it was.'

Heaney looked at his watch. 'It's now half past eight.' He didn't elaborate, but Grace read his meaning easily enough. The boys would have been in the water for hours.

'Sarge.' One of the male SES volunteers was leaning out of the bus door. Grace and Gerard moved aside to allow Heaney through. He stepped inside.

Sarah held up two space blankets and this time Grace accepted one, as did Gerard.

'There was a helicopter,' Grace said. 'Channel Seven.'

'What?' Sarah couldn't hide her surprise.

'Fifteen minutes ago, maybe.' Grace looked to Gerard for confirmation, and he nodded.

'Shit!'

When Heaney returned, he pulled the SES volunteers and teachers into a tight circle in front of the bus. The wind was still up, and everyone hunched inside their clothes, hands in pockets. 'Here's the plan,' he began. 'You'll take the boys back to Wheelers Bay. Bill will go with you.'

One of the SES crew raised his head and nodded. 'Bill Shackleton,' he said, extending his hand to Gerard like they were meeting at a backyard barbeque. Then he shook hands with Grace and Tom.

'The rest of us will wait here for the other crews to arrive,' Heaney continued. 'We'll mount a full-scale search at daybreak.'

'Daybreak?' Grace said, shocked at how matter-of-fact Heaney was about the likelihood of finding the boys.

'Grace,' he said, softening his voice. 'After this amount of time, we're most likely looking at a recovery operation.'

'But . . .'

'We know the conditions pretty well here, love,' Sarah said. 'We've been here before.'

Grace only heard the word *love*. Sarah was standing next to her, the only other woman in the group.

'Tomorrow morning,' Heaney continued, turning to Grace, Tom and Gerard, 'we'd like one of you to come back here and help us piece together what happened and where.'

'That should be me,' Grace said as strongly as she could. 'I'm the teacher in charge. It's my class.'

'Gerard? Tom?' Heaney seemed to be looking for support from the two men.

'I dunno, Grace,' Gerard said. 'Maybe it'd be better if . . .'

'No,' she said, firmly. 'You've been great with the boys. They need you.' She knew she was dismissing the idea of Tom coming back without them even considering it.

'Regardless,' Heaney said, 'you can sort that out in the morning.'

'I'm staying here,' Grace said. She left the statement hanging in the freezing air for a few seconds before continuing. 'At least until the other crews arrive. I can go back later.'

'I don't think that's . . .' Sarah began.

'That would be very helpful, if you are up to it,' Heaney interrupted. 'It would be good to get some of the details around what happened. Maybe just an hour, then we could get you back to Wheelers Bay.'

Grace didn't wait for a consensus. She walked to the trailer and pulled her pack out. When she lifted it, both the shoulder straps gave way. She didn't bother investigating why; she needed to appear strong and in control. She picked up the pack by the loop on top and carried it back to the group.

'Sarah said you'd seen a chopper,' Heaney said to Grace.

'Media,' she replied. 'Channel Seven. They blasted me with their spotlight then just flew off.'

Heaney was shaking his head. 'None of you, obviously . . . called them?' He drew the sentence out, knowing how absurd it sounded.

'The only people we've spoken to are triple O and Jim Sheridan, our principal,' Gerard said.

'You might just have been unlucky,' Sarah said. 'The premier was in Wheelers Bay this afternoon, opening the new community centre. There was media everywhere.'

'But how did they know about the accident here?' Grace asked.

No one had an answer.

6

After the bus had left, Sarah shepherded Grace towards a small picnic area next to the car park. The SES crew had a fire going, and extra bench seating had been fashioned roughly from a couple of crates and lengths of timber. Grace leaned into the warmth of the fire. She had put her waterproof jacket back on, and now she pulled the space blanket tight around her shoulders. Heaney was propped on a crate opposite her, looking uncomfortable in his uniform and police-issue boots. Sarah directed her volunteers to begin unloading their search equipment, then sat down next to Grace on the bench. The fire blazed against the night.

'Are you up to answering a few questions?' Heaney asked Grace. His voice was soft, encouraging.

Grace's confidence had leached away now that she was alone with the rescuers. She didn't care about Tom, but she would have loved to have Gerard sitting next to her. Someone to support her, to help her fight through the fog and remember exactly what had happened.

'Is this an interview?' Grace asked. Smoke blew into her eyes, and she turned away.

'Nothing official,' Heaney replied. 'We just find it's good to get some details while the order of events is still clear in your mind.'

Clear, Grace thought. Things were anything but clear.

'So, here's what we know,' Heaney began. 'You've lost three boys. Is that right?'

'*We*,' Grace corrected him. 'We've lost three boys, yes. They ran into the sea.'

'And what time was this, Grace?' He had perched a notebook on his knee and was jotting details as he went.

'I —' She paused, suddenly conscious of how quiet it was. The wind had dropped away and all she could hear was the crackling of the fire. 'I'm guessing, but around four, maybe a bit later.'

'Okay, but you're not sure about that?'

'Sarge?' Sarah said. 'Can I have a word for a minute?'

They moved away a few metres, but Grace could still pick up most of the conversation.

'What's the point of this, Pete?' Sarah whispered.

'I need to —'

'You realise she's probably still in shock?' Sarah pointed back towards Grace.

'I know. I know. But first impressions are important,' the cop said. 'We need to get the facts.'

'She can't even remember what time it happened. We need to get her warm and fed.'

Grace stood up and walked the few paces to them. 'I'm fine. Really. I want to help.' She made a determined effort to sound strong.

Heaney and Sarah looked at each other.

'I'm warming up,' Grace continued before they had time to argue. 'And I've got some food in my pack.'

Sarah stood in front of her and held her by the hands. 'Are you sure?'

'Yes.'

'That would be a great help to us, Grace,' Heaney said. 'What'd you think?' he asked, turning to Sarah.

As best Grace could tell, Sarah was in her mid-forties, maybe younger. Her hair was pulled back into a severe pony-tail to accommodate her SES cap, and her face showed the weathered lines of someone used to being outdoors. She was medium height and stocky, though that could just have been the effect of the coveralls. Regardless, Grace felt she was on her side.

'Okay,' Sarah said. 'But first we need to get some food into you, Grace. When did you last eat?'

Grace couldn't remember, but she wasn't going to tell them that. 'Lunchtime. About one thirty.'

Sarah looked at her watch. 'That's nearly eight hours ago,' she said.

They moved back to their seats at the fire. Sarah pulled a thermos from her pack and handed Grace a cup of warm tea. 'Get that into you, love,' she said.

Grace gulped it down, but the tea was milky sweet, and it seemed to line her throat without finding its way to her stomach. She lurched away from the fire and vomited. 'Sorry, I don't usually drink tea,' she lied.

In twenty minutes, Sarah had heated soup on a small portable stove. It was too hot to drink quickly, so Grace took tiny sips, allowing her stomach to get used to the salty taste. She'd found a crushed packet of crackers in the side pocket of her pack, and she sprinkled them into the soup. She was still aware of the tension between Heaney and Sarah: one wanting to get on with his job, the other more concerned with Grace's welfare. In a strange way, she didn't mind this friction. It shifted the focus from her and created an ally in Sarah. The break to prepare the soup also allowed her space to put the events of the day into some sort of order. She tried to recall the time she'd left the car park. Feeling for her phone in her jacket pocket, and keeping it hidden under the space blanket, she tapped the 'Photos' icon and brought up the picture she'd taken from the lookout. *Today 2.19pm.* She guessed she'd walked for about an hour and a half to get to where she saw the boys at the track head. Then she remembered the river crossing and added another fifteen minutes. She'd told Heaney it was mid to late afternoon. She estimated now that it must have been about four o'clock.

When she finished the soup, Heaney fitted a headtorch and

turned the beam to the notebook resting on his lap. Sarah moved closer to Grace.

'If it's okay with you,' Heaney began, 'we'd like to get some basic details now.'

Grace drew a heavy breath. 'Sure,' she said.

Heaney glanced at his notebook, found what he was looking for and said, 'Gerard told us you weren't walking with the boys. Is that right?'

She took her time to answer. Her heart was thumping in her chest, but she wanted to appear calm. 'Yes. I helped pack the camp at Crayfish Bay this morning and saw them off. We were going to stay here at Juliet tonight, and someone had to bring the bus around.'

'Can I just clarify something?' he asked. It wasn't lost on Grace that he hesitated slightly before continuing. 'You said earlier that you were in charge of the trip? The lead teacher?'

'Yes,' she said. 'It's my outdoor ed class.'

'So —?'

'So why didn't I walk with them? Is that what you're asking?'

'It seems a bit strange, that's all.'

Grace tried to see it from his perspective, as someone who'd probably never operated in a school, who wouldn't understand how the hierarchy was often turned on its head to make things happen.

'It's a linear track from Crayfish Bay to here,' she said, trying not to sound defensive. 'You can't get lost. I knew Gerard and Tom could handle it.'

Heaney took his time to reframe the question.

'By the look of Gerard and Tom, they'd both be more senior than you, wouldn't they?' he said.

'I'm the outdoor ed teacher,' Grace said again. 'I was best qualified to run the trip.'

Heaney's every movement was betrayed by his headtorch. He glanced at Sarah then quickly returned the beam to his notebook. 'So, neither Tom nor Gerard are outdoor ed teachers?' he asked.

'No.' She knew how odd that sounded.

'Have you thought more about the timings, Grace? The question I asked you before.'

'Yeah, I have. I got to the car park at about quarter past two.'

'You're sure about that?'

'Yes.'

'Why did it take so long to get there? Crayfish Bay's only, what, thirty k's by road.'

'The boys were slow to get going. That's not unusual on the second day of a trip. I had to walk back out to where the bus was parked, and I took a detour up to Lavers Hill to get petrol.'

Heaney did the calculation in his head and nodded. 'So, once you got to the car park at Juliet, you walked straight out onto the beach?'

'Pretty much, yeah.' She didn't tell him about stopping on the platform to take the photo.

'Was there anyone else there? Did anyone see you?'

Grace noted the slight change in his tone. He was struggling not to interrogate her.

'I don't think so, no,' she said.

'So, then you walked up the beach. What did that take you – an hour and a half?

'A bit longer.' She told him about the river crossing. 'Like I said before, I got there by about four o'clock.'

'And to the best of your knowledge, the boys were already gone by then. In the water?'

Grace wondered how much Gerard had told Heaney. They must have talked before the bus left, while she gathered wood for the fire.

'No,' she replied, conscious of the effect that one word had on both Heaney and Sarah. The sergeant stopped writing and jerked his head up, blinding her with the torchlight again. Beside her, Sarah leaned closer to the fire and turned to look at Grace.

'No?' Heaney asked. 'I understood from Gerard that . . .'

Grace took a deep breath and closed her eyes, trying to conjure the image of the boys, stripped to their underwear, their skin white against the darkened background, their arms swinging wildly beside their young frames. 'I was about fifty metres away, maybe a bit more, when I saw them running into the water.'

She could feel their eyes on her. Something crackled and spat in the fire. The breeze swirled and lifted smoke into her face again.

'I didn't think they were our boys at first. They shouldn't have been there yet.' She paused and hugged the blanket tighter around her shoulders. 'I recognised Jake first – he's so tall, with that long hair.'

She rocked backwards and forwards. As much as she tried to hold them back, tears welled in her eyes. Sarah looped her arm through Grace's.

'And what happened then?' Heaney's voice was little more than a whisper. His words seemed to break up as they crossed the fire to Grace.

'I ran towards them, waving my arms in the air, screaming. But the rain was so heavy, the waves so loud.' She felt herself tilting towards Sarah, towards comfort.

Heaney waited. He put his pen down and stared at the page. 'What did you do, Grace?'

Grace's body convulsed. Sarah had her arms around her now, pressing, trying to contain her. Tears streamed down Grace's cheeks, and she buried her face in her hands. 'I couldn't do anything,' she managed to say. 'I couldn't save them.'

'But you went in after them?'

'No. I didn't.'

7

The fire spat and popped, the wood giving up its life-time store of carbon. Grace felt its heat and energy. She composed herself, pulling the hair back off her face and looking directly at Sergeant Heaney. He sat with the pen poised above his open notebook.

'I ran as fast as I could to where they'd gone into the water,' she said. The need to defend herself sent her searching in the fog that had obscured her memory of the accident.

'You ran?' Heaney asked. 'With your pack on?'

She couldn't recall taking her pack off.

'I think so, yes. The boys couldn't have picked a worse place to go in. There was a gutter, a runout, murky with sand and debris. I could see one of them about thirty metres out, maybe more. He was trying to tread water, but the swell was so big waves were breaking into the rip. I never saw the other two once they went in the water. They were gone.'

Telling the story didn't give her the relief she thought it might. She was hoping it would spread the burden somehow, allow others to carry it with her, but Heaney and Sarah stayed quiet.

Grace could feel it coming: the question she'd been waiting for since the moment the bobbing head was swamped by a huge wave, erasing it from the surface of the sea.

'So,' Heaney said, 'can you explain exactly what you did when you reached the spot they'd gone in?'

Grace closed her eyes and tried to put herself back in the place she'd never wanted to be. What happened next had drifted in and out of focus all evening. She would remember some parts vividly, but then she'd question them until they became vague again.

'I think —' she began, then stopped. Her thoughts were confused, and she felt like hitting her forehead to somehow rearrange them. Everything was blurred, and the moths were back, humming inside her head again. 'I remember running to the water, but —' *What was the sequence?* 'No, wait,' she said, acutely aware of how she sounded. 'I had to get my boots off. The laces were wet and tight, and my fingers didn't seem to be able to grip. I was looking out to sea, trying to keep track of the boys.'

'At this stage, then, you could still see all three of them?' Heaney said. 'So, it's before two of them disappeared?'

'Yes. No. I'm not sure.' Grace raked back through the coals of those brief couple of minutes. 'I just remember struggling to get my boots off.'

'Intending to do what? When you got them off?'

She knew where this was leading. She shook her head. 'It just seemed like the logical thing to do.'

'Okay.' Heaney's voice was taking on the tone of an interrogation again, but Grace was so deep in the moment, she hardly cared. 'What did you do when you got your boots off?'

Grace intertwined her fingers and squeezed them together until they hurt. 'I think I took my jacket off.'

'Anything else?'

'What do you mean?'

'Did you take anything else off?'

'Yes. My shorts.'

'So, you stripped off to your underwear?'

'No, I left my shirt on.'

'Where's this going, Pete?' Sarah had been quiet. Her voice seemed to break a spell, bringing Grace back from the midst of the event.

'Just trying to get the details straight,' Heaney snapped. He turned back to Grace. 'What happened then? After you took your boots and your clothes off.'

Grace's focus had been thrown to the wind. She had to work her way back into that place, on the sand, with the sea raging, the boys out there somewhere. *What did I do?*

'I ran to the water,' she said, wanting to believe she had.

'*Into* the water?' Heaney asked.

She slid her hand under her jacket to touch her shirt, thinking it could still be wet, proof of her action, of having tried. But she'd changed her clothes since then.

'Did you go into the water at all, Grace?' Heaney persisted. 'Did you wade out? Did you try to get to them?'

She lifted her head, and everything around her seemed to have a new clarity: the outline of the cars, the tree line against the clearing sky.

'No,' she said loudly. 'I didn't. First rule of rescue: don't create another casualty. I'm not a strong swimmer. I would have drowned, too.'

The strength of her statement struck Heaney dumb. He slid the headtorch off and stared at her across the fire, his eyes wide, the low flame reflecting in them. He mumbled something so low Grace couldn't hear.

'What did you say?' she asked.

'Nothing.'

Sarah's silence only provoked Grace further. She stared at Heaney, daring him to drop his gaze. 'Yes, you did. You said something. What was it, Sergeant?'

He sighed deeply. 'Are you a parent?'

Grace jumped to her feet. 'Fuck you,' she said. 'You weren't there.' She stormed off towards the wide expanse of the empty campground.

She walked in circles until exhaustion overtook her rage. Finally, she dropped to her knees and rolled onto her back. The clouds had cleared completely, and the Milky Way splayed gloriously across the sky, south to north. The quiet of the surrounding bush descended on her. The wind had eased, and it murmured through the she-oaks at the edge of the paddock. Looking up, she remembered a story her dad had told her when her mum died. He'd said that when you passed away, you became a new star in the sky, and that her mum would always be there, looking down at her. Which of those stars was Harry, she wondered now? Which one was Jake? Which one Roberto?

Torchlight flicked across her line of sight. She hoped it wasn't Heaney. He'd already judged her for not having gone in after the boys. She heard it in his voice, saw it in his look, his movements.

'Hey,' Sarah said as she approached, breathing heavily. 'Bloody smokes,' she said. 'Should have given 'em up years ago.'

Grace sat up.

'He's just doing his job,' Sarah said, nodding her head back towards the fire.

'He was judging me,' Grace replied.

'I've known Pete for ten years. He's a good cop. Don't be too hard on him.'

'He wasn't there. He doesn't know what it was like.' Grace was ashamed of how small her voice sounded. How defensive.

'Come on,' Sarah said, extending her hand to Grace. 'Let's get you back to the motel.'

Sarah's hand felt strong against hers, but there was something soft about it, too. Maybe it was just the touch of another human being.

'I want to stay here tonight,' Grace said. 'One of us will have to come back tomorrow to show you where it happened anyway, won't we? And I'm so tired. I've got my tent and all my gear.'

'I don't think that's a good idea,' Sarah said. They walked slowly up the incline towards the car park. 'A good night's sleep is what you need.'

'Well, I'm not going to get that at some dodgy motel, am I? I'll be better off here. You're all staying, aren't you? And who's going to drive me back? You'll be down a vehicle *and* one volunteer.'

'We'll certainly need one of you back here in the morning . . .'

'So . . .'

Sarah sighed, looked at her watch. 'I'll talk to Pete.'

Grace found a protected spot on the edge of the campground to set up her tent. Heaney hadn't taken much convincing. She got the feeling he would have liked to question her all night. Sarah and her SES crew had walked to the beach to begin a shoreline search, and Heaney had gone out to the platform to make some calls. For the time being, Grace was alone.

When she had collected her pack from the picnic area, she had forgotten that the straps had given way earlier. It was an old pack, one she had taken on dozens of trips, but both straps breaking at the same time was hard to believe. Pulling it closer to the fire, she'd rolled it towards the light. The straps hadn't given way through wear and tear; the heavy-duty webbing had been cut clean through.

Grace had gasped. 'What the fuck?' she said aloud.

Too tired to think it through, she had lifted the pack as best she could and carried it down the slope to the campground.

Now, the simple tasks of pegging out the tent and inflating her sleep mat were weighted with exhaustion. Her body was stiff with cold, every joint complaining as she finally undressed and slid into the sleeping bag. There was comfort in the way it enveloped her, close and warm after the expanse of the beach and the limitless sky. She wanted Lou's arms around her. They'd shared this tent a few times, zipping their sleeping bags together and holding each other as the rain beat on the fly, whispering plans, skin touching skin until they drifted into blissful sleep.

Not tonight.

Grace tossed and turned, unable to find a comfortable position for her head on the fleece jacket she used as a pillow. Her brain fevered over her every movement from the time she locked the bus to laying here now. She wanted to find a chronology she could adhere to when Heaney continued his questioning. She tried to remember what she'd already told him. He'd have notes, even though he said it wasn't an interview – and a witness in Sarah. An image was trying to emerge from the fog of the calamity, something she couldn't see clearly, something she'd done but hadn't mentioned yet. Or something she'd told him she'd done but now doubted. What was it?

When she finally slept, she dreamed of throwing herself into the sea, allowing herself to be taken. It pulled her down, and she did nothing to resist. The currents twisted her body into disjointed shapes, pushing her arms behind her back, her legs above her head. Her face was hit by fast-moving fish, their sharp fins cutting at the flesh until she bled. And there, below her, through the plumes of blood, she saw the boys, all three of them somehow breathing underwater. They laughed, pushing and shoving each other, their hair wafting like halos around their heads, beckoning to her. She uncurled her body and stroked towards them, but the deeper she swam, the tighter her chest became and the further away they seemed, until they vanished into the darkness.

Three students are missing, believed drowned, on a school camp in Victoria's south-west. Circumstances surrounding the tragedy are unclear, but Channel Seven is reporting it has spoken to a parent from a large Catholic boys' college in Melbourne's northern suburbs who said that the students drowned late this afternoon.

The ABC understands police rescue and SES volunteers have travelled to the site of the tragedy this evening. Unconfirmed reports have stated the boys, who were on an outdoor education excursion, were swimming at a remote beach on the Great Western Walk, near Moonlight Head, when they got into difficulties.

The area is known for its dangerous and unpredictable surf. Weather conditions in the south-west this afternoon were described by the Bureau of Meteorology as severe, with strong to gale force winds and rain.

The principal of the boys' college has been contacted for comment, but the school has yet to issue a statement. The ABC has chosen not to name the school.

More details to come.

8

Grace woke in the half-light of predawn. She took a few minutes to gather herself, hoping she'd dreamt the events of yesterday – that she was still at Crayfish Bay, the boys stirring in their tents, calling out crude jokes to see who else was awake. But only the sound of a currawong came to her as she pushed out of the sleeping bag and started to organise her gear.

Finding her phone, she noted the low battery warning and checked the time: *6.30*. She had been vaguely aware of the arrival of more vehicles during the night, the movement of headlights across the campground and the rumble of diesel engines. Grace emptied the tent and methodically took it down to fold away. The familiarity of this little ritual was reassuring. She had forgotten again about the severed straps on her pack, and when she tried to pick it up it fell away from her. Having time to think about it now, she realised it could only have been one of the boys who'd cut them. But why? And who had carried a knife sharp enough to do it?

When Grace crested the rise above the campground, she hardly recognised the car park from the previous evening. It was dominated by a police bus, next to which half a dozen uniformed officers stood around a fold-out table, a map spread between them. There were three more SES vehicles, one of which was a van with a fold-down side, distributing food and hot drinks to volunteers. And beyond that, in a roped-off corner of the car park, at least a dozen media cars and vans were parked at skewed angles. People huddled in small cabals, all wrapped warmly in puffer jackets and most holding cups of something hot. Few noticed the young woman carrying her pack awkwardly and heading towards the beach.

Grace couldn't see Sarah or Heaney, so she dropped her pack by Sarah's ute and followed the path out to the platform. When the beach came into view, it looked entirely different from yesterday. The swell had dropped away, with small, even waves replacing the maelstrom from the previous afternoon. The wind had swung offshore, feathering the peaks as they pushed towards the sand. The shoreline was dotted with orange and dark-blue uniforms. Half a dozen searchers immediately below her were climbing the rocks at the western end of the beach.

Sarah stood on the platform. 'How are you doing, love? Did you get some sleep?' she asked.

'A bit, yeah. Have they found . . .?

'No,' Sarah replied. 'Not yet. We've got a chopper coming from Geelong and two boats from Wheelers Bay. They're more likely to . . .'

As Grace rested her elbows on the railing, her phone vibrated in her jacket pocket. She pulled it out and checked the screen. *32 messages. 18 missed calls.* Notifications on Twitter, WhatsApp and Instagram.

Sarah looked at her. 'No time for that,' she said. 'We've got to get moving.'

Grace ached to call Lou and her dad, just to hear their voices, but she remembered Jim's instructions about not speaking to anyone but him. Reluctantly, she slid the phone back into her pocket.

'What happens now?' she asked Sarah. She was talking about the next couple of hours but could just as easily have been referring to the rest of her life.

'Food first,' Sarah replied. 'Then Pete – Sergeant Heaney – wants you to take us down to where it happened. From what you told us last night, it's right at the other end of the beach,' she said, pointing. 'Is that right?'

'Yeah. Where the track comes out.'

'There's no other way but walking, I'm afraid.'

'That's okay,' Grace said. 'Walking I can do.'

Sarah smiled.

'How are the boys?' Grace asked. 'Have you heard?'

'All okay. It took a while to check them out at the hospital, but they slept at the motel.'

'Will Tom or Gerard come back here?'

'No, love. They'll take the boys back to Melbourne. And you'll be able to head off, too, just as soon as we get this business over this morning.'

Grace knew her own insistence on staying last night had led her to being the only person on the beach directly connected to the tragedy, but now she wished again that one of the other staff were with her. Tom, not so much, but Gerard would have been a solid support, someone to back her up, to deflect the attention from just her.

'Come on,' Sarah said. Back in the car park, she shepherded Grace into a small space between her ute and a fence. Reaching into the back seat, she pulled out a pair of SES coveralls and handed them to Grace. 'The media are here already,' she explained. 'And they'll be looking for you. Best you blend in.'

Grace took off her boots and stepped into the coveralls. When she stood, Sarah wedged an orange cap onto her head.

'Perfect,' Sarah said. 'Now, wait here while I grab us some breakfast.'

'Just coffee for me,' Grace said.

The walk along the beach took them a little over an hour and a half. The low tide made the river crossing easy. Sarah checked in on some of her crew as they passed, their grim faces telling Grace all she needed to know. None of them took any notice of her. For all they knew, she was part of a different team, assigned to Sarah as well. A hundred metres before the trailhead, police tape had been strung up to restrict access to the eastern end of the beach. At the tape, TV crews had set up tripods for their cameras, while other reporters clustered in nests of puffer jackets, long-lens cameras swinging on straps from their shoulders.

Sarah nodded at the police officer guarding the tape, and she and Grace ducked underneath.

When they arrived at the trailhead, there were about twenty people standing in a large circle. Most were in the familiar SES uniforms, but about a dozen wore the dark-blue coveralls of Police Search and Rescue. Grace noted at least half their number were women. Heaney was addressing the group. They all turned to look at Grace and Sarah as they approached.

Anxiety had built in Grace the closer they came to the site, and now that she was back here – albeit in conditions a world away from yesterday – the weight of what had happened bore down on her again. Sarah took her by the arm and led her towards the assembled group. Grace wondered how long this woman would be around to guide her through the chaos.

Heaney had stopped talking. 'All right, everyone,' Sarah said. 'This is Grace. As you know, she was here yesterday when the boys ran into the water. She will be assisting Sergeant Heaney and I for an hour or so.'

The eyes of the searchers fell on Grace, and she didn't know what to say. Some of them turned away quickly, others shifted their boots in the sand. When she looked back up the beach, all the cameras at the police tape were now pointed in their direction. Sarah broke the awkward silence by nodding towards the trailhead and leading Grace away.

Heaney finished his instructions, then followed Grace and Sarah. There was a small campfire on the edge of the sand. Sarah lifted a billy from the coals and poured cups of tea.

'How are you feeling this morning?' Heaney asked Grace.

'Like shit,' she said, which made him smile.

'That's understandable.'

His voice sounded gentler, kinder than it had yesterday. He looked older in the daylight, greying at the temples, deep lines furrowing his forehead. Last night, Grace would have picked him as being about forty, but lack of sleep and the morning light had added ten years to that guess.

'We'll make this as quick as we can,' Heaney said. 'The chopper will be here any minute.'

'What do you need from me?' Grace asked.

'I want you to show me exactly where the boys went in, where they ran from, that sort of thing. Should only take a few minutes.'

'And then?' Grace said.

'We think it's best we get you away from here. Home,' he replied.

Sarah handed her a muesli bar. 'Here,' she said. 'Get that into you.'

Grace thought it strange how her body had forgotten its most basic needs. She wasn't hungry, but she knew she should be. She'd barely eaten since yesterday afternoon, but she wasn't light-headed or lethargic. What was her body functioning on? What was keeping its myriad fibres moving?

They heard the rhythmic *foomp-foomp* of the helicopter

before they saw it. They walked out onto the sand and waited. It eventually rounded Moonlight Head and flew directly towards them. A woman in Search and Rescue coveralls stood on a high point of the beach, earmuffs in place, her arms stretched horizontally. The blue-and-white police chopper hovered twenty metres offshore, spray pushing sideways and lifting from the surface of the water. As Grace drew closer, she saw the small microphone attached to the woman's earmuffs.

The pilot, having received their instructions, banked and flew parallel to the shore. They turned out to sea for a small distance and did another slow pass where Grace stood with Sarah and Heaney.

'Let's get this done,' Heaney shouted above the roar. 'Then you two can get going.'

Grace took her bearings from the trailhead and led the way down to the water. The rip was still visible, a deep gutter running diagonally towards a bank where waves were breaking about forty metres offshore. She pointed it out to Heaney.

'What am I looking at?' he asked.

'That's the runout where the boys went in. They were swept . . .' She stopped herself. *They were swept away.* 'It was flowing much faster yesterday. Waves were breaking into it from both sides.'

Grace glanced at Heaney. He seemed to be struggling to grasp what she was saying. Surely, a cop in a coastal town understood what a rip was. Or was he playing dumb to get her to talk more?

'Look,' she said, pointing into the middle of the gutter. 'It's deep. Fast flowing, even with a small swell.' She tried not to sound like a teacher, but she couldn't help herself.

'And where were you?' Heaney asked. 'Now that you can see it in daylight, I mean. How far away?'

Fifty metres, Grace thought. *Is that what I told him last night?*

Grace looked back towards the line of cameras, then up at the dunes that towered over that part of the beach. 'About where that lump of kelp is,' she said, pointing.

Heaney squinted in the light, assessing the distance. 'So, fifty metres. Sixty, maybe?'

'Yes.'

'And that's where you first saw the boys?'

'Yes. Three of them running straight for the water,' she said.

'All together or strung out?'

Grace conjured the image in her head again: the lanky Jake in front, then Roberto, gaining on him. Harry was a good way behind. Was he chasing them? Trying to stop them? If he was, why had he stripped off, too?

'In a line,' she said. 'Jake, Roberto then Harry.'

Heaney swung towards her. 'It was raining, wasn't it? You said that yesterday. But you could still make out who they were?'

They were interrupted by Sarah. 'Pete,' she called. She was standing next to the woman in the earmuffs. 'They've got something.'

As Heaney and Grace walked towards them, the woman lifted one muff off her ear.

'How far away is the boat?' she asked.

'About an hour,' Heaney replied.

'Okay.' She relayed the information to the chopper crew.

Heaney and Grace waited. The helicopter beat its rotors against the morning air, hovering above the water. All the SES and Search and Rescue crews on the shore stopped to watch.

The woman lifted her earmuff again, pushing the microphone away from her mouth. 'They think an hour's too long,' she said to Heaney. 'They could lose it.'

Grace didn't understand what that meant, but Heaney nodded.

A rappel rope dropped from the open door of the helicopter, and a figure in a wetsuit was winched slowly down until their feet touched the surface of the water, which was whipped into a white frenzy. They seemed to hold there for an age. Grace stood rooted to the spot, with Heaney beside her. The sun had crept above Moonlight Head and flooded the beach in inappropriately soft light.

The diver was winched lower until they entered the water. Everything paused; even the wind seemed to wait, expectant. Along the beach, all the cameras were trained on the rescue. The diver was in the breaker zone. *So close*, Grace thought. *I could swim that easily on a day like today.* The swell was only small, but every now and again, the bigger waves at the back end of a set would break over the area where the diver was working. Finally, two shapes rose above the surface: one, the diver, had his arms around the other, which was bare and white, hanging limply in a double loop harness.

Grace's hand went to her mouth and tears welled in her eyes. She could barely breathe.

The winch stopped halfway up, and the diver made some adjustments to the harness before continuing. They spun slightly when they got to the open door of the chopper. An arm reached out and pulled them inside.

Grace felt an emptiness in the pit of her stomach. Who was it? She couldn't tell from this distance.

The woman with the earmuffs held up her hand. 'There's a second one,' she said.

Grace couldn't bear to watch another boy lifted from the water – one who had been alive and breathing this time yesterday, folding up his tent and pulling his pack on as he joked with his mates. She turned away.

'They're going to land in the campground,' Sarah said to her back.

Grace looked up the beach. A pair of hooded plovers darted along the sand, creating a diversion to protect their nest at the base of the dunes. She'd seen their eggs on her trips down here before, little brown-and-black speckled ovals that looked so vulnerable in their exposed nests. They were an endangered species; thousands of years of evolution were unable to protect them from feral cats and surfers' dogs.

'Grace?' Sarah was beside her.

'Sorry, yeah, what?'

'Sergeant Heaney just has a few more questions, then I think we should head back.'

Grace felt a familiar numbness spreading through her body.

Her boots were intolerably heavy, and it seemed to take all her strength to lift her hand and pull the hair from her face. Sarah's voice echoed, like it was coming from a great distance.

Sarah was beside her again. 'Come on,' she said. 'Let's get you away from here. Pete's questions can wait. You'll be needed back in the car park when the chopper lands.'

She walked over and spoke briefly to Heaney. They exchanged some terse words, but the sergeant eventually nodded, before directing his attention back to the helicopter.

When Grace and Sarah reached the police tape, the media was distracted by the rescue. Grace pulled the cap down tightly over her forehead. Sarah nodded at the cops guarding the tape, ducked underneath again, and walked higher up the beach. They were almost past the throng when someone called out.

'Is it the boys?' A woman walked towards them, holding her phone out. 'Rose Cotter. *Melbourne Star*.'

'Dunno,' Sarah replied without stopping. 'You'll have to talk to the sergeant in charge.'

The reporter kept walking. Sarah shielded Grace from her. 'Keep going,' Sarah whispered, before turning and confronting the reporter.

'What can you tell us about the teacher?' Cotter asked. Grace slowed.

'The teachers and students were all evacuated yesterday,' Sarah said, sounding authoritative.

'Why were the boys unsupervised on the beach?' Cotter asked. 'This was negligence, wasn't it?'

Grace froze.

'We don't know that they were unsupervised, and you should be very careful about what you report.' Sarah snapped. 'Now if you don't mind, we've got work to do.'

Grace waited for her to catch up, and the two of them trudged towards the river crossing, putting space between themselves and the threat of the media pack.

'Thanks,' Grace said, after they'd walked another few minutes.

'What for?'

Grace didn't reply. Her steps grew heavy again. She suddenly found it hard to keep moving, like her legs were cramping. She'd been holding herself taut – every muscle trying desperately to give the appearance of strength. The muffled thumping of the chopper merged with the beating wings of the moths in her head. She stopped.

Sarah stood in front of her, pitching a look back at the cameras to make sure they hadn't turned their way. 'Shit happens, Grace,' she said quietly. 'I've seen it over and over: accidents, people in the wrong place at the wrong time. You can't guard against stupidity.'

Grace looked at her. 'What am I going to do?' she said, wiping snot from her nose with her sleeve. 'I lost my boys. The parents, the school, everyone, they're going to blame me.'

'The boys ran ahead of the group. How could you predict that?'

'It's my job to predict it,' Grace said.

'Come here,' Sarah said, offering her hands. She pulled Grace into a hug. 'You're strong, love. I can see that,' she said into Grace's hair. 'It's going to be tough, but you'll make it through. I know you will.'

Grace stepped back and dusted the sand off her uniform.

'Come on, then,' Sarah said. 'Anyone sees this, we'll be giving the SES a bad name.'

Grace almost smiled.

9

Tim Simpson slid into the seat on the bus and rested his head against the window. It felt like he hadn't slept, but he must have. They'd been hours at the hospital, and the motel beds were small and uncomfortable. All he could think about was getting home, hugging his parents, closing the door of his room and falling into his own bed.

He'd given up on hiding the tears. All the boys were the same, huddled inside hoodies and coats, slumped in their seats. Mister Kruger was driving. Before they left Wheelers Bay, he had walked down the aisle, checking on each of them. Or maybe he was doing a head count, after what happened on the walk yesterday. Half the boys had phones and were using them openly, knowing the teachers wouldn't confiscate them now. Everyone'd already spoken to their parents and mates anyway. The story was out.

The walk back to the car park at Juliet had been long and slow, though Tim had managed to stick with the lead group. He wanted desperately to get away from the beach. Even so, the closer they got to the car park, the more he felt he was deserting Jake. They'd stayed as long as they could, watching and waiting and scanning the ocean for any sign of their three mates. Tim had fully expected Jake and Roberto and Harry to reappear, pissing themselves at having made the teachers panic. But they never came.

Tim had watched the teachers try to hold everything together. He couldn't believe they let Disher take charge. It should have been Kruger. A bloke. He was the one looking after Daniel, keeping an eye on the boys, always asking how they were going. Winter had totally lost it, sitting on the sand with his head in his hands. But Disher, she was all business, telling people what to do and when to do it, like three boys drowning was just something to be dealt with so they could all move on. It was an act, though. Jake had been right about her all along; she was useless. She'd fallen for the phone trick when they'd left school on Monday morning, making out she was all strict and organised. They'd just handed in their old phones and kept their good ones hidden.

So easy, Jake had said.

Now the bus inched its way down a tight laneway at the back of the motel. There had been a police car at the main entrance all night, and this morning it had been joined by a posse of TV crews and reporters. A makeshift screen – a big green tarp – had been held up to shield the boys as they boarded the bus.

Tim leaned forwards, elbows on his knees, and checked his phone. They were the lead story everywhere. He was usually only interested in sport. But now the spotlight was on *his* school, *his* mates. When he started scrolling, it was so frustrating; most of the news sites were pay-for-view. There'd be a clickbait headline about the boys drowning, then it'd lead straight to the log-in page.

The bus eased out onto a small back street and slowly picked up speed. Mister Kruger was a shit driver. The bus lurched each time he tried to change gear, losing revs and struggling as he missed second and went straight to third. Tim thought about his dad, Gus. He was an ace behind the wheel. He reckoned he could feel the engine when he planted his foot in his Commodore. Tim wished he were here now. They'd be home in half the time.

Tim's phone buzzed. His mum. He'd spoken to her last night, when he'd got a signal up near the toilets at the car park, but he hadn't had time to say much. She had cried, asking over and over if he was all right. Like he wouldn't be, even though he was talking to her on the phone. She was friends with Jake's mum, Celine. They went everywhere together. The DFO terrorists, his dad called them. Always planning another shopping trip. He had no idea what they did with all the shit they bought.

Tim pushed the buds into his ears and answered. 'Hi, Mum.'

'Hello, darling.'

He winced.

'How are you this morning? Did they give you breakfast? I'll have a big lunch ready when you get home. I've made an egg and bacon pie.'

This is how she spoke when she was stressed. Like when he broke his wrist playing footy last season: she'd taken him from the ground to the hospital and hadn't stopped talking the whole way, all about how she was going to take time off work to look after him.

'Thanks, Mum. That'd be great.'

'It's everywhere on the news,' she continued. 'Poor Celine! She's a mess. And Rick. He's gone down to the search site.'

Tim didn't miss the tension in his mum's voice when she mentioned Rick. He and Celine had split up, and Tim's mum was firmly on her side. Jake reckoned his dad had been screwing around for years. He'd hated being shunted from one place to another, his parents always fighting about who should pay for what.

'Timmy, love, what happened at the beach? There're so many stories on Facebook. They're saying there weren't any teachers supervising. That can't be right. Where were they?'

Tim had tried last night to tell his mum what had happened, but she'd kept interrupting, asking if he was okay, was he warm enough, were the teachers looking after him?

'The whole thing was a stuff-up, Mum. Jake and Robbie and another boy you don't know, Harry, they got a long way ahead of the group. The teachers were useless.'

'Who?' his mum snapped. 'Which teachers?'

'Mister Kruger, you know, the PE guy I had in year eight, and Mister Winter. He's an IT teacher. I've never had him.'

'And what about the other teacher, the bossy one at the bus on Monday morning?'

'Disher,' Tim said. 'Yeah, she was in charge. I dunno why.'

'What do you mean?'

'Should have been Mister Kruger. He's a PE teacher. Everyone likes him. He's funny.'

'Miss Disher was on the news. Doing weird stuff. Running away from the rescue helicopter. Why would she do that?'

Tim's mind raced. 'No one in the class likes her,' he said. 'She thinks she's king shit. And she was always picking on Jake. She made fun of him at our camp on Monday night. Tried to make him look like an idiot just cos he was being a bit of a smart arse.'

'The teachers had been picking on Jake? Is that why he ran away from them?'

'Disher hated Jake. I reckon that's why she let him drown.'

He heard the intake of breath on the other end of the line.

'Wait. What?' his mum said. 'She *let* him drown?'

Tim hesitated. 'That's what I heard,' he said.

'Oh my God, Timmy. Are you sure about that?'

'Like I said, Mum. That's what I heard. She was the only one there when we all got to the beach.'

'They haven't said anything about that on the news.'

'They wouldn't, though, would they? They're protecting her, but when the real story gets out . . .'

His mum was momentarily lost for words. 'I'm posting this,' she eventually said.

'I dunno, Mum. Maybe you should wait.'

'Someone has to speak up, Timmy. Otherwise, stuff like this gets swept under the carpet. And three boys are dead.'

The bus was snaking along the Great Ocean Road, and Tim was starting to feel carsick. He'd only had some toast and orange juice for breakfast. 'I gotta go, Mum,' he said. 'We'll be home in a couple of hours. I'll see you then.'

'Love you,' she said before Tim ended the call. He hoped his dad would be there when they got back. His mum would make a scene, but his dad would be solid as ever, probably give him one of his famous man hugs and a shadow punch to the jaw.

Tim eased the window open a few centimetres and breathed in the salty air. It was cold, but it distracted him from his growing nausea.

Danny Lombardi sat across the aisle, his arms drawn tight around his chest, his hoodie shielding his face. Tim thought he was asleep, but every now and again his body shuddered. Tim undid his seatbelt, pulled the buds from his ears and slid across the aisle to sit next to him.

'How you doin', bro?' he asked. He'd hardly spoken to Danny. Mister Kruger had been great with him, though, supporting him all the way back up the beach, carrying his pack as well as his own. And he'd stuck with him when they got to the motel later.

Danny pushed his hood back, but he couldn't look at Tim.

Tim reached out and gently fist-bumped Danny's shoulder. 'Hang in there,' he said. 'We'll be home soon.' It would be hard enough losing a brother, Tim thought, but a twin – that had to be worse.

'I don't know what I'm going to do without him,' Danny mumbled.

Tim didn't know what to say. He'd never had to deal with anything like this. His nana had died when he was in primary school, but she was old, and you expected that. This was something completely different, and he had no idea how he should behave. He wanted adults to handle the grief for him, to take charge like Mister Kruger had.

Danny turned to look directly at Tim. 'How did it happen?' he asked, as though Tim might be able to provide him with an answer.

'How would I know?' Tim replied, a little too sharply. He moved back to his own seat, replaced the buds in his ears, leaned his head against the window and closed his eyes.

10

When Grace and Sarah arrived at the car park, everyone was moving towards the campground. One of the volunteers recognised Sarah and waved. 'The chopper,' she called to them. 'It's coming back.'

Sarah led Grace to the food van. 'I'd kill for another coffee,' she said. Grace nodded, keeping her head down, the cap hiding her face.

'Hey, Sarah,' the man in the van called. 'How's it going down there?' He nodded towards the beach.

Sarah didn't answer. 'Caffeine first, thanks Watto. And something warm to eat.'

'Sure,' he replied looking quizzically at Grace. 'You're new, aren't ya, love? Haven't seen you before.'

Grace forced a smile.

'Come on Watto,' Sarah interrupted, 'or I'll come in there and make it myself.'

'Alright. Keep your shirt on,' he said. 'I've been flat out this morning.'

The approach of the helicopter removed the need for any further conversation. Watto handed them coffee in paper cups and two beef rolls. The beating rotors of the chopper filled the air around them as it rose over the last dune and began to circle the open ground where Grace had camped. It hovered for a few seconds before the pilot eased it to a soft landing.

Sarah ushered Grace into the lee side of one of the SES trucks, hiding her from the activity in the paddock. 'Probably best you wait here,' Sarah said. 'I'll find out what's next for you.' She touched her arm again. 'And eat,' she commanded.

Grace sat down against one of the big tyres. She was wedged between the truck and a wire fence that protected the vegetation at the back of the dunes. The ground was littered with bark, dead leaves and cigarette butts. She scuffed the heels of her boots into the loose soil and made two parallel tracks. Unwrapping the beef roll, she tried to eat, but it made her gag. Maybe the coffee would be better than the one she had had earlier. It burned all the way down, but at least she was able to swallow it.

The chopper's engines ground to a halt and an empty silence fell over the car park. Grace jumped when she heard her phone buzz. It pinged again and again. She fumbled to find it in her pocket. More messages and missed calls. More notifications on socials.

There was one bar showing in the top left-hand corner and the battery was low, but she couldn't resist anymore. She scrolled to Lou's number and called. It rang twice before she answered.

'Gracie?'

Just the sound of her voice, the way she said her name like no one else, choked Grace again. 'Hey,' she whispered.

'Oh, Gracie. I've been so –'

'I'm okay,' she said. She inhaled deeply and tried to hold the breath in her chest for a moment to steady herself. 'Has anyone spoken to you?'

'Yeah, we all know. Ah, babe, those poor boys.'

Grace struggled to respond. The mention of the boys seemed to constrict her breathing even further. 'I know,' was all she could say.

'I'm on my way down. Jim gave me the go-ahead, wanted someone with you. I'm taking the inland route. I'll be there in about an hour.'

'Oh,' Grace replied.

'Are you still at the beach? Are you safe? Have you eaten? Is there someone with you?' This was so like Lou, ever the practical one.

'Yeah, I'm at Juliet car park.' Grace found it easier to talk practicalities. 'It's a clusterfuck here: police, rescue, SES, media. I'm hiding behind a truck.'

'Why are you still there? Gerard, Tom and the boys are on their way back to Melbourne.'

Grace thought of the limp body hanging in the sling above the water. 'They've found two bodies, Lou.'

Louise didn't respond.

'I might need to identify them,' Grace continued.

'Isn't that up to the families?'

'They need to know who's still missing, I guess.'

Sarah appeared from the back of the truck and nodded, waiting for her to finish her call.

'I have to go,' Grace said. 'See you soon.'

'Love you,' Lou said.

'Me too,' she replied, and hung up.

'Boyfriend?' Sarah asked.

Grace nodded.

Sarah slid down next to her. 'You haven't eaten,' she said, looking at the ants crawling over the discarded roll on the ground.

'I couldn't get it down.'

'Listen,' Sarah said. 'The Colac uniforms are here. They want to know if you're up to identifying the boys. It's just preliminary, the families will do the proper ID later.'

'Do I have to?'

'No. But –'

'The parents,' Grace said.

'Yeah. We could let them know, then.'

Grace nodded. She couldn't imagine the anguish of the parents waiting for news. Her own grief paled in comparison. The idea of identifying the bodies terrified her, but it was the least she could do for them.

'Take your time,' Sarah said. 'Get yourself together. I'll lead you round the back way so we can avoid the cameras.'

Grace pushed herself to her feet. 'Let's get it over with,' she said.

They skirted the food van and followed the fence line away from the car park. Fifty metres along the road, Sarah directed her through a rough track under a stand of moonah. It brought them out at the back of the chopper. They squeezed through the strands of a wire fence and signalled to the police officer guarding the open door. He waved them across.

'This is Grace,' Sarah said. 'One of the teachers.'

'Senior Constable Mercer,' he replied. He was in his mid-thirties, stocky but athletic, his chest pushing at the dark blue flight suit. 'You can identify the boys?' he asked.

'Yes, they're in my class,' Grace said, though that statement seemed redundant now.

Mercer spoke quietly, carefully. 'There are two of them,' he said. 'They are covered, but I'll show you their faces. It can be quick. We just need to know who they are so . . .'

Grace finished the sentence for him. 'So you know who else you're looking for.'

'Yes,' Mercer said. 'They've been in the water for quite a while, but they're' – he paused – 'intact.'

Grace was struck by a horrible thought. *What if I don't recognise them?*

'Can you . . .?' Grace asked Sarah, taking her hand.

Mercer stepped up into the chopper and helped the two women board. The door on the other side had been closed, but Grace could see the phalanx of cameras through the window. They were being held at bay, twenty metres away.

Two grey bags with thick zips down the middle lay on the floor.

'Are you ready?' Mercer asked Grace.

She nodded.

He reached down, undid one of the zips and pulled the flaps aside to expose a face. Grace's hand went to her mouth. It was Roberto. His tight ringlets were still wet, and a single droplet clung to his cheek. His olive complexion had washed away, and he looked like a pale imitation of the boy she knew. His lips were open as if he were about to speak, and there was a trail of water leaking from one side of his mouth. His eyes were closed, but she half expected them to spring open if she could just touch him. Without thinking, she moved her hand towards his face.

Mercer took a gentle hold of her wrist. 'Best not,' he said.

'Can you identify him?' Sarah asked.

'Roberto,' she whispered. 'Roberto Lombardi.'

Mercer pulled a pad from his pocket. Grace spelled out the surname for him.

The bag was rezipped before Grace could think to say anything more. Like *I'm sorry*.

Mercer shuffled across and opened the second bag. It was Harry. He looked so different from Roberto, his jaw set in a half-smile, like it had been in life, his brow smooth and his long, brown hair swept back off his face. But he had a long scratch down one cheek that had been washed clean, hollowed out by the sea. Water pooled under his head.

Harry, you were so smart, Grace thought. *Why did you follow them in?*

'Harry Edwards,' she said.

It was only then that something cracked in her, as the smell of the bags hit her from up close. She lurched towards the door, leaned out and tried to vomit. There was only coffee to bring up, but she dry-retched over and over while Sarah held her hair off her face and stroked her back.

'Let it out, Grace. Let it all out.' Her voice was matter of fact, like she'd done this a hundred times before.

Grace looked up to see a photographer training his lens on her from the stand of moonah they'd walked through. The shutter clicked again and again.

Sarah jumped out of the chopper and walked towards the photographer with her arms outstretched, but he backtracked before she reached the fence.

Grace peered through to the front of the chopper to see if she could escape that way. The rest of the cameras had been distracted by a large, blue four-wheel drive entering the car park at speed. It skidded in the gravel and came to a halt within a couple of metres of the media pack. Sarah seized the chance to start moving towards the truck without being noticed. She hurried Grace around the front of the chopper and across the open space.

The door of the four-wheel drive flew open, and Rick Bolton pushed his way through the throng.

'You!' he yelled, pointing at Grace. 'Where's my boy? Where's Jakey? What've you done?'

Three boys from St Finbar's Catholic Boys' College in Darebin are missing, believed drowned, on a school bushwalking trip in the state's south-west.

The boys, all sixteen years of age, were swimming at Juliet Beach, thirty kilometres west of Wheelers Bay, when they got into difficulties yesterday afternoon around 4pm.

Teachers on the beach were unable to rescue the students.

First responders reached the site yesterday evening. A spokesperson for Victoria Police said it is unlikely the boys could have survived, but rescue teams are continuing to search beaches in the area. Water temperatures are believed to be as low as 14 degrees.

The principal of St Finbar's, James Sheridan, released a brief statement late last night saying the school was in shock and that they would be doing everything they could to support the grieving families.

'We are a Catholic school, and we will rely on our faith in God's grace to help us deal with this tragedy,' Mr Sheridan said.

A spokesperson for the Wheelers Bay Surf Life Saving Club, Stephen Murdoch, said conditions at Juliet Beach yesterday would have been treacherous. 'There was a big swell running and we had a thirty-knot westerly wind with heavy rain,' he said.

'I don't know why anyone would have been swimming there,' he told *The Star*. 'Juliet is one of the most dangerous beaches in the state. There are strong rips and currents, and it's open to huge ocean swells.'

The remaining students and teachers on the trip were transported to Wheelers Bay last night where they were treated at the local hospital for hypothermia and shock. *The Star* understands they will return to Melbourne today.

The names of the missing boys have not yet been released.

11

Grace stopped abruptly enough for Sarah to run into her. The attention of the media swung between Rick Bolton and Grace as they tried to make sense of why he was yelling at an SES volunteer.

'Who's he?' Sarah asked Grace.

'He's a parent of one of the boys,' she replied. She was riveted to the spot. They were at the bottom of the low grassy slope that led up to the car park.

'One of those boys?' Sarah asked, nodding towards the helicopter.

'No. The other one. Jake. The one they haven't found.'

Three police now formed a line in front of Bolton, their arms outstretched.

'I'm sorry, sir,' one said. 'This is a restricted area. There is a police operation in progress.'

Bolton's eyes moved wildly around the car park, as though he might find his son there somewhere. Then he slumped against the side of his car. 'My boy,' he said, his voice high and broken. 'Please. Jakey.'

Sarah had Grace by the arm again and was pulling her towards the food van. While everyone's attention was on Bolton, she hustled Grace up the steps and through the door.

'Watto,' she said. 'Can you look after Grace here for a bit?' Then she disappeared, shutting the door behind her.

'No problem,' Watto replied. He directed Grace to a stool in the corner, where she'd be out of view.

Grace could feel everything spinning out of her control. Like a puppet, she had people pulling her strings every which way. And now Jake's dad was here to add to the chaos. She held her head in her hands and ground her thumbs into her temples.

'Here,' Watto said, squatting in front of her. He held a steaming cloth in his hands. He shook it a couple of times and handed it to her.

It seemed the strangest thing to Grace, but once she opened the cloth out and allowed it to cool a little, she buried her face in it. She rubbed at her skin, closing her eyes and feeling the washer warm her cheeks. Then she lifted her hair and scrubbed at the back of her neck. She couldn't think of a single act of kindness that had ever felt so right.

'Don't ask me why,' Watto said, 'but a good face wash always makes you feel better.'

'Thank you,' Grace said, looking around the inside of the van. It smelled of toast and instant coffee and old grease. 'What's happening out there?' she asked.

Watto leaned across the counter. 'That fella's in a bad way,' he said. 'A parent, huh? Poor bastard, I reckon he's going to need some coffee.'

'You know I'm . . .'

'Yeah, I guessed. Didn't think you were SES.'

'Where's Sarah?'

'She's talking to Pez. Search and Rescue. He's the copper in charge. Good bloke. I've been on a few jobs with him.'

Grace tried to build a picture from the staccato information Watto relayed. Just then, the whirring of the helicopter's rotors began, a *woosh woosh,* before the engines took over and the van vibrated with the noise and wind. Grace thought of Roberto and Harry, their wet bodies enclosed in the waterproof bags, zipped up and airless. She didn't know if they were still in the chopper, or if they'd been transferred to an ambulance she'd seen arrive earlier. Either way, they had been her responsibility, under her care, and she would never see them again. She stood up just as the helicopter lifted from the paddock, flattening the grass with its downdraft. It banked quickly and disappeared behind the line of trees at the top of the ridge.

Grace ducked a little lower and looked for Rick Bolton. His car was still there. He stood with his back against the side panel, a policewoman next to him and a broad-shouldered copper in front. Bolton leaned forwards, hands on his knees, and the woman rubbed his arm. They were twenty metres away, but Grace heard his crying turn to body-deep sobbing. The media crews had been forced further back towards the car park entrance, but they still had their cameras trained on Bolton.

Sarah was speaking to the big copper. When she pointed at the van, he nodded, said something to the policewoman and walked towards Grace. Rick Bolton straightened and followed with his eyes.

There was a soft knock on the door, and Watto undid the latch. Grace slid back down onto the stool.

The policeman entered the van and stuck out his hand. 'Watto, isn't it? You were at the rescue up at Macedon last Christmas.'

'You've got a good memory. Coffee?'

'No, thanks, but Rick over there could do with one. Strong,' he said. He looked around the van.

'On it,' Watto said, then gestured towards Grace on her stool. 'This is Grace, one of the teachers.'

The policeman did a double take as he took in the SES uniform, then squatted in front of her. 'Senior Sergeant Mario Pezzementi,' he said formally. Then, seeing the way Grace stiffened, he added more gently, 'Call me Pez.'

Grace leaned back. Pez seemed to take up all the space in front of her.

Watto poured coffee from the urn into a paper cup, added milk and sugar then squeezed past Pez to hand it to the police-woman who had come up to the van.

'Grace,' Pez said, 'Can you come with me? We'll find some-where more comfortable for you.'

He held out his hand to help her up. She took it. For the first time, she felt weak from lack of food.

They walked around the back of the van and crossed behind two police cars to a large tent that had been set up in a side bay of the car park. It was protected and private, but cold. There was a trestle table and a scattering of chairs. Two uniformed police, a woman and man, tapped at laptops. They stopped and looked up when Grace and Pez entered the tent.

'Boss,' they said in unison.

'How're you battling?' Pez asked them.

'Connection's wafting in and out,' the woman said. 'But the booster's helping.'

'Comms team,' Pez explained to Grace, as though she might understand.

Grace nodded. She sat down, undid her boots and stepped out of the SES coveralls. 'I don't want to hide,' she said.

'Okay.' He sat next to her, rested his elbows on his knees and intertwined his fingers.

Grace had no idea how she should act, whether to show how broken she was or hold strong.

'Is there someone you'd like to call?' Pez asked. His voice was soft for a big man. 'Have you spoken to anyone?'

'One person from school,' Grace said. 'She's on her way down here now.'

'And who's that?' Pez asked, taking a notebook and pen from the table.

'Louise Chan. She's on the executive team.'

'I understand you've spoken to your principal already. What's his name?'

'Jim Sheridan. Yes, last night. It was brief, just the details of what had happened.'

'Alright. This is going to sound harsh, Grace, but I have to caution you about who you speak to and what you tell them. There's a been a tragic accident here, and three young boys have died.'

Grace seized on the word *accident*. He had called it an accident.

'I assume you're on social media?' he asked.

'Yeah, of course.'

'Then I'll caution you even more strongly not to engage with anyone on there. This is just the sort of incident they feed on. You might want to consider closing your accounts. In the meantime, this Louise, would she be the best person to drive you back to Melbourne?'

'Yeah, she'd be good,' Grace said.

'We have our own counsellors,' Pez said, 'but I'll check with the school and see what they can provide.'

'Don't you want to . . . I mean, when will I make a statement? Don't you want to know what happened?'

'We've got as much information as we need for now from Sergeant Heaney. You're tired, and you've been through a terrible ordeal, something no one should have to witness. We'll get you back to Melbourne, make sure you have a proper night's sleep, get some food into you. I want you to take time to think through exactly what happened yesterday. Write it down. Get the events in order. Then we'll talk.'

She could have hugged him – leaned over and buried her face in his chest. 'Thank you,' she said.

'Just remember,' Pez said. 'Nothing you can do will change what's happened. Focus on what you can control. And – I know I'm repeating myself – write it all down.'

'What about Jake's dad? Should I speak to him?'

'I'd advise against it, Grace. He's angry and grieving – not a good combination.'

Grace tried to think it through. She knew she would be inextricably linked to Jake's family – and Roberto's and Harry's – for a long time; she was the last person to see their boys alive. She wanted to begin in the right way, not running and hiding from them. Her fogged mind had cleared enough for her to understand that. It wouldn't assuage the guilt that had racked her since yesterday afternoon, but maybe she and Rick Bolton could connect over their shared loss of Jake.

'I'd like to speak to him,' Grace said, more forcefully. 'Can we talk in here?'

Pez glanced at the two officers at the tables, then back at Grace. 'Not on your own,' he said. 'We'd have to be here.'

'Witnesses,' Grace said.

Pez grimaced. 'Can I make a suggestion?' he said. 'Keep it short. He won't hear most of what you say anyway. Comfort him if you can. It's probably the best you can hope for.'

Pez left her with the two uniforms, who busied themselves

on their laptops. Grace wondered what they were doing. Were they watching her, taking notes?

When Grace heard low male voices outside the tent flap, she stood up. She didn't want to look diminutive against Rick Bolton's height and bulk. The two constables stopped their typing and waited. A drop of condensation from the tent's roof fell into the mess of Grace's hair.

Bolton stepped through the flap and stopped a metre from Grace, his eyes on the ground. He looked smaller than she remembered. Maybe it was because Pez was standing next to him, or maybe it was what grief did, shrink a person somehow. She waited for him to speak, but he scuffed his black leather shoes on the gravel and pushed his hands deeper into his jacket pockets.

Grace realised she was holding her breath. She let it go and stepped towards Bolton. Finally, he raised his eyes and looked at her. They were bloodshot, red-rimmed and puffy. Capillaries close to the skin fanned out across his cheeks and lost themselves in the thick stubble on his chin.

'I'm so sorry for your loss,' Grace said, reaching both her hands towards him, her palms turned up. Her eyes welled again.

An unreadable expression flashed across Bolton's face, but then it was gone. His jaw moved slightly from side to side as he ground his teeth. He looked at her hands but kept his own wedged in his pockets.

'What happened?' he asked. His voice was so low, so lost, Grace could hardly hear him. But his words carried weight. No threat, but weight just the same.

Pez loomed behind Bolton. 'Do you two want to sit down?' he asked.

Bolton shook his head. 'I just want to know what happened,' he said.

Grace dropped her hands and then didn't know what to do with them. She'd envisioned hugging him, comforting him, sharing his grief. She knew it would look defensive, but she folded her arms across her chest. She needed to contain herself, to hold herself up.

'They ran ahead of the main group,' Grace began. She kept her voice soft, gentle, searching for understanding.

Pez shot a glance at Grace. A caution.

'They?' Bolton interrupted.

'Jake, Roberto Lombardi and Harry Edwards,' Grace replied. Speaking the boys' names was enough to conjure the image of Roberto and Harry's faces inside the body bags. Grace felt bile rise in her throat. She swallowed hard to force it back down.

'Where were the staff?' Bolton asked. It wasn't a neutral question.

'Gerard Kruger and Tom Winter were with the main group of boys. Like I said, Jake, Roberto and Harry somehow got a long way ahead of the others.'

'You're saying they did the wrong thing, then?'

'The instructions were . . .'

He blew air from his puffed cheeks. 'Get on with it,' he said.

Pez moved slightly forwards so he was almost shoulder to shoulder with Bolton. He stared at Grace, then nodded.

Grace braced herself again. 'They got to the beach first, and for some reason, we'll never know why, they ran into the ocean.'

'And where were you in all this?'

The conversation wasn't going where Grace had intended. 'We'd agreed on a rendezvous time, that I'd come from this end of the beach and meet them where the track came out.'

'So, were you there?' Bolton said again. 'When they arrived.' He was bouncing slightly on his toes, rocking backwards and forwards.

'I was within sight of them,' she said.

Bolton waited.

'They ran across the beach and threw themselves into the water. I yelled at them, waving my arms, screaming for them to stop.' She immediately regretted using the word *screaming*. He'd be thinking, *a bloke wouldn't have screamed*.

Now Bolton threw his head back and looked at the ceiling of the tent. He breathed in heavily, flaring his nostrils. 'None of this makes sense,' he said finally.

Pez interrupted. 'Grace, can I have a word? Privately.' He didn't wait for an answer, taking her by the arm and leading her outside into the sunshine. Grace wanted to stand in it, turn her face up to its warmth.

'Sorry, Grace, I shouldn't have let that happen,' Pez said. 'Neither of you are in a good place emotionally. He's going to explode at any minute. I'm going to shut it down.'

Grace nodded. She was happy to be out of the dank confines of the tent, away from Jake's brooding dad. Pez was right, it had been a mistake.

Bolton flew out through the flaps, closely followed by one of the constables. Pez instinctively placed himself in front of Grace, but Bolton didn't stop. He pushed past them and walked another ten metres before he turned back. Grace saw it all in his face: fear, loss, anger, disgust, the crippling angst of not knowing how to respond when your life has been stripped raw. She knew because she recognised all that in herself, too.

'Cunt!' he spat.

12

Grace's phone vibrated with a new message: *Please call me as soon as you can. Jim Sheridan.*

Bolton had stormed off, but Grace still felt the sting of what he'd said, the way he'd hurled it like a weapon. *Cunt.* She knew it was anger fuelled by grief but that didn't mean it hurt any less.

Pez stood next to her. He hadn't said anything to Bolton, but he'd moved a step closer to Grace.

'Are you okay?' he said. It seemed he had asked her that a lot in the last hour.

She shrugged. 'I've got to make a call,' she said, holding up her phone. 'Jim Sheridan, my principal.'

Sarah approached them, carrying Grace's backpack in front of her. She nodded at Pez, who moved off towards the van.

'What happened to this?' Sarah asked, dropping the pack at her feet and pointing at it.

Grace shook her head. 'I dunno. I only saw it last night.'

'Weird,' Sarah said, bending to look at the harness. 'The straps have been cut.'

'I know. I think it was one of the boys.'

'Grief does strange things to a person.'

Grace had no answer to that.

'How did it go with the parent?' Sarah asked.

'It was a train wreck.'

'I figured as much,' Sarah replied, then continued. 'I'm sorry, love, but I need those coveralls.'

'They're in the tent,' Grace said.

Sarah nodded. 'I have to go.'

'Thank you,' Grace said. 'For everything.'

Sarah pulled her into a tight hug. 'Stay strong, girl,' she said. Her voice was firm, even a little gruff. 'And take shit from no one, you understand?'

Grace never wanted to let this woman go.

Sarah stepped away and held her at arm's length, as though she were sizing her up. 'Better get going,' she said. She walked briskly into the tent, remerged with the coveralls bundled under her arm and walked off towards the beach.

'Hey,' Grace called after her. 'What do you do? I mean. when you're not with the SES?'

Sarah stopped and turned. 'I run a trawler out of Wheelers Bay,' she said. 'I know the sea.'

Grace picked up her pack and dropped it just inside the tent.

She gave Sarah a couple of minutes then followed in the same direction, relieved to be turning her back on all the activity in the car park. She headed along the track to the platform, then turned and climbed to the top of the dune, where she found a protected spot between the tussocks. The chopper had left, replaced in the search by a police boat that was moving slowly, parallel to the beach, beyond the line of the breakers. A zodiac zipped in and out of the wave zone, making wide sweeps and leaving a wake behind.

They hadn't found Jake yet. *Jake's body.* The body of the boy whose father was waiting in the car park.

Grace looked at her phone. The battery was very low. She hoped it would hold out. She found Jim's number and pressed *call*.

'Grace?' Jim answered.

'Yeah.' It was more a breath than a word.

'Whereabouts are you?'

'Still at Juliet.'

'Is Louise with you? Has she arrived yet?'

'Not yet, but I've spoken to her.'

'I'm sorry, Grace, I don't have a lot of time. It's bedlam here, but I want to know how you are going. Are you okay?'

Everyone wanted to know if she was okay, but what did that word even mean? *Am I breathing?* Grace thought. *Barely. Am I alive? Just. Am I coping? How would I know?*

'Grace,' Jim continued. 'What have the police told you about what's going to happen today?'

'They said Louise could drive me back to Melbourne.'

Lou, who she just wanted to hold, to fold into. Lou, who always made things feel right again.

'That's good,' Jim replied. 'Probably best that you get away from the scene of the . . .'

'Accident.' Grace finished his sentence for him.

'Yes,' he said. 'The accident.'

'We'll come to the school,' she said.

'That's not a good idea, Grace. There's media everywhere. You're probably a bit isolated down there, but it's blown up overnight.'

'There are media here, too,' Grace said.

'I want to reassure you, Grace. The whole school is here to support you. But brace yourself, okay?'

She wasn't sure what that meant.

There was a paternal note to his voice now. 'We're all dealing with the loss of the boys. There are counsellors here at school for you, Tom and Gerard.'

He hesitated.

'Right now, though, Grace, I need some details myself.'

Grace felt the breeze gust a little. Strands of hair that had escaped her ponytail wafted across her face, catching on her lips. She tucked them behind her ear.

'Just a couple of things,' Jim said. 'Are you okay with that?'

That word again. 'What do you want to know?' Grace asked.

'For now, it's just around supervision on the beach. The media are reporting the three boys who went into the water . . .'

'*Ran* into the water,' Grace interrupted. 'They ran.'

'Right, yes, the boys that ran into the water . . .'

'Jake, Roberto and Harry,' Grace said.

There was a pause on the other end. *The mention of Harry,* she thought.

'Grace, I really need to know whether there were staff with the boys on the beach. Were they being supervised?'

Grace didn't answer for a few seconds. She ran the film in her head one more time: the rain lashing at her legs, the wind lifting the sand in plumes, her screams lost in the fury of the pounding ocean. The film kept drifting in and out of focus.

She began slowly. 'I was coming towards them from the other end of the beach when they ran across the sand. They were racing each other.'

'So, you were with them? They were under your supervision?'

'It was so windy and noisy. The surf was huge. And the rain . . .' Her voice was beginning to fray.

Jim allowed her a few seconds before continuing. 'How far away were you, Grace? Take your time to answer. Think it through. This is very important.'

'Sixty metres. Maybe less. Fifty.' She tried to fix on what she'd told Heaney. The kelp on the sand. It was a story she would have to tell again and again. And not just *a* story, the *same* story. It felt like parts of a jigsaw were being forced into place to build a picture they could all agree on. But there were pieces that would never fit: her overwhelming sense of failure, Harry and Robbie's faces in the body bags, the devastation in Rick Bolton's eyes.

'Is it possible they saw you coming?' Jim asked. 'That they deliberately ignored you?'

This hadn't occurred to Grace, but yes, it was possible. They knew she would be coming. Even with the rain and the sand and foam in the air, they could have seen her. But something didn't quite fit with this explanation. She could imagine Jake and Roberto ignoring her – but not Harry.

'Maybe,' she said, despite her misgivings.

Jim again. 'Was there anyone else on the beach other than you and the three boys?'

'No.'

'Surfers? Fishermen? Walkers from other groups?'

'No, just us. We didn't see anyone else on the track for two days.'

'Right. So, no one saw what happened. There were no other' – he paused before using the word – 'witnesses?'

'No.'

'Can we agree, then, that you were fifty metres from the boys? And that they could have seen you even if they couldn't hear you?'

Grace left a long silence. She understood what that small detail meant: if the boys had seen her, Jim could say they were under her supervision. That they had chosen to ignore her. That the blame could be shifted onto them.

'Yes, they could have,' she said, finally.

'Right. Thank you, Grace. That helps enormously.'

She slid further into the tussocks until she was almost lying down.

'Grace, I'm cautious about doing this on the phone. I don't want to cause you any more pain, but – now we have established you were there – can you tell me what happened next, after the boys ran into the water? What did you do?'

Grace rubbed her face with her fingers. She wanted the warm washer Watto had given her in the van. Gathering her strength again, she told Jim exactly what she'd told Heaney.

'So, you didn't attempt a rescue?' Jim asked.

'No,' she said.

She knew how this must sound to Jim. One of his teachers had watched three of her students drown. He would be thinking of what he would have done, whether he'd have tried to save them, swum out knowing he might drown, too.

But his response surprised her. 'First rule of rescue,' he said. 'Don't create another casualty.'

She remained silent.

'You did the right thing, Grace.'

This stirred something inside her, a flicker of light in a deep chasm of despair. Someone understood. She *had* done the right thing.

Grace could hear another voice in the background. Jim was being hurried up. She couldn't imagine the things he must be dealing with.

'I'm sorry, Grace, I have to go,' Jim said. 'But there are just a couple more things. I'll be quick.'

'Sure.'

'We're having some difficulty finding the paperwork you submitted for the trip. Did you upload it onto the server?'

Fuck, Grace thought. She'd meant to do it on Sunday night.

'It's on my laptop,' she said finally. 'Everything was such a rush because of the last-minute staff changes. I was waiting to see who I could get.'

'Okay,' Jim said. In the pause that followed Grace could see him thinking through the ramifications. 'And where's your laptop?'

'It's in my car. At school.'

'And you have the keys?'

'Of course.'

'Right. We'll need to get those off you as soon as we can. Maybe you could give them to Louise. We need that documentation.'

Grace considered the forms she had filled out. There had been dozens of questions about escape routes, communications, first-aid experience, risk management. This was the first time she'd overseen a multi-day trip.

'Okay. I'll give my keys to Lou. To Louise,' she corrected herself.

'Good. And one last thing, Grace.' Jim hesitated. 'We have to have all our ducks in a row. Do you understand what I'm saying?'

Grace scratched at a midge bite on her ankle. 'Yeah,' she said, finally. 'I understand.'

'You're not obligated to talk to the police until you're ready. By then, we'll have someone with you.'

'Who do you mean?' she asked.

'Grace, the executive team have discussed it, and we think it best you have a college representative with you. A legal representative.'

'What? Why?'

'It's just . . .'

'Gerard and Tom, will they have legal representation, too? Or is it just me?' Grace had sat up without realising, her shoulders tense.

'No one here is thinking of anything but your welfare, Grace. Trust me. It's the best thing. It doesn't mean you are in any . . .' She knew he was trying to think of a better word than *trouble*. 'That this is anything more than a tragic accident.'

'You didn't answer my question.'

'We'll be offering support to Tom and Gerard as well. Of course.'

'Support? You mean legal support?'

'We haven't spoken about that yet, but probably, yes.'

'Probably?

Jim was silent long enough to remind Grace she was a junior staff member and he was her principal. 'We just don't want you to say anything you might regret later,' he said eventually. 'This is us throwing our arms around you, Grace. Trust me.'

'Around me – or the school's reputation?' Grace didn't know where that had come from, and she immediately regretted saying it.

Now there was a much longer pause at Jim's end.

'I'm going to pretend I didn't hear that, Grace. You've been through a terrible ordeal, and you must be very tired, but can I say again, our first concern is for you and your welfare. You just have to believe that.'

'Right,' she said, a little too abruptly. She winced. 'Is that all?'

'Yes, that's all for now,' he said. 'I have to go. Is there anything else you need right now?'

'Have you heard from Tom and Gerard?' she asked. 'How are the boys?'

'They're on their way back to Melbourne.'

'To the school?' Grace asked.

'No. To St Jude's. Away from the cameras.' St Jude's was their sister school in the next suburb. 'We'll have counsellors there to meet them, to support the families, the boys, Tom and Gerard.'

So, Grace thought, all the others were being brought back together, given immediate support, while she'd been asked to stay away.

'You need to know, Grace. Some of the boys had phones with them. They contacted their parents, who spoke to the media before we could get a lid on the situation. There's a lot of wild talk out there.'

'Directed at me?' Grace had the feeling of everybody – Jim, the school, Tom and Gerard, the parents – all receding, inching away, leaving her on her own. And then the thought struck her: *what if they found out about Perth?*

'We'll deal with it, I promise,' Jim said.

13

Grace looked at the time on her phone: *8.45.* It felt like half the day should have been over by now. She would have liked to stay there, hidden up in the dunes, feeling the morning sun on her skin. To lie down between the grasses and sleep. Fatigue was deep in her bones, and the conversation with Jim had drained her further. She was groggy, but she knew exactly what he was doing. Support would be available from the school, and that was reassuring. But he was positioning himself, too. If the boys were under her supervision, if they had seen her, the focus would turn to the stupidity of their actions. But it would also place her there and force her to defend not attempting a rescue. There was a fine line between protecting her and protecting the school's reputation – and she was beginning to understand how blurred that line might become.

Her phone's battery was almost dead. She opened her messages and quickly typed: *Hi dad, could you give me a call as soon as you get this message. Love you.* She pressed send.

When Grace stood, she could see inland to where the gravel road wound its way through the farmland to the gates of the national park. She watched as a vehicle made its way between the impossibly green pastures. As it drew closer, she recognised Louise's big Pajero SUV. They'd joked about it when she'd bought it – Grace called it an urban assault vehicle.

Louise took some time to get past the police at the gate, rounding the food van just as Grace emerged from the back of the dunes. Pez waved the car past the police vehicles and tent, directing her into a bay in front of the toilet block. Grace waited by the track head, staying out of sight of the group huddled around the campfire near where the chopper had set down. Rick Bolton would be there somewhere.

Louise was much more cautious about public intimacy than Grace. She had a terrace house in Fitzroy, a dozen suburbs across town from the school, away from the prying eyes of students and parents. But even at that distance, Louise still wouldn't walk hand in hand with Grace. She chose the back stalls in the bars they frequented and was always wary someone might recognise them. They had been together for just over three months, and as far as they knew no one at school was aware of their relationship.

Louise stepped down from the four-wheel drive and looked around at the people in the car park before spotting Grace, who gave a furtive wave. Pez was caught up talking with another cop. Grace nodded towards a stand of tea trees that formed an alcove near the track through the dunes.

Just the sight of Lou walking towards her made Grace feel parts of her body were falling in on themselves, like her muscles were disconnecting from her bones, no longer able to keep her upright. She grabbed the wire of the fence at her back for support then leaned forwards, clutching at her stomach. Louise broke into a run and caught her before she fell.

'Ah, Gracie, Gracie, Gracie,' she whispered, pulling her back to her feet. 'I'm here now. I'm here.'

Grace buried her face in the soft folds of Louise's fleece jacket and wept. Her body heaved and shook, hanging onto the only solid thing in her life at that moment.

'It's okay, let it out,' Louise said over and over. 'Let it out, babe.'

'The boys,' Grace said, her voice breaking as she tried to catch her breath between sobs. 'I couldn't get to them. They couldn't hear me. I screamed and screamed.'

'I know, I know,' Louise said, but Grace knew she never could.

Pez cleared his throat and Grace looked up to see him standing behind them. Louise stiffened a little and turned so she could loop her arm around Grace, hold her up.

Grace swiped at her face with her sleeve. 'This is Pez,' she said.

'Senior Sergeant Pezzementi,' he said, offering his hand. 'You're from the school?'

'Louise Chan. I'm part of the executive team at St Finbar's.' She shook Pez's hand.

'Grace has been through a terrible ordeal,' Pez said, his eyes fixed on Louise. 'We think it'd be best if she went back to Melbourne. We haven't taken a formal statement yet. We'd like to give her some time to recover physically.'

In a strange way, Grace didn't mind the way they talked as if she wasn't there. It was why she wanted Louise with her, to deflect some of the attention, to make decisions she was incapable of making on her own.

'We're liaising with your principal.' Pez said.

'Jim Sheridan,' Louise said.

'That's the fella. We'll be here for a while,' he continued, nodding towards the beach, 'but I'll send everything I've got to the Melbourne team. They'll be taking over the investigation once we're finished here.'

Investigation. Grace knew it was probably part of Pez's everyday vocabulary, but to her ears it carried another meaning. In her experience – informed by police dramas on TV and true crime podcasts – it was usually preceded by another word: *criminal*.

'And we've got the coroner coming down from Melbourne this afternoon,' Pez continued.

'Of course,' Louise replied.

'It's standard procedure in incidents like this,' Pez explained.

'Deaths, you mean.' Grace said, inserting herself back into the conversation.

'Yes,' Pez said.

'It's okay,' Grace said. 'You can say it. Three boys have died. Their names were Jake, Roberto and Harry.'

Louise shot a concerned glance at Grace, then back at Pez. 'I'd like to see the beach for myself before we go,' she said.

'The main search area is down towards Moonlight Head,' Pez said. 'But you get a good view from up there.' He pointed towards the platform.

'Come with me?' Louise asked Grace.

Grace hesitated. She didn't need to see the beach again – in fact, she wanted to erase it from her memory – but she also wanted to be alone with Louise. They'd be driving back together, but that wouldn't allow them to hold each other. She nodded and turned towards the track.

When they were out of Pez's sight, Louise stopped and opened her arms to Grace. They fell into a desperate embrace, like each was trying to pull the other into her body. Grace was the stronger of the two, thanks to the twice-weekly gym sessions and her obsession with running, but Louise was taller.

Grace gripped Louise with a fierce intensity, her fingers clutching at her clothes, hanging on as though she might be ripped from her at any moment. More than anything, she needed to be held. Since yesterday, a desolate sense of aloneness had taken hold of her.

Louise's hand found its way under Grace's clothing and onto her bare back. This touch, this human connection of skin on skin, was something Grace knew she should welcome, but it was strangely disconcerting. She knew it was well-meaning, but after what she'd been through – what she'd seen and done – the intimacy of fingers on her skin felt wrong. Jake, Roberto and Harry would never feel fingers on their skin again.

She reached around, took Louise's hand and pulled it up to her lips.

'I just . . .' she began, before realising she had no words to explain.

'It's okay, babe. Things are going to be weird for a while. Just keep talking to me. Promise?'

'Promise.'

'Come on,' Louise said, looping her arm through Grace's and leading her towards the platform.

Grace shook her head. The moment was over. 'Actually, I might wait in the car.'

'Sure,' Louise said, handing her the keys. 'I'll have a quick look. Then I think I should speak to Rick Bolton.' She left a pause. 'On my own.'

'I don't want to go near him,' Grace said.

When Louise left, Grace diverted up the steps to the toilet block. She desperately needed to piss, though she'd only drunk Watto's milky coffee since last night, and most of that she'd spewed out the side of the chopper. The building had five partitioned cubicles with gaps at the top and bottom to allow airflow. As soon as she closed a door, her phone started vibrating in her pocket again. She checked it for calls or messages from her dad, but there were none. Putting the phone away, she sat on the cold metal seat. Her clothes were dirty, and she felt stale in them. She reminded herself to pick up her pack before they left.

A wasp had built its nest, a thin cylinder of mud, in the corner of the cubicle. Grace watched as it buzzed around the entrance before disappearing inside.

Someone was coming, climbing the gravel steps towards the toilets. Heavy boots. Two people. Doors swung open on rusty hinges and closed. Latches clicked into place. Grace held her breath.

'I hate it when there are kids involved.' A woman's voice.

'Me too,' a man replied.

A steady stream of piss hitting metal.

'At least we've found two of them,' the man said.

'Poor bastard, the bloke down there. How do we tell him we might never find his son?'

'Or if we do, he could be in pieces.'

'Did you hear the rescue boat spotted a shark?'

'Ah, Jesus.'

Grace clamped her hand between her teeth.

'What do you make of the teacher?' the woman asked.

'I feel sorry for her. From what I gather, the boys ran way ahead of the other teachers. How do you guard against that?'

Two toilets flushed and doors opened. Water ran into the hand basin outside Grace's cubicle.

'You know what Heaney said?' the man asked.

'No. What?'

The man hesitated. The tap turned off. The sound of hands being wiped on pants.

'The teacher, she saw them in the water, but . . .'

'What? I thought they were gone by the time she got there.'

'Apparently she could see them. But she didn't go in after them.'

'Faark! You're kidding me.'

'The surf was huge yesterday. I think she made the right decision. We would have been looking for four bodies today.'

The woman was silent.

'First rule, Mandy. How many times have we had that drilled into us?'

'Yeah, I know. But I'm a mum. I don't think I could live with myself if I didn't try.'

They moved off down the steps and their voices faded.

Grace waited a couple of minutes before pulling her pants up and flushing. She couldn't remember pissing, but she must have. Her bladder was empty. Sticking her head out the toilet block door, she checked the way was clear to walk to the police tent. She didn't look at who was inside, just grabbed her pack and made a beeline for Louise's car. The remote made its beeping sound, loud enough to be heard across the car park, but she kept her back to anyone who might be watching, opened the hatch and threw her pack in. Then she walked to the passenger side and climbed in.

The car was spotless. A deodoriser in the shape of a pine tree hung from the rear-view mirror and filled the car with its unnatural scent. Grace tilted the seat back and kept her head below window level. For once, she welcomed the bulk of the four-wheel drive. It felt like a fortress.

After a few minutes, Louise tapped on the driver-side window. Grace opened the door.

'I'm just going to talk to Rick Bolton,' Louise said. 'Is there anything else you want before we head off? Food? Coffee?'

Grace shook her head.

'Sit tight. I won't be long,' Louise said.

She was gone for half an hour. Grace fiddled with her phone, but the signal was gone again. She plugged it into the car's charger.

Finally, Louise walked to the driver's side, got in without saying a word and held her hand out to Grace for the keys. With a cursory look over her shoulder, Louise reversed quickly, swung the wheel and drove a little too fast out of the car park.

Grace brought her seat up and touched Louise's arm.

'What's happened?' Grace asked.

Louise exhaled heavily and stared straight ahead. 'Fucking hell!' she said finally, as she negotiated the dirt track back to the gates. 'Rick Bolton. He's all over the place. He's got no right . . .'

'What? What did he say?' Grace asked.

'He threatened me. Threatened you. Threatened the school.'

'Did the police hear him? Did they step in?'

'Yeah, Pez did. I mean, I get it; Bolton's lost his son. But he should never have been allowed to come down here.'

They were waved through the gates, and Grace felt the relief of finally leaving everything behind: the beach, the police, search and rescue, the stares and conversations. She wanted the drive to last forever now. Just her and Louise. Like they could be heading home from Daylesford again, after a decadent weekend of food and wine and fucking, or from the hot springs down on the Mornington Peninsula.

Louise carried the confrontation with Rick Bolton in the set of her shoulders, her grip on the steering wheel, the way she looked too intently at the road.

'There's stuff I have to tell you,' Louise said, her voice low. 'About what's going on in Melbourne.'

Grace sat back in her seat. 'What stuff?' she asked.

'Stuff you won't want to hear. What did Jim tell you?'

'Just that it's a shitstorm and I shouldn't come back to the school. That I should go home.'

'We lost control of the information right from the start.'

'Jim said some of the boys had phones. I can't believe it. I mean, I know how they did it – handed in old ones and kept their real ones. But what was I supposed to do, frisk them in front of their parents?'

'Don't beat yourself up about it,' Louise said. 'Honestly, if there's one thing I've learned at Finbar's, it's that I'd like to wring the necks of half the parents. Even when they know their boy's in the wrong, they'll still go in to bat for him. And with the phones, it's as much about them needing reassurance from their son as the other way around. Some of them never severed the umbilical cord.'

'So, what am I in for?' Grace asked.

'You know socials as well as I do. There's already a shitload of misinformation.'

As the road ascended into the hills, Grace's phone began to ping again. Still nothing from her dad. She ignored the other messages and missed calls and went straight to Twitter, aware she was ignoring Pez's advice.

Louise took her eyes off the road, slid her hand down and covered the screen of Grace's phone. 'Don't,' she said. 'There's nothing to be gained by looking at that rubbish. And you've got calls to make. Have you rung Colin?'

'I've messaged him,' she said, 'but I'll try calling.'

She opened her contacts, scrolled to her favourites and called her dad. It went straight through to his voicemail. She was relieved not to have to explain herself just yet.

'Hey Dad, it's me. Not sure if you've seen the news but, the boys down at Juliet, the ones who . . .' She paused and drew breath. 'The ones who drowned. I was with them. They were in my class. I know you'll want to come straight up to Melbourne, but just wait. Please. Call me back. Love you.'

Grace turned away from Louise, hit the Twitter icon again and scrolled. It didn't take long to see the story was trending. The oldest tweets were from last night, all thoughts and prayers and offers of condolences to the families, but by this morning the mood had turned.

@davos5792 *Something not right about all this, who was in charge? What happened to duty of care?*

@hyperskye3131 *So many unanswered questions. Someone's gotta be held responsible.*

@distillerybender *Fucking disgrace! This should never have happened.*

@wilsonshack20 *Check this video, it says it all. Guilty as.*

Grace stared in horror at footage from the Channel Seven

helicopter the previous night. In it, sand blasted into the air as she ran down the dune, her arm raised to protect her eyes from the glare of the spotlight. She looked so small, so frightened, so desperate.

'Fuck!' she seethed. 'I was trying to lead them to the car park. You don't know anything.'

Louise pulled Grace's shoulder, forcing her to turn towards her. 'You're right,' she said. 'They don't know. So don't give them the satisfaction. Don't respond. You could block them, but there'll only be more to take their places. Use that brain of yours. Be smarter.'

Grace threw her phone onto the carpet in the footwell. It bounced up and hit the glove box lid.

'Hey,' Louise said. She pulled to the side of the road and switched the motor off. 'Look at me.'

'I can't,' Grace said. Her whole body was shaking. 'I let three boys drown. That's what everyone thinks, isn't it?'

'Please, Gracie.'

Grace kept her chin on her chest but turned to look up at Louise.

'Are you listening?' Louise said. 'We've got three hours to work out a plan. Three hours until we get back to Melbourne. It's going to be awful regardless of what we do, but we've got a choice about how we respond.'

Grace lifted her chin. She could hardly hear what Louise was saying, but she understood one thing. The most important thing. Louise had said *we*.

14

Fiona Knowles sat in her office, eyeing the blanket on the couch and trying to work out if she had slept at all. She desperately needed coffee. She had pulled an all-nighter, having been called back to school after the finance committee meeting, along with the rest of the executive, as the scope of the tragedy unfolded.

Fiona had been deputy principal at St Finbar's for five years. At fifty-two, she knew she would have been a principal by now if she were male. The Catholic system was like that. Once the nuns and brothers had grown too old to run the schools, they had been replaced by men. Some of the girls' colleges had appointed female principals, but the boys' schools remained bastions of masculinity, even when they had more female teachers than male.

She had a good working relationship with Jim Sheridan. He was a strong leader, in a blokey sort of way. Fiona thought they complemented each other well – her with her take-no-prisoners attitude to discipline and student welfare, and him with his easy connection with the staff and boys.

She had a lot less time for the other deputy, Luke Thomas. Fiona struggled to understand how someone with such limited leadership experience had made it to deputy principal. But Luke was an old boy of the school, a former state basketballer and champion athlete, the kind of person that schools like St Finbar's loved to celebrate – and reward. As best Fiona could tell, his skills lay in avoiding responsibility at every turn and disguising his laziness by delegating to those below him while staying on good terms with Jim.

Last night's crisis meeting with the executive team – Jim, Louise Chan, Luke, Minh Tran and Erin, Jim's PA – had been an exercise in futility. Not through any fault of theirs: the story had broken almost before they had sat down in the boardroom. They had an emergency management plan, but it was redundant before they had even had time to read it through.

Minh was the school's legal counsel and parent representative on the executive. He'd just begun to talk about the need to control the information flow when their phones started pinging.

Fiona's was the first to ring.

'Who?' Jim had asked.

'Ally Simpson,' Fiona answered.

'Who's she?' Louise asked.

'Tim Simpson's mum,' Fiona said. 'He's on the trip. I negotiated special conditions for him. He's had three detentions this term. Wasn't supposed to go.'

'What do you think?' Jim asked the group. 'Answer?'

Fiona handed the phone to Jim and nodded. 'Speaker,' she added quickly.

He'd laid the phone flat on the table. 'Hello,' he answered. 'This is Jim Sheridan.'

There was a pause on the line, then a harried voice, 'Is Miss Knowles there, please? It's urgent.'

Fiona had leaned into the phone. 'I'm here, Ally. We're in a meeting of the executive at school. You're on speaker.'

That confused Ally for a few seconds, but then she continued. 'I'm worried, I'm so worried,' she said. 'My son, Tim, he's called me from that trip they're on, the outdoor education one . . .'

Jim froze. He looked around the table. *Fuck*, Luke mouthed.

'He says three boys have drowned. Three boys! I've rung some of the other parents, no one's been told anything. What's going on? Please, we need to know.'

Jim had steepled his fingers and rested them under his chin. He looked to the ceiling, then back to the phone.

'Mrs Simpson – Ally,' he began, 'there's been an incident on the outdoor education trip, but details are still very sketchy. They're in quite a remote area and communications are difficult.'

'But Timmy rang me,' she interrupted. 'He said the boys had drowned.'

'Yes, we've heard that, too,' Jim replied, trying to keep his voice calm. 'But Ally, please, we're waiting on information from the police before . . .'

'*Police!* It's true, isn't it. Three boys, oh my God, oh my God.'

'Ally, please,' he tried again. 'Here's what I want you to do. Are you listening?' He could hear her talking to someone else in the background. 'Ally, are you there?'

The line went dead.

Now, sitting in her office, Fiona checked the online news reports, becoming more alarmed the further she scrolled. The media was on a feeding frenzy, poring over what scant detail the police had released and filling out the rest with conjecture. You knew a journalist was struggling for content when they included Twitter posts in their articles.

Jim had delegated the morning staff briefing to her. The head of the CSD, the Catholic Schools Directorate, had arrived early to meet with Jim, and the police would need to speak with him after that. Fiona had caught up with him briefly after he'd spoken to Grace Disher again. He'd had a couple of minutes to fill her in on the details of what was happening at Juliet.

There were a hundred and ten full-time teachers at St Finbar's, and another twenty part-timers and sessional staff. It was rare that they all met together, but every staff member had been asked to come in today. The hubbub of conversation in the Davidson Room dropped away as Fiona entered. She was confronted by a wall of grief and incomprehension.

Staff held hands; some had arms around shoulders, others were openly crying.

Luke sat at the front, but off to the side, his arms folded across his chest and his eyes on the floor.

Fiona stood at the front with a woman Erin had introduced her to when she arrived – Juanita, from the Headspace counselling team.

Fiona was acutely aware of how much relied on her being able to reassure everyone in the room. They would all gauge how today would go by how she spoke. She had written two words on the sheet in front of her: *clarity* and *purpose*.

'Good morning, everyone,' she said, keeping her voice strong and even. 'This will be a brief meeting. If you could hold any questions until the end, that would be appreciated.

'Three of our year ten students – Jacob Bolton, Roberto Lombardi and Harry Edwards – went missing at Juliet Beach while on the outdoor ed trip that left here on Monday morning. Two bodies have been found this morning. They have not been formally identified, but we believe they are Roberto and Harry.'

A wave of anguish swept the room. There were loud sobs and heavy intakes of breath as confirmation shattered any hope of the news having been exaggerated in the media.

'The rest of the boys in the class, along with Tom, Gerard and Grace, are safe and doing okay. All of them, apart from Grace, spent the night in Wheelers Bay and will be returning to Melbourne around lunchtime. We have arranged for them to go to St Jude's, to avoid the media scrum you will all have seen at the gates when you arrived this morning. The boys' parents will meet them there and take them home.'

Fiona paused to take a sip of water from the glass Erin had left on the table for her. She didn't need a drink, but she wanted to give the staff time to comprehend what she'd told them before she moved on.

'Today is going to be very difficult for all of us, staff and students alike. Jake, Roberto and Harry were part of the St Finbar's family. Many of you will have taught them, coached them or encountered them in other ways. We are all grieving, all hurting, but we have an obligation to our students and their families. This is what makes today, and the weeks ahead, so very hard. Each and every one of us needs to lead. We shouldn't hide our own grief, but we have to be strong for our boys.'

Fiona knew how clichéd she sounded as soon as the words left her mouth. She'd been determined not to fall into the worn phrases they would expect to hear, but who knew the right words to use in a situation like this?

'I'll introduce Juanita from the Headspace counselling team in a minute, but first I want to emphasise the need for structure and routine today. We'll begin with Home Rooms as per normal. The counselling team will set up in the library, and the chapel will be open all day. Encourage the boys to avail themselves, but make it clear it's optional. Of course, these services are there for staff as well. Classes will continue according to the normal timetable apart from period four, when we will all come together in the auditorium for a mass led by

Father Nguyen. At the end of the day, I invite anyone who would like to stay to meet back here for an informal debrief.

'Before I hand over to Juanita, it's important when we leave this room that we turn our focus to the boys. They'll be arriving as we speak. Don't overwhelm them – the usual teachers on duty, plus any who want to support them. Just be there. Be open and supportive.'

Fiona eyed the clock on the back wall. They had ten minutes before Home Room. Lesley Fergus had her hand in the air. Ever since Lesley had been overlooked for a position on the executive, she had found ways to put Fiona on the spot. She'd call it holding her accountable. Fiona called it being a pissed-off meddler.

Reluctantly, Fiona turned to her. 'Yes, Lesley. You have a question?'

Fiona was ready to shut her down if this was about herself and not the pall of grief that had descended on the school.

Lesley stood up. She was a big woman with an imposing presence.

'We've all seen the news,' she began, her eyes roaming around the room. 'And I think we have a right to know the facts.'

'I'm sorry, Lesley,' Fiona interrupted. 'I'm going to stop you there.'

Lesley's eyes widened in mock horror. 'Oh, come on . . .'

'No,' Fiona said firmly. 'We are gathering the facts about the accident and how it happened. Conjecture is very unhealthy at this point.'

'But' Lesley said, puffing herself up and squaring her shoulders, 'our boys, their parents, the whole world has seen the footage of Grace on the beach. She was running away. And it's all over the news that the boys were unsupervised. How do we respond to that?'

Small conversations broke out around the room. Lots of heads nodded.

'The answer,' Fiona said, 'is that we don't respond. The media are guessing. We all know they thrive on tragedies like this. Any, I repeat *any*, conjecture on our parts will only add fuel to that fire.'

She wanted to add *now would you please sit down and shut up*, but she had to content herself with staring Lesley back into her seat. She'd sat for only a moment before she was on her feet again.

'I've spoken to Gerard and Tom this morning,' Lesley said loudly.

Fiona should have expected this, but it caught her by surprise.

Lesley filled the gap. 'Somebody had to support them,' she continued, puffing herself up again.

Fiona's hands clenched into fists by her side before she released them, stretching her fingers and pressing them onto the table in front of her.

'Thank you, Lesley,' she said. 'That was very thoughtful. We'll all need to close our arms around the boys and the staff.'

Lesley hesitated.

'But let me make something absolutely clear.' Fiona paused to emphasise the importance of what she was about to say. She wanted it to sound authoritative without being threatening. 'None of you are to talk to the media, or any families, without speaking first to myself, Luke or Jim. And that extends to social media. I know a lot of you are on Facebook or are part of WhatsApp groups, but I urge you to refrain from commenting there, too.' She knew this was a stretch. Any of them could post anonymously. 'Our focus should be on honouring the boys we've lost, supporting their families and friends. We don't need the added distraction of speculation about how the accident happened.'

It didn't escape Fiona's attention that several staff were now looking at Lesley.

'Jim has spoken to Grace this morning,' she continued. 'And I can assure you the facts are very different to what are being reported.'

Lesley looked around the room, then reluctantly sat down.

'Now, we only have a few minutes,' Fiona continued. 'So, I'm going to hand you over to Juanita Sanchez, who'll quickly speak to you about the counselling available to students and staff today.'

Fiona felt a tap at her elbow. Erin.

'Sorry,' Erin said quietly. 'But I thought you'd want to know. Bruno and Maria Lombardi are here.'

Fiona nodded to Juanita to take over and left the room. Erin walked beside her.

'Jim should talk to them,' Fiona said.

'I told him they were here, but he said he'd be tied up for another half an hour. I didn't think we should keep them waiting.'

Fiona stopped in the middle of the hallway and composed herself. She felt the weight of responsibility building on her shoulders. Especially as Luke was back there in the Davidson Room, sitting on his arse.

'Where are the Lombardis?' she asked.

'I've put them in the interview room.'

'Good. Can you bring coffee?'

'I'm on it.'

Fiona turned down the passageway towards the interview room while Erin headed in the other direction, skipping into a half trot. Fiona stopped for a second, pressed her hands to her diaphragm and took three deep breaths. She had never dealt with anything on this scale before, and she was surprised at how much it was affecting her physically. Lack of sleep wasn't helping either.

Bruno Lombardi was a short, thick-set man in his early fifties. His black curly hair was streaked with grey. Fiona had worked with him on school council and had always found him efficient and organised without being overly friendly. His wife, Maria, who looked several years younger than her husband, was dressed in black. Fiona had only met her briefly at a social function.

They sat on a sagging two-seater couch, hanging onto each other like some great force was trying to pull them apart. They struggled to their feet when Fiona entered the room.

'Bruno, Maria,' Fiona began. 'I'm so sorry this has happened.'

Bruno didn't meet her eyes, but he shook her hand firmly then looked behind her to the doorway.

'Is Jim coming?' he asked pointedly. 'We'd like to speak with Jim.'

'I'm sorry,' Fiona replied. 'He's meeting with the police. I'm sure you understand. He'll be with us as soon as he can.'

Bruno didn't hide his disappointment, but he sat back down on the couch with his wife.

Maria had a set of rosary beads wound around her hands, and she clutched at the cross, rubbing it between her fingers.

Fiona reached over and rested her hand on top of hers.

'Thank you for seeing us,' Maria said, her voice low and broken.

Fiona only needed one look at their eyes to know they hadn't slept since getting the news. Bruno held Maria's arm. On the other side, he braced himself against the couch and tried to sit a little more upright.

Fiona gave them time to collect themselves.

'Thank you for your call last night,' Bruno began. Jim had made the calls to the parents at around nine. 'Please, can you tell us what happened?'

'The police are obviously investigating,' Fiona began. 'And the facts are still unclear. Jim has spoken to the teacher in charge, Grace Disher, this morning. She's still in shock, but he was able to glean some information from her. Could I just say, what's being reported in the media is not only unhelpful, it's wrong.'

Fiona hadn't spoken to the police about what she should and shouldn't tell the families. She didn't know whether they'd been told about the bodies, but she was here now, so she'd just have to feel her way through it.

'I don't trust the news,' Maria said. 'They don't know anything.'

'We've spoken to Daniel,' Bruno said.

The twin, Fiona remembered. *Of course, they would have spoken to Daniel.*

'How is he coping?' she asked.

'He's broken,' Bruno said. 'He told us he feels like he's lost his other half.'

Maria unwound the rosary beads from her hands then rewound them.

Erin arrived with tray of hot drinks and a box of tissues. Smelling the instant coffee, Fiona left her cup on the tray and waited for Erin to leave before continuing.

'We have counsellors from Headspace here today,' Fiona said, wanting to move things along. 'And Father Nguyen will arrive a little later. If you would like to talk to someone . . .'

'The only person we want to talk to,' Bruno said, a sliver of anger creeping into his voice, 'is Grace Disher. We want to know exactly what happened, how it happened. Why were those boys there on their own?'

Fiona raised her hand. 'Sorry, Bruno. I can't imagine how hard this must be for you, but the boys weren't on their own. Grace was on the beach when the boys ran into the water.'

'That's not what Daniel said,' Bruno replied. 'He said the three boys ran ahead and –'

'With all due respect,' Fiona replied firmly. 'Daniel wasn't there when the accident happened. There were just the three boys and Grace.'

Bruno didn't answer. He looked at the floor and shook his head. 'We know they ran ahead,' he said, eventually. 'And they did a stupid, stupid thing.'

'What were they thinking?' Maria said.

Fiona sensed this was a conversation they had had on repeat since last night. The how and the why of senseless loss.

'Bruno. Maria,' Fiona said. 'Can I ask you not to draw conclusions until we are across all the facts? I *know* there was a teacher on the beach when the boys arrived there.'

'Then why did my son drown?' Bruno said loudly, his voice breaking. 'Why was he allowed to die?'

Maria buried her face in her hands. Fiona placed the box of tissues on the couch next to her. The meeting was spiralling, and she needed to pull it back.

'Can I just say . . .' Fiona said, leaning forwards towards the grieving parents. 'I know you want answers, and I promise you I will get them for you.'

'Thank you,' Bruno said, composing himself. 'But no answer will bring our boy back.'

'It's not the same as losing a son,' Fiona said, searching for some common ground. 'But Harry Edwards was Jim's nephew. He understands what you are feeling. His family is grieving, too. And they want answers.'

It was clear Bruno and Maria didn't know of Jim's connection to Harry.

'Oh, I'm so sorry for his loss,' Maria said. The opportunity to extend sympathy to someone else seemed to release some-thing in her.

Bruno and Maria pushed to their feet and arranged their clothes.

'Here's my card,' Fiona said. 'You can contact me at any time.'

Bruno took the card and held it at arm's length, like he needed glasses to read it. Fiona knew he'd be contacting Jim, not her.

'You know the boys will be returning to Melbourne by lunchtime?' Fiona said, immediately wishing she had framed it differently. Not *all* the boys would be returning.

'Yes, we've been told,' Maria said. 'We'll be there to meet Daniel.'

Fiona shook hands with Maria and Bruno and shepherded them to the door. Bruno whispered something to his wife, and she went ahead down the hall. She didn't notice the front desk staff pause their work and watch as the automatic doors closed behind her.

Bruno turned back and blocked Fiona's way. He leaned into her. Fiona was taller and she had to stoop to hear what Bruno was saying.

'If it was negligence that caused our son to die,' he said, 'it won't be a priest or counsellors we'll be talking to. It'll be our lawyer.'

Then he turned his back, shrugged his shoulders like a boxer and followed his wife out into the car park.

15

As they drove away from the coast, through the foothills and into the thick ash and messmate forest, Grace took a notepad from the console, found a pen in the glove box and started to write down everything she could recall. She opened the window a couple of centimetres, allowing the cold mountain air to rush over her. She inhaled deeply, then closed the window, reluctantly casting herself back to the beach, to the boys and the sea that had swallowed them.

Louise drove without disturbing her until they reached the outskirts of Colac. When Grace looked up from her notes, the deep colonnades of the forest were behind them, and the flat farmland stretched across the plain to a horizon shrouded in mist.

'We have to get petrol,' Louise said. 'Do you want something to eat?'

'I haven't been able to hold anything down,' Grace said, her eyes returning to the notepad resting in her lap. She had filled five pages with scribbled notes.

Colac was one of the few towns of its size that hadn't been bypassed by a freeway. The big transports and tourist buses crept through the shopping strip on their way west. Louise turned onto the main street and scanned the shops for a café that looked half decent. The only prospect, a neat place called the Hub, was closed. The bright green sign of a BP station beckoned from the bottom of the hill. She pulled in and drew up to a bowser.

'Might have to be servo coffee and a sausage roll,' Louise said.

'Whatever,' Grace replied, knowing how much Louise hated that response to anything.

As Louise stepped out of the car, closed the door and lifted the nozzle from the bowser, a white station wagon swung in behind them, stopping only inches from the SUV's back bumper. A woman with a phone in her hand stepped out of the front passenger side, and a man with a professional-looking camera emerged from the back door.

'Hey,' Louise called. 'What are you doing?'

They ignored her and moved quickly to Grace's side of the car. The photographer stood close to the window, pushing the lens against the glass.

'What happened at the beach, Grace?' the woman called, holding up her phone, recording. 'How did the boys drown? Were you there, Grace? Why didn't you try to save them?'

Grace was too stunned to do anything other than turn away from the camera. *How did they know her name?* People on the street stopped to watch. A man on the footpath stepped closer, filming with his phone.

The woman from the van pulled open the passenger door and thrust her phone in Grace's face. 'What have you got to say to the parents, Grace?'

It had all happened so quickly that Louise barely had time to respond. Petrol spilled as she fumbled the nozzle back into its slot.

Inside the car, Grace covered her face with her arm and lifted herself over the console into the driver's seat. But the woman pushed closer, firing more questions. Panicked, Grace opened the driver-side door and stepped out. Her boots slipped on the petrol-wet concrete at Louise's feet, and she fell.

The station attendant emerged through the automatic doors and ran towards them. He had one arm in the air. 'Hey,' he called. 'Be careful. You can't do that here.'

Louise picked Grace up off the ground and shielded her from the photographer, who had come around to their side, the staccato shutter of his camera whirring.

Grace pushed away. She ran blindly into the man filming with his phone and knocked him over, then took off along the footpath. Shouting continued behind her but when she looked back, no one was following. She turned into the first street she came to and saw a park that ran along a riverbank on the opposite side. Crossing without looking, she was almost hit by a ute towing a trailer. The driver blasted their horn, coming to a stop centimetres from Grace, who held up both her hands in apology. The driver was a young tradie in a hi-vis shirt. He looked more relieved than angry and waved Grace on.

She sprinted across to the park and took cover behind some low bushes that screened her from the road. A little further along, closer to the riverbank, she found a picnic shelter with a table and a coin-operated barbeque. She slid down behind its brick wall, brought her knees up and buried her face between her thighs. She was trembling again. Sweat trickled down her neck and her breath came in short gasps. Her heart raced.

She wasn't sure how long she waited before she heard Louise calling her name. Grace composed herself as best she could, stood up slowly and peered around the corner of the shelter. Louise was standing by the door of her car.

Grace looked up and down the street then walked across. 'Jesus!' she said, closing the car door behind her.

'I should have picked it,' Louise said. 'They'd been following us. It was the only road into Colac, though. They could have been anyone.'

Grace felt around in the footwell. She reached under the seat, her hands moving frantically.

'What is it?' Louise asked.

'My phone. It's gone.'

'Are you sure?' Louise looked in the console. 'Check again.'

'What happened after I ran?' Grace asked.

'They got in their car and left,' Louise said. 'I put in enough petrol to get us home and went inside to pay. When I walked out, they were gone. But . . .'

'But what?'

'Your door was still open.'

'They took it!' Grace exclaimed. 'They stole my phone.'

'Let's not panic,' Louise said, though she looked panicked.

They both got out of the car, opened the back doors and checked the floor space thoroughly. No phone.

They drove back to the petrol station and looked everywhere, even in the bins. Louise tried calling Grace's number, but they couldn't hear it ringing anywhere close. The call eventually went through to voicemail.

Louise spoke to the attendant, who promised to contact his boss to access the CCTV footage.

'Should we go to the police?' Grace asked, after they had left the petrol station and parked on the main street.

'And tell them what?' Louise replied.

'Exactly what happened! We were ambushed, and that reporter stole my phone.'

'We don't know she took it,' Louise said.

Grace glared at her.

'We'll call Pez,' Louise said. 'Ask him what we should do.'

Grace exhaled heavily and nodded.

The conversation was a short one. Louise put her phone on speaker and relayed the details of what had happened.

'Leave it with me,' Pez said, sounding distracted. 'I'll call it in and see if we can get hold of the CCTV. Don't hang around in Colac, though. Best you get back on the road.'

Reluctantly, Grace and Louise drove out of town towards Melbourne, the road opening out into a two-lane highway that ran between rolling hills to the south and farmland to the north.

They didn't speak for a few minutes. Grace was still trying to work through the consequences of the lost phone. She hadn't heard back from her dad. He must have seen the news by now.

'What's the security like on your phone?' Louise asked, eventually. 'Tell me you have a passcode.'

Grace's eyes stayed fixed on the rolling bitumen of the highway. 'Yeah, of course I do,' she said,

'How random is it?'

Grace didn't answer.

Louise asked again. 'Grace, how random is it?'

Grace stayed silent.

'Tell me it's not your birthday.'

'It's my birthday.'

'Oh, fuck!'

'They can't possibly know it,' Grace said, defensively.

'Your socials, what are your settings? Are they on private?'

'You know I'm only on Twitter and Insta, right?'

'Yeah, I know.'

'Twitter's open slather but my Insta's set to private.'

'Thank Christ for that.'

Grace put her feet up on the dash and buried her chin in the fleece of her jacket.

'What aren't you telling me?' Louise asked.

Grace hesitated. 'I never shut down my old Facebook account. I haven't used it for years, but it's still up.'

'And?'

'There might be posts from birthdays when I was a teen.'

Louise took a few seconds to process this. 'So, it won't take Sherlock Holmes to work out your date of birth.'

'What can we do?' Grace asked.

'Here,' Louise handed her phone to Grace. 'Start with your bank details. Lock your accounts.'

Grace took the phone.

'What's your passcode?' Grace asked.

Louise grimaced.

'It's your birthday, isn't it?' Grace said, tapping the date into the phone. Her hands were shaking. She couldn't remember her banking password. Numbers and letters streamed through her head. She knew all the fuss about internet security but usually fell back on familiar passwords. The third attempt worked, and she put a freeze on her accounts.

'Okay, what's next?' she asked.

'You've got Find My Phone?'

'Yep, of course.'

'I think you can disable your phone without wiping everything.'

Grace's fingers fumbled with Louise's phone, almost dropping it.

'I need my iCloud password for that.'

'And?'

'I'm not sure what it is. I've tried three. It'll lock me out.'

'Okay. Close down all your socials, then.'

'Why do I have to shut them down?' Grace had logged into her Twitter account.

'If they get into your phone, they can hit the app and post as you.'

'Shit, I hadn't thought of that.' Grace's fingers worked the screen for a few seconds, then she stopped. 'Photos,' she said. 'They'll have all my photos. All *our* photos.'

'Jesus.' Louise puffed her cheeks and exhaled. 'What's on there?'

'Everything. The Daylesford weekend. Sydney at Easter. Joel and Amara's wedding.'

'Is there anything . . . compromising?'

'Not that I can think of.'

'Nothing you took without me knowing?'

Grace turned her head to the side and looked out the window. 'A couple,' she said, quietly. 'But they're in a secure folder.'

'What are they of?' Louise demanded.

'You were asleep. At your place. You looked so . . . fuck, I don't know why I took them, but I did.'

'Could anyone tell it's me?'

'Not unless they recognise the mole at the bottom of your back.'

Louise thumped the steering wheel. 'Okay,' she said, after a while. 'Let's think this through. They have photos of us together. As a couple. What else could they use?'

'Like what?' Grace asked.

'Pics of your place or mine. Anything that might identify where we live.'

Grace had a sudden sense of falling, of not being able to control the rolling disaster her life had become in the last twenty-four hours. Everything was crowding for space in her head: the deep, dark grief at losing the boys and the horror of watching them die; the helicopters *foomp-foomp*ing overhead; the questions, the endless, relentless questions; the cameras shoved in her face. And now Louise was going to be dragged into it, too.

'Pull over,' Grace cried. 'Pull over!'

Louise checked the rear-view mirror and crossed lanes before easing into the gravel.

Grace had the door open before the car stopped. Louise grabbed her arm, but she shook free. Grace scrambled out, stepped over the roadside barrier and crossed the verge to a low wire fence. She was moving fast and tried to jump it, but the top strand caught her boot and she fell into the paddock, sprawled in the wet grass.

Louise got out of the car and stood at the barrier. There was nowhere Grace could go that she couldn't be seen. The paddock stretched away towards a railway embankment, its iron stanchions marching parallel to the road.

Grace rose onto her knees and pounded the ground with her fists again and again. She screamed long and loud into the empty morning air.

Cars flew by on the highway.

Louise waited.

Eventually, Grace climbed to her feet and brushed herself down. Her clothes were wet, and they smelled of fertiliser and petrol. She turned and looked towards Louise, who was no more than twenty metres away.

Grace opened her arms, like she was preparing for cruci-fixion. 'Go,' she yelled. 'Leave me. You don't need this. Everything is my fault. I should have gone in after them. I failed them. I should have drowned, too.' She stood, arms stiff, waiting for Louise to say something.

'Are you finished?' Louise called.

Grace shook her head. 'It's not only the boys I lost. It's mum, too. That was our special place, the last place I remember her as whole person before the cancer started to eat at her. And now I can't go back there.'

Her hands fell to her sides.

Louise walked calmly to the fence and beckoned Grace to her. 'Come on,' she said. 'This is getting us nowhere.'

Grace trudged through the ankle-high grass and took the hand Louise offered. 'I don't deserve you,' she whispered.

A cattle truck blasted its horn, making them both jump. The bulk of its trailer sucked at the air, buffeting their car and leaving the stink of cow shit in its wake.

'That seems apt,' Louise said.

Grace's lips formed a grim smile.

They walked arm in arm to the car. Inside, they sat for a minute without speaking.

'Can we make a deal?' Louise said, finally.

'What sort of deal?'

'No matter what happens, we stick together. We don't turn on each other.'

'That's a bit of a one-sided deal, don't you reckon?' Grace said. 'I'm the one they're coming after. You don't need to be involved.'

Louise leaned over and slid her hand behind Grace's neck, pulling her gently towards her. Tears ran down Grace's face, and Louise kissed them away.

'I guess we knew we couldn't stay a secret forever,' Louise said.

'You could lose your job,' Grace said.

'I doubt it would come to that. But if the media gets hold of the stuff on your phone, I'll be outed with you.'

'Deny everything. It's nothing compared to what's going to be thrown at me. And it's irrelevant.'

'No, it's not, babe. They'll dig into every aspect of your life. Being gay has nothing to do with what happened at Juliet, but they'll find a way to use it against you.'

'Jesus,' Grace said.

'Jesus, indeed.'

'No, I mean . . .'

'What?'

'If they go digging, there's something else they might find.'

Louise let go of Grace and leaned her back against the driver's door, creating distance between them. 'What?' she asked again.

'Perth,' Grace said, and exhaled slowly.

'Perth?'

'I never got around to telling you what happened there. Why I left.'

'Go on. I'm listening.'

'I'm sorry. I should have told you.' Grace stared through the windscreen. 'There was' – she paused, her chest tight again – 'an incident at my old school.'

Louise said nothing.

'A boy made an allegation against me. It was a complete fucking lie.' She raced to get the words out. 'He was in year eleven, a big strong kid, a footballer. I remember how he stank of sweat. I'd failed him on an assignment, and he waited back after class. It was a set-up. His mates guarded the door outside, and he moved in close to me, wanting to know why I had marked him so hard. I backed up against the whiteboard, but he kept coming closer – so I pushed him away. He claimed later that I'd tried to put my hand inside his shirt.'

'That's it? That's all it was?' Louise asked. 'Your word against his.'

'His parents took it to the principal,' Grace continued. 'She stood by me, but you know what schools are like. Pretty soon everyone knew about it – kids, teachers, parents. I was the young, female teacher hot for the boys. By the end of the year the principal said it would be best if I' – she made air quotes with her fingers – 'looked for another opportunity.'

'And then the job was advertised at Finbar's.'

Grace nodded.

Louise shook her head. 'They may not find out. The media, I mean. I think we keep this to ourselves and hope no one digs that deep.'

'Should we tell Jim about us, though?' Grace asked.

'I think we should. It's going to come out, and it's best he hears it as soon as possible.' As Louise turned the key to start the motor, her phone buzzed in its cradle. Jim's name lit up on the screen.

'Speak of the devil,' Louise said, then touched the button

on the steering wheel to accept the call. 'Hi Jim. You're on speaker here. I'm with Grace.'

There was a pause at the other end. 'Okay,' Jim said, eventually. 'Where are you now?'

'Just the Melbourne side of Colac.' Louise eased back out onto the highway and floored the accelerator once the tyres hit the bitumen.

'Grace. How are you?' Jim asked.

'I'm okay.' She leaned towards the phone as she spoke, conscious her voice sounded small against the thrum of the engine.

Louise glanced at Grace, then back at the road. 'We had a bit of an incident in Colac,' she said.

'What sort of incident?' There was a weariness to his voice Grace hadn't heard on their call earlier.

Louise explained what had happened at the petrol station.

'Okay, so you've lost your phone,' Jim said matter-of-factly.

'No. They *took* the phone,' Grace said. 'And they'll have access to what's on it.'

'Sorry,' Jim said. 'But that doesn't sound like a big deal right now.'

'Actually, it *is* a big deal, Jim,' Louise said. 'There's something you need to know.'

WEDNESDAY 24 MAY 11.00AM

SCHOOL IN SHOCK AFTER STUDENTS DROWN ON CAMP

Police have confirmed two sixteen-year-old boys from St Finbar's College in Darebin have drowned at a remote beach in south-west Victoria yesterday. A third boy is missing, presumed dead.

The students were taking part in a school excursion along the Great Western Walk as part of their outdoor education course. The boys, whose names have not yet been released, became separated from the main group of students and teachers on Tuesday afternoon.

Police Search and Rescue recovered two bodies from the water before 8am this morning. Senior Sergeant Mario Pezzementi, who is coordinating the rescue operation, said search efforts had been focused on the coast to the west and east of Juliet Beach this morning in the hope that the third boy may have made it back to shore. However, hopes for his survival are fading. 'It is unlikely a swimmer could have survived in the water any longer than half an hour,' he said. 'The water is very cold and the seas on Tuesday afternoon were extremely rough.'

The Principal of St Finbar's, James Sheridan, said the school was in shock. 'Each of these young men was a valued member of our school community, and our thoughts and prayers are with their families and friends as we try to come to terms with this tragedy. These boys had their whole lives in front of them. We are offering support to the families and to our students and teachers.'

Sergeant Pezzementi also said police were concerned at

conjecture on social media about the circumstances surrounding the boys' deaths.

'This sort of speculation – including the naming of the teachers involved – is uninformed and dangerous.'

He said the trip had been well organised and that the teachers were cooperating fully with police.

The ABC has chosen not to name the female teacher in charge of the camp. Footage from a Channel Seven helicopter, aired last night, appears to show her running away from the site of the drownings.

The State Coroner will travel to Juliet Beach this afternoon.

16

Grace lapsed in and out of sleep. Louise had the radio on a low murmur, but it didn't escape Grace's attention that she turned it off whenever the news bulletins approached. As they crested the West Gate Bridge, Grace brought her seat upright and looked out across the docks and the Yarra River, its muddy water pluming into the Bay after the rain. A huge cruise ship was docked at Station Pier, and the sails of half a dozen yachts caught the sun further up towards St Kilda.

Everything looked exactly as it should in the city she had called home since her return from Perth at the beginning of the year. The traffic slowed by never-ending roadworks, the office towers on the skyline reflected the early afternoon sun. For everyone else, life went on just as it had yesterday and the day before, and its humdrum routines tugged at Grace. A car passed as they descended the bridge; a woman driving with two kids in booster seats in the back. Grace watched as the mother talked over her shoulder to the children and handed one a juice pack. Why did such a simple action now seem like the most beautiful and graceful thing she had ever seen? She wanted to be her, to hide in that woman's life for a while: drive to her home, unpack the shopping, feed the kids and watch them play in the backyard. She could almost picture the house somewhere in the snug eastern suburbs: big front lawn, a dog like in those paint ads and fruit trees.

'You alright?' Louise asked as she shifted lanes to exit onto the Bolte Bridge.

Grace was pulled back into the shambles of her own life. She shook her head.

'I was thinking,' Louise said, 'we should go to school and pick up your car. We can park a couple of blocks away to avoid the media. I'll take your keys and you drive my car home.'

'The laptop's in my car. Can you give it to Jim?' Grace asked.

'Sure.'

Grace picked up Louise's phone. 'Do you have Gerard's number?' she asked.

Louise nodded. 'I put it in this morning before I left. Tom's, too.'

Grace wasn't sure she wanted to talk to Tom. He hadn't been as supportive as Gerard back at Juliet, more concerned about getting his story straight than looking out for the boys.

She thought the number was going to ring out, but eventually Gerard answered. 'Hello,' he said, tentatively.

'Gerard. It's Grace.'

'Sorry,' he said. 'I didn't recognise the number.'

Grace could hear traffic noise in the background. He was on speaker. 'Long story,' she said. 'How are the boys?'

'We dropped them at St Jude's. Their parents were all there. Robbie's mum and dad . . .' He struggled to keep himself together. His voice wavered. 'Jesus, Grace, how did this happen? How did we end up here?'

Grace had already pictured the scene in her mind. Distraught parents holding their sons, relieved but feeling survivor's guilt at their boy returning safely while the Lombardis collected two backpacks, but only one of their twins. Boys being shepherded away to waiting cars. Counsellors hovering. St Jude's girls looking on from a distance.

Grace didn't have an answer for Gerard's questions. 'Where are you now?' she asked.

He paused for a few seconds, gathering himself. 'On my way home. Tom's with me. I'm dropping him off.'

'Hello, Grace.' Tom's voice sent a brief shiver through her.

'Tom,' she said, trying not to sound surprised. 'How are you doing?'

It was Gerard who answered. 'We just want to get home, Grace. Talk soon, eh?'

'Of course, yeah. Look after yourselves.'

The line went dead.

Neither of them had asked how she was coping.

★

Grace didn't like driving Louise's SUV; its bulk was completely unsuited to the inner suburbs, with their narrow streets and tight roundabouts. She hit the gutter a couple of times as she wound her way home through the back streets of Flemington, praying she wouldn't sideswipe a parked car. Grimshaw Avenue was a one-way street that led to the train station. It was always hard to find a park. Grace eased into the kerb fifty metres from her front gate and sat for a while to survey the street. It seemed quiet, but she'd been spooked by what had happened in Colac and wanted to make sure no one was going to ambush her again. She grabbed a hoodie of Louise's off the back seat and pulled it on, left her pack in the car and began walking towards her house. It was rubbish collection day, and the footpath was a maze of bins. She wound her way through them, checking over her shoulder to make sure she wasn't being followed. As she approached her gate a dark van slowed, keeping pace with her.

She jumped when the driver spoke.

'Excuse me,' he said. He was young, twenty-ish, clean-shaven.

Grace ignored him and kept walking, past her own gate, towards the laneway three doors down. She pulled the hoodie up to cover her face.

'Hey,' he called again. 'I've got a delivery for number twenty-two.'

That was her house.

'Is that you? Grace Disher?'

'Nah, sorry,' she said, trying to sound casual.

The guy didn't respond as Grace turned into the laneway. Her heart was pounding but she kept her pace even, unaffected.

She leaned down to pick a small flower growing up through the cobblestones and ventured a look back to the street as she came up. The van had stopped, the driver watching her. There was a back entrance to her place off the intersecting alleyway ahead. She just needed to get around the corner before the van tried to follow. The afternoon sun reflected off the corrugated iron fences. She was overdressed and sweating. Finally, she reached the corner, breaking into a run as soon as she was out of the driver's sight.

Grace fumbled with the gate. There was an old combination bike lock looped between two holes in the corrugated iron. *1960.* The year her dad was born. She hadn't used it in months, and it was stiff with dirt and rust.

The van must have turned into the laneway. She could hear it approaching the corner.

'Come on!' she seethed. 'Fucking open.'

Finally, it snapped apart and Grace pushed her shoulder into the gate. The bottom of the frame scraped on the concrete, but it opened enough for her to squeeze through. She leaned all her weight against it while she threaded the lock back into place.

The van had stopped outside the gate.

'Grace,' the man called over the sound of the engine. 'We just want to talk to you.'

'We're on your side, Grace.' A woman's voice this time. 'We want to give you the chance to tell your version of the story, okay?' A hand reached through the hole in the gate, holding a card. 'We'll pay, Grace. Ten thousand for the exclusive. *A Current Affair.* Prime time. We can do it here if you like.

Or in the studio. What do you say? A chance to set the record straight. They're saying terrible things about you, you know. That you let the boys drown.'

Grace had her back to the gate. She put her hands to her ears and pressed. 'Go away,' she yelled. 'Please. Just go away.'

'No one's going away, Grace.' It was the man now. 'Three boys have died on your watch. The public's got a right to know what happened. And the parents. Have you spoken to them?'

'Are you okay, Grace?' Vic Spinoza, her next-door neighbour, stuck his head over the side fence. 'What's goin' on?'

'Can you help me?' Grace pleaded. 'Please?'

Vic was a former boxer, built like a brick shithouse. He and his wife, Thel, were forever giving Grace fruit from their trees. Now, he lowered himself awkwardly over their shared fence and into Grace's yard.

'I don't want them here,' Grace said pointing at the gate. 'Can you get rid of them?'

'She's big news, mate. Best not to get involved,' the man called from the alleyway. 'We just want to talk to her, that's all.'

Grace shook her head. Vic nodded and climbed onto a crate to look over the gate.

'Right,' he said. 'Fuck off. Or I'll call the cops. But not before I come down there and shove that camera up your arse.'

'Alright, mate, no need to get narky,' the man said. 'We're going, we're going.'

'You've got my card, Grace' the woman called. 'Ring me any time. And remember what I said. Ten grand is a lot of money.'

'I won't tell you again,' Vic said, making as though he was going to climb over the gate.

Grace heard the van doors close and the rumble of the engine as it took off.

'Are you okay, love?' Vic asked.

She looked at him. Vic was shorter than Grace. His wide shoulders and boxer's nose made him look more dangerous than he probably was, now that he was in his mid-sixties. Still, Grace thought his first half a dozen punches would be lethal.

'Have you seen the news?' Grace asked, leaning hard against the gate.

'Don't watch that shit,' Vic replied. 'But Thel saw it on *The Morning Show.* I'm so sorry, love. What can we do to help?'

'Shoving that bloke's camera up his arse would have been a good start,' Grace half joked.

'They got no right,' Vic said. Grace saw something flicker in his eyes, maybe the memory of standing toe-to-toe with an old opponent.

'I'll be okay, now that I'm home. Thanks, Vic.'

Grace could feel the pull of a hot shower, the comfort of familiar smells and carpet warm under her feet. She'd been in the open too long, too long under the gaze of strangers, too long being asked questions she didn't have answers to.

'You're sure?' Vic asked. 'I could stand guard out the front. I've got nothing else on today.'

Grace gave him a cursory hug. 'I'll be fine.'

Vic nodded towards the fence that separated their properties. 'Do I have to climb that again?'

Grace had forgotten herself. 'No, of course not. Come through.' She lifted the pot by the back door to retrieve the key and let herself into the house.

Vic followed, assessing the place as he walked down the passage to the front. 'You should get onto the landlord about those stumps,' he said. 'The place leans like a ship.'

'Sure, Vic,' Grace said wearily. 'I'll do that.'

She opened the front door and Vic stepped out to check the street. No one rushed at them. No car screeched to a halt, spilling photographers onto the footpath.

'All clear,' he said. 'Sing out if you need anything.'

Grace summoned the energy to nod before she closed the door and slumped against the wall. The hallway was dark, but light shone through from the kitchen. She couldn't remember when she'd last eaten or when she'd last vomited; the two had become one and the same in her mind. It was as though all the signals she needed to stay alive had been muted, numbed by grief. She lifted her top to run a fingertip along the ridge of her appendix scar, to reassure herself she was still Grace, still the same woman who'd walked out the front door on Monday, excited about the trip ahead.

Louise would be here soon, but Grace wasn't even sure that's what she wanted. Maybe she needed time on her own, without the pressure of being watched and assessed and asked how she was feeling. Her pack was still in the car, and she'd have to get it at some stage, but for now she pushed herself off the wall and tried to stand upright. She corrected her posture, pushing her shoulders back until she heard the familiar crack in her spine.

Then she rolled her neck to free the kink from it, threaded her fingers and stretched her hands above her head. Feeling slightly looser, she walked down the hall to the kitchen. The cereal bowl from Monday morning's breakfast was still in the sink, crusted with dried muesli.

Grace knew she should eat, but the familiar ritual of making coffee, even if she couldn't drink it, was calling. She flicked the switch on the grinder and pushed the button on the coffee machine. The smell of ground beans filled the kitchen. She packed the portafilter, tamped it hard and slotted it into the head. It felt good not to have to think, to do something that was entirely muscle memory. The dark brown crema trickled into the cup.

The backyard faced north, and it was now filled with afternoon sunshine. Grace opened the door and stepped outside. She had found the small wrought iron table and chairs on a hard rubbish night the previous month and positioned them near the back door to make the most of the light. The chairs weren't particularly comfortable, but they forced her to sit upright, not to slump. The concrete yard was filled with potted plants and herbs. Everything was moveable, to suit the transient life of the inner-city renter. She and Louise had talked about moving in together, but Grace didn't mind having a little bit of geography between them. It gave her space to breathe. And she liked her own company.

The coffee was strong, with just a dash of milk. She looked at it, steaming on the table in front of her, and hoped she could hold it down. All day, her body had betrayed her when she needed it to be strong. Her muscles ached for no reason. She hadn't done anything more strenuous than walk the length of Juliet Beach with Sarah. But the lack of sleep and food was catching up with her. She needed more than coffee, but that would mean cutting, toasting and buttering bread, and all that would require energy.

The coffee swooped through her. She almost gagged but swallowed hard and breathed deeply through her nose to keep it down. When the cup was empty and she hadn't vomited, she felt a tiny sense of achievement. Only then did she allow herself to think, to worry again. The last forty-eight hours spooled through her mind like a movie. She didn't want a part in this film, but there she was, front and centre, in every shot.

And there, too, were Jake, Robbie and Harry, glowing in the full flush of youth, their bodies lithe and strong, their smiles broad at the prospect of the future. Grace wanted to reach out to them, hold them, reassure them. Apologise to them. Grief and failure melded together in her mind to form a block she couldn't see past.

Grace leaned her elbows on the hard metal table and ran her hands through her hair. It was knotted and ropey. She scratched at her scalp and felt granules of sand catch under her fingernails. Right at that minute – and she realised she was living minute to minute – her most overriding need was for a shower. When she stood, she was overcome by dizziness and had to grab the table's edge for balance. She left the coffee cup on the table and went inside.

The bathroom floor was uneven, the lino tiles unable to hide the slump in the foundations. Grace shed her clothes and piled them in the corner. She didn't want to look at herself in the mirror, but there was no avoiding it. Her hair stood on end like a scarecrow's, and her face was drawn and lined in places it hadn't been on Monday morning. She consciously drew her shoulders back again, but her spine refused to yield another crack.

There were bruises on her upper arms. She remembered Tom's vice-like grip when he had grabbed her on the beach.

She reached over the bath to turn on the taps. The pipes let out a groan and shuddered inside the wall before the water began to flow. As it warmed, Grace stepped in and turned her face up to the shower rose. Without deciding to do so, she eased down into the bath and curled her knees up to her chest, feeling the steady stream cascade over her body – and she wept. As much as she tried, she couldn't fend off the waves of guilt that now assailed her. No one had said it out aloud – not Gerard or Heaney or Pez – but they were all thinking the same thing. She had a duty of care to protect Jake and Robbie and Harry, even from themselves. She had been scared and alone, but she hadn't even tried.

Grace didn't know how long she sat there, but eventually she climbed to her feet. She quickly washed her hair, then took a bar of soap and scrubbed at her skin, leaning over to clean the sand and dirt from her legs. Her body felt heavy in a way it never had before. She made the effort to stand upright again and rinse the conditioner from her hair.

Turning the taps off, she pushed the shower curtain aside. Her reflection was muted by condensation on the mirror. She didn't wipe it with the towel, preferring the image of the ghost woman she had become since the accident. She dried herself quickly, tied her hair in a turban with the towel and walked naked down the hallway to her bedroom. The unmade bed beckoned. She had slept poorly in the tent and sporadically on the trip back to Melbourne with Louise. Fatigue overwhelmed every muscle in her body, but still she wasn't sure she could sleep. She regretted the coffee.

She freed her hair from the towel, dried it a little more then slipped between the sheets and pulled the doona up to her chin. Instinctively, she drew herself into the fetal position and closed her eyes. She expected the movie of yesterday to begin its relentless spooling again, but behind her eyes there was only black. Blessed, empty black.

17

In the semi-conscious zone between sleep and wakefulness, Grace felt a hand on her skin. A slow, familiar caress. The tips of soft fingers touched the side of her face.

'Hey,' Louise whispered.

Grace rolled towards the warmth of the hand and allowed it to brush against her hair.

'Sorry,' Louise said. 'But you need to get up now. There's someone here.'

Grace rubbed her eyes, bringing the room into focus. 'What time is it?' she asked. She had no memory of falling asleep. The room was dark but for a sliver of light coming under the door from the hallway. She felt the weight of Louise sitting on the bed.

'Seven thirty,' Louise said.

'Morning or night?' Grace wanted to believe she had slept for fifteen hours.

'Evening,' Louise said.

'Who's here?' Grace asked.

'Fiona, the DP from school.'

'Why is she here so late?'

'She's checking in on you, Grace. It's what they do.'

Grace switched on the bedside lamp, pushed the covers back and stood up. She was still naked, and her hair fell in clumps over her face.

Louise reached out and touched her bare hip. 'You might need to tidy yourself up a bit, babe.'

In any other circumstance, any other time during the few short months they'd been together, Grace would have teased her, taking her hand and placing it between her legs or pushing her body against Louise's and kissing her. But tonight, she stumbled to the wardrobe and pulled out a pair of tracksuit pants and a windcheater. She drew her hair into a ragged ponytail and found a tie on the dresser to hold it in place. Leaning closer to the mirror, she rubbed at her face as if that might make her more recognisable to herself.

'This is going to be . . .' Grace began.

'Uncomfortable?' Louise finished the sentence for her. 'Yeah, I know. But we're out now, you and me. Fiona knows.'

Grace reached out to hold her hand.

'Come on,' Louise said, gently leading her into the hallway. 'Let's get this over with.'

Grace hadn't had a great deal to do with Fiona Knowles since arriving at St Finbar's. They were on the staff welfare committee together, so Grace knew she was a stickler for detail, always prepared, always persuasive. Maybe that's why Jim had sent her instead of coming himself. Then Grace remembered that his family would be dealing with their own grief.

Louise was on the executive with Fiona. While she and Grace had a tacit policy of not bringing their work home, it was almost impossible not to when they both taught at the same school, so Grace knew Louise didn't have a high opinion of Fiona. She found her too driven, too hard, thought she'd lost connection with the kids by not having a teaching load on top of her admin duties.

Fiona was dressed for work. Grace guessed she hadn't been home yet. It would have been a long twenty-four hours for her, too.

'Hello, Grace,' Fiona said, extending her hand then pulling her into a short, awkward embrace. 'How are you holding up?'

'Ah, you know . . .' was all Grace could say. She wanted to gauge the tenor of the meeting before she gave anything away about how she might be coping.

Louise put the kettle on without asking whether anyone wanted tea. It was too late for coffee. Grace sat opposite Fiona at the kitchen table, an old Laminex top on uncertain metal legs. Grace had chocked one side with folded cardboard, to keep the surface even.

Fiona reached for the bag at her feet, a slim leather briefcase, and pulled out a notebook. She opened it at a page with a series of dot points.

'Jim would have come himself,' Fiona began, 'but his family needs him tonight.'

'I understand,' Grace said.

'It's a very difficult time for him.'

Most of what Grace had been dealing with since the accident had been focused on the boys: the panic, the searching, the police, the bodies in the chopper. But now, with the benefit of distance and a few hours' sleep, she could see more clearly the ripple effect of those few catastrophic minutes on the beach at Juliet. The families, the parents, the brothers and sisters, uncles, aunts, friends: everyone who knew the boys. Jim included.

'Is there any news from Juliet?' Grace asked. 'Have they found . . . anything more?'

'We've had police liaison at school all day,' Fiona said, 'and they've kept us updated. When I left half an hour ago, they hadn't been able to locate Jacob's body. They're not hopeful of finding him now.'

Grace held tight to the edge of the table. As much as she tried not to, she couldn't help but think of Jake floating in the cold sea. It had been a small mercy that Roberto and Harry had been found so quickly, before they were too damaged, before the sea and its creatures *got to* them. The man she'd overheard at the toilets said a shark had been sighted. Grace could almost hear the tearing of flesh, see the plume of blood in the water. She thought of the woman in Sydney a few years ago who'd been identified by a foot in a shoe, washed up on a beach. In that moment, she hoped Jake wouldn't be found.

Grace let go of the table as Fiona continued. 'I'm here first and foremost to make sure you are okay and to reassure you of the school's support.'

Grace thought it sounded as though Fiona had practised this bit. Her voice wasn't warm or empathetic, even though she was probably aiming for that tone. It was a little too clipped, formal.

'Thanks,' Grace replied, still wary of where this might be going.

'Beyond that . . .' Fiona said.

We moved beyond that pretty quickly, Grace thought.

'Beyond that, we are obviously dealing with grieving parents, the police, the media, the coroner and the whole student cohort. This is a massive blow for the St Finbar's community. We have excellent support from the CSD and from Headspace and we're coping as best we can, but we've been besieged today. The media has been ahead of us all the way. Louise told me what happened at the petrol station in Colac and that Jake's father travelled down to Juliet. I'm sorry. That should never have been allowed to happen.'

'The media were here when I got home, too,' Grace said.

'What?' Louise was aghast. She placed cups of tea in front of Grace and Fiona and sat down at the table. 'How . . .?'

'I don't know,' Grace said. 'But they were here.'

'Bastards,' Louise said.

Fiona looked around, as though there might be cameras

prying through the window from the backyard. 'I'll let the police know,' she said.

'What can they do?' Grace said. 'We've all seen it on the news a thousand times. Media camped outside some poor victim's house while they hole up inside.'

She hadn't meant to say *victim*.

Fiona didn't seem to notice. 'Let's not confuse the movies with real life, Grace,' she said.

'Easy for you to say. They're not ambushing you at every turn.' Grace replied, a little too sharply. 'They offered me ten thousand dollars for an interview.'

'They don't waste any time, do they?' Fiona couldn't hide her surprise. 'Of course, you can't do it. Promise me you won't.'

Grace nodded.

'Okay,' Fiona continued. 'We need to find you somewhere else to stay for a few days, at least until the media attention dies down. Do you have family in Melbourne?'

'She can come to mine,' Louise said.

'Yes. Um . . .' Fiona flicked over a page in her notebook. 'Jim told me about your conversation this morning. That you two are in a relationship.' She closed her notebook and spread her fingers on the tabletop. 'This is an added complication.'

'It has nothing to do with the school,' Louise said.

Fiona took her time to answer. 'Of course, you are entitled to your private lives, and I want you to know we respect that.'

'But?' Grace said.

'But we are dealing with a tragedy,' Fiona replied. 'And with the media, nothing will be off limits.' She paused then, dropping her gaze to the tabletop as though embarrassed about what she going to say. 'Not to mention the parents, who have an expectation we employ staff that reflect our Catholic values.'

Grace pushed back from the table. 'So,' she said, cautious now not to sound too aggressive, 'does that apply to all the staff? The maths teacher having an affair. What about him? And the cleaner with an AVO out against him?'

Fiona tried not to react, but her eyes gave her away. 'Anyway,' she said eventually, 'we've spoken to representatives from the diocese today . . .'

'About us?' Grace interjected. 'About Lou and me?'

'I'll put this to you bluntly, Grace,' Fiona said, clearly growing impatient. 'We have an entire management strategy, but the fact that you two have kept your relationship secret has thrown a spanner in the works.'

'A spanner in the works!' Grace exclaimed. 'Jesus, Fiona. How about you start thinking of something other than the school's reputation? Three boys have died, and you're worried about two of your staff being gay?'

Louise squeezed Grace's arm. The kitchen fell quiet. Fiona looked at her hands.

Grace thought about apologising, but decided against it.

'You've had a tough couple of days, Grace,' Fiona said quietly. 'You should talk to the counsellors – in fact, we insist you do. We've got to deal with the situation head on. We can't be seen to be hiding or obfuscating.'

'What about Tom and Gerard?' Grace asked. 'Are you saying the same to them?'

'We spoke to them when they arrived at St Jude's this afternoon.'

'And . . .?' Grace asked.

'They'll come into school tomorrow. And we'd like you to do the same. We can arrange for everything to be dealt with there. Police, counsellors, the CSD. Honestly, Grace, we are with you every step of the way.'

'And tonight?' Grace asked.

'If the media know you are here, you should go to Louise's place,' Fiona said. 'It'll be safer.'

'What about the cameras outside the school tomorrow?' Louise said. 'They were feral today.'

'We've got security on every gate, but the media are mostly out the front, on Grant Street. Go to the Fitzgerald Road entrance, the one that leads to the sports ovals. Park by the pavilion and walk up from there.'

'What time?' Grace asked.

'First thing. Before the students arrive.'

'Okay.'

Fiona stood up to leave. Grace kept the table between them. She didn't want another half-hearted hug.

'I'll see you in the morning,' Fiona said.

Louise walked her down the hallway, and they had a short conversation just out of Grace's hearing. When they opened the front door, a riot of flashing lights burst through. Cameras. Louise closed the door quickly and retreated to the kitchen, with Fiona following.

'Where did they come from?' Fiona exclaimed.

'I told you,' Grace said, unable to hide the smugness in her voice. 'Just like the movies, huh?'

Louise rolled her eyes. 'There's a time and a place, Gracie.'

'There's a back entrance onto the alleyway,' Grace said. She quite liked the idea of Fiona being chased along the cobblestones in her heels.

'We should all get out of here,' Louise said, ever the organised one. 'Grab what you need, and we'll work out how we do it.'

Grace nodded and left them in the kitchen. She slid out of her windcheater and trackpants and dressed for a quick exit in black jeans, t-shirt and puffer jacket. She grabbed her runners from under the bed and pulled them on. Then she threw some less casual gear into a bag – clothes for the sessions with counsellors and police tomorrow – and headed back to the kitchen.

Fiona was on a call, while Louise was checking the backyard.

'Good news,' Fiona said, hanging up. 'The Colac police have found your phone.'

'Where?' Grace asked.

'A kid handed it in. Found it on her way to school.'

'Had anyone got into it?' Grace asked. 'I mean, accessed anything? Did the police say?'

'The kid was ten. Came in with her mother. Seems unlikely.'

'Is the SIM still in it?' Grace asked.

Fiona shrugged, her frustration growing. 'I don't know. We've only just heard from the police. They're sending it back to school. It should be there tomorrow.'

'Okay,' Louise said, coming back into the kitchen. 'The alleyway is clear. Let's make a run for it.'

'Are you sure?' Grace asked. 'They knew about it this afternoon.'

'Here's what we'll do,' Fiona said. 'I'll go out the front door, make some bland statement to keep them distracted, while you two exit out the back.'

'We'll have to go the long way around to your car,' Grace said to Louise. 'Do a lap of the block and get to it from the other end of Grimshaw.'

Without waiting for agreement, Fiona marched to the front door, opened it and stepped outside, pulling it closed behind herself.

Louise reached inside her bag, which was sitting on the kitchen bench. 'Here,' she said, handing Grace her laptop.

'Thank you,' Grace replied, feeling as though part of her life had been restored. 'Did you show it to Jim?'

'I uploaded the trip forms on the server myself. That's all they wanted.' Louise didn't look at Grace as she spoke.

'What?' Grace asked, sensing something more.

'Nothing,' Louise replied.

'Don't do this, Lou,' Grace said. 'We stick together. Isn't that what we agreed?' She stood in front of Louise now, holding her gaze.

'Come on, we have to go,' Louise said, shepherding Grace towards the back door.

Grace pushed her away.

Louise took a deep breath and exhaled. 'We backdated them,' she said.

'You what?'

'Jim said it would be best.'

'Jim said! Since when did Jim get you to lie for him?'

Louise grabbed Grace by the wrists. 'Do you understand what's going on, Grace? Do you know how bad this could get?'

'How bad? You mean worse than watching three of my students drown in front of me? Worse than being chased by the media and having every part of my life turned over like I'm some specimen in a jar?'

Grace shrugged her arms free and turned her back on Louise. They rarely fought. Disagreements usually slipped into long silences because neither of them was good with confrontation.

'We don't have time for this now,' Louise said. 'We need to get out of here.'

Grace briefly considered staying, but the thought of being watched all night and then having to escape in the morning was worse than going with Louise. She put the laptop in her bag and walked out the back door.

The alleyway was clear. They scurried like rats in the dark, looking back every few steps to make sure they weren't being followed. When they got to the end of the laneway, they turned towards Grimshaw Avenue. At the corner, Louise peered along the street to the front of Grace's place. There was a dark huddle of people, all their attention focused on Fiona.

They walked on the bitumen, keeping low until they reached Louise's car. The car remote beeped loudly and the lights flashed, but no one noticed. Louise edged the SUV out onto the road, and they cruised past the crowd.

It was only a fifteen-minute drive to Louise's place in Fitzroy.

Wednesday nights were quiet in the inner city; the corner pubs glowed their welcome, but most of the restaurants were either half full or closed. Neither woman spoke. Grace stewed on what Louise had told her about the risk management documents. If she accepted Jim's decision, she would be complicit. If she didn't, she would be guilty of not doing her due diligence before taking students on a trip along one of the most dangerous beaches in the country. She did know *she* would never have asked him to change the date – would never have even thought of it. She and Gerard and Tom were responsible for the fuck up and, one way or another, they would be held accountable.

18

Rick Bolton hunched over his beer at the Wheelers Bay Hotel. His half-eaten parmigiana, the cheese congealed and cold, had been pushed to the side of the table. The bistro was as empty as expected on a Wednesday night, with a smattering of pensioners snapping up the mid-week specials (with extra chips) and a few backpackers sharing kids' meals between them. He could see through to the bar, where drinkers huddled in small groups, their voices rising and falling. He knew what the topic of conversation would be – the drownings at Juliet Beach, twenty kilometres west of town.

Bolton had stayed at the beach until the copper in charge, Pezzementi, told him they were shutting the search down for the day. The rescue teams had made their way back to the car park, unable to look at him, the parent of the one boy they hadn't been able to find. The one body. Bolton had retreated to the warmth of his car. The campfire was still going, but he had grown tired of the sympathetic nods and pats on the shoulder, tired of the endless offers of tea or shit coffee, tired of the reassurances they were doing everything they could to find his son.

Before he left the beach, he'd walked out to the viewing platform one more time, like he might see something the rescuers had missed. It was still light, but the sun had dropped behind the dunes and, even with the wind having backed off to a breeze, the air was cold. His eyes had watered as they moved up and down the beach, then out to sea.

'Where are you, Jakey?' he'd said aloud. 'What did they do to you, those teachers? Why did you run away from them?'

There was no answer, just the restless roll and dump of the waves, the eternal sounds of the sea.

Now, in the pub, his phone buzzed on the table in front of him. It was Celine, Jake's mother.

'Hello,' he said.

'Why haven't you answered your phone?' she began without returning his greeting. Her voice was frantic, desperate. 'I've called a dozen times.'

Bolton let her wait a few seconds while he took a sip of his beer. 'Been out at the search site. There's no reception out there. They haven't found him yet.'

'Where are you now?'

How many times had she asked him that over the last three years? *Where are you? Who are you with? Whose turn is it to have Jake this weekend?*

'I'm back in Wheelers Bay.'

'Where on earth is that?'

He smirked. 'It's the nearest town to the search area.' Celine had no knowledge of anywhere west of Highpoint Shopping Centre.

'Rick, can you please tell me what's going on down there?' she pleaded. 'We're dying here. The media are saying all sorts of crazy stuff. They say the boys weren't even supervised when they went swimming.' Her voice broke and she began sobbing. 'And worse.'

'What do you mean, worse?'

Sniffs came down the line. 'On Facebook. They're saying the teachers didn't try to rescue the boys. They let them drown.'

'Disher,' he said, through clenched teeth.

'Who?'

'Disher. You know, the young one. The one Jakey never liked. I spoke to her today.'

'And . . .?'

Bolton thought back to his conversation with the teacher in the tent, the big copper watching him like a hawk, pulling him up when all he wanted to do was strangle her.

'She wanted a hug. Can you believe it?' he said.

There was silence on the other end.

'You still there?' he asked.

'I can't bear to think of him out there in the sea. Do you

think he could have made it back in? He's such a good swimmer. All those lessons.'

Rick had been asking himself the same questions. He fought the instinct to give her comfort. She'd given him none for years; all through the separation she'd taken the moral high ground.

'I dunno,' he said, finally. 'The police aren't saying much, but there's still gotta be a chance.'

'Don't you dare leave until they find him, Rick. He needs someone there who knows him.'

She hadn't been there all day, watching the boats and helicopters – hadn't seen the looks on the faces of the SES and rescue teams. They'd given up on finding Jake alive.

Bolton took another sip of his beer. 'I'll go back to the beach in the morning,' he said.

'And you'll stay there until they find him. You've abandoned him before, Rick. Don't do it again. Not when he needs you the most.'

'Fuck off,' he seethed. An older couple at a nearby table turned to look at him. He'd been trying to keep his voice low. He raised his hand to them apologetically.

'What? You don't think it's true? What about his presentation night last year? Where were you then, Rick? Oh, that's right, I remember. Up on the Gold Coast fucking a woman half your age.'

He stabbed his finger at the phone, ending the call. One of the bar staff, a girl who couldn't have been eighteen, had walked towards his table then backed away.

'Sorry,' he said to her. 'It's been a long day.'

'That's okay, sir,' she said. 'Are you finished with that?' She pointed at his plate.

'Yeah, thanks.' The girl took his plate quickly and retreated to the kitchen. He watched her every step of the way, noting the line her underwear made under her tight black jeans.

He pulled his eyes back to his phone when it buzzed with a message.

Just keep me updated, Rick. You owe me that.

His anger had subsided, cooled by the last few mouthfuls of beer. He didn't owe her anything; she was as much to blame for the separation as he was. But Jake was her son, too.

He took his time and walked to the bar. He ordered a double scotch, knocked it back and straightaway ordered another. The alcohol was barely touching the sides. He craved the dulling of the senses it usually gave him. He wanted to sink into oblivion.

But first, he relented and punched his fat fingers at the phone. *I'll stay here for as long as I need to. Keep you updated. R.*

It felt like another one of her little victories from the last few years, always predicated on his mistakes. If only he'd been more discreet, smarter. He could still have had his half of the house, all his superannuation. Maybe Jakey could have forgiven him, too.

A woman entered the bistro. She looked vaguely familiar, smartly dressed, and Bolton followed her with his eyes. He was sure she had been at the Juliet car park. She ordered a drink at the bar, picked it up and walked towards him.

'Mr Bolton?' she said.

'Who's asking?'

The woman stood beside his table. She wore a tight-fitting puffer jacket over black slacks. There were flecks of mud on the bottoms of the legs, and her boots were scuffed and dirty.

'Rose Cotter. *Melbourne Star.* I wonder if I could have a word with you?'

He thought about brushing her off, but she was cute, and he didn't mind the company. He nodded for her to sit down.

'I'm so sorry for your loss,' Rose said.

'They haven't found Jake yet,' he replied.

'Of course.' She sipped at her lime and soda. 'Have they . . .' she hesitated. 'Have the police spoken to you about the circumstances of the accident? It's just that there's so much conjecture. It feels like they're hiding something.'

As Bolton watched, she undid her puffer jacket and slipped it off. She wore a white shirt that stretched so tightly across her breasts that a button had popped open, revealing her bra. If she noticed, she did nothing to fix it.

'They're hiding *something* alright,' Bolton said. 'The teacher in charge, Grace Disher, she fucked up.' He felt the anger rise in his chest again, fuelled now by the whiskeys.

Rose placed her phone on the table, tapped at the screen. 'Do you mind if we record?'

'Go for it,' Bolton said.

'How do you mean, she fucked up?'

'First, the boys were somehow allowed to get way ahead of the rest of the group.'

'From what I understand,' Rose interrupted, 'Grace Disher wasn't walking with the group.'

'She wasn't. She was supposed to be there when they arrived at the beach, but she was late. And then . . .' Bolton thought back to the conversation with Celine.

Rose waited.

'She let them drown,' Bolton said, his voice laced with disgust. 'She watched while they drowned.'

Rose's eyes widened. 'You're sure of that?' she asked.

'I spoke to her today,' he said.

'And she told you she didn't try to save them?'

'Not in as many words, but . . .'

'Go on.'

'So, she says she was there when the boys ran into the water, right? But then, nothing. She just screamed at them. She didn't even try.'

'Jesus,' Rose said. She buttoned her top as if she'd just realised it was open, pulled her puffer jacket back on and zipped it up. 'I have to go,' she said, standing abruptly.

'You don't want another drink?' Bolton said. 'Maybe something stronger?'

She shook her head, looking past him towards the door. 'There is one more thing.' She paused. 'There are posts on social media suggesting Jacob and Miss Disher didn't get on, that they'd had some sort of argument on the trip. Can you comment on that?'

Bolton took his time to answer. 'Jake could be cheeky, sure, but he wasn't a bad kid. Some teachers just couldn't see the good in him. He never liked Disher.'

Rose Cotter tapped the phone to stop the recording, thanked him and left through the side door.

The bistro had emptied out and the staff were giving hurry-up hints: wiping down the tables, cleaning the specials off the chalkboard, dimming the lights in the vacated sections. He wanted to tell them who he was, what had happened to him today. It hadn't occurred to him that they might already know.

He'd lost count of the number of drinks he'd had, but he felt the effect of the alcohol when he finally left the bar. The cold night air assaulted him as he grabbed for the rail to guide himself down the steps. His hand slipped and he stumbled, falling and rolling onto the footpath. The street was deserted, and if the bar staff had noticed, none came out to help him. He lay still for a minute, feeling for anything broken. Satisfied he hadn't injured anything other than his pride, he pulled himself to his feet and leaned against the wall of the pub.

It was a ten-minute walk to the motel, but it felt like an hour. The Happy Wanderer was a half-circle of dogboxes around a fenced pool. Bolton had thought the police might pay for his room at least, but they'd just asked where he was staying and said they'd keep in touch.

Lying on his bed, Rick scrolled through the photos and videos on his phone. They were nearly all of Jake. Pivoting to shrug off a tackle while surrounded by opposition players, shooting hoops in the backyard, with his first trailbike, cleaning cars in the yard on his holidays. He wore the same grin in most of them, like he was in on a joke only he and his dad understood. There were dozens of pics of the two of them standing next to each other, fingers pointed like cocked pistols across their chests. It was their signature move. Rick's eyes welled with tears. What would he do without his boy? He had poured everything into him, every ounce of love and care and protection. Jakey-boy. The Jakemeister.

He tried not to think of his son out there in the sea. What had been running through his head as the waves took him down? Had he thought of his dad? Or was he so terrified he didn't have time? What about the other boys? Had he tried to help them? Rick liked to think he would have.

Bolton watched the Channel Seven helicopter video on his phone. He'd viewed it a dozen times because it reinforced everything he wanted to think about the accident. Only guilty people run. He scrolled further and found another video he hadn't seen. It was filmed at a petrol station somewhere. Those same two teachers. Reporters trying to talk to them. Thank God the media were doing their job for once. Disher was acting crazy. She ran at the person with the camera. Must have knocked them over. Next minute, she disappeared down the street.

Fucking guilty as hell, Bolton thought. It was written all over her face. And the other woman from the school, the older one, he couldn't remember her name. Another bitch. Hard as nails. Gave him nothing, just fucking platitudes when he wanted answers. Why did they send women, anyway? This sort of situation is men's work. The coppers seemed to know that. They put men in charge, though that Pezzementi was a prick. Kept defending Disher, protecting her.

Well, she'd only be able to hide for so long. He vowed, on the life of his boy, to find her and get answers for himself. For Jakey.

19

Grace found it hard to believe it was still the same day as when she'd woken in the campground at Juliet. It felt like a week had passed. The ache across her shoulders bore the weight of every minute she had spent lurching from one crippling situation to another. The people who had populated her day flashed before her as she lay in Louise's bed, staring at the ceiling: Sergeant Heaney and his pointed questions; Sarah, who she'd hardly had a chance to thank; Pez and his big, assertive presence – empathy in a uniform; Jake's father, with his fury and grief; Watto's warm face washer and awful coffee.

It was close to midnight, but Grace couldn't find a way of switching off the stream in her head. Louise slept beside her. They weren't touching, but Grace felt her warmth.

Louise had cooked mushroom risotto when they arrived at her place. Grace had pushed it around her plate but eventually eaten half. The backdating of the risk management plan had been the elephant at the table. Now, the risotto sat heavily in her stomach. She hoped she could keep it down because as best she could remember it was all she'd eaten for the day.

Grace listened for the rhythmic sound of Louise's breathing before pushing the covers back and slipping out of the bedroom. Even in the dark, she knew this place almost as well as her own – the long central hallway with its polished timber boards, leading to the back of the house and what Grace called the Spartan kitchen: white walls, white benchtops, white cupboards. Everything about Louise's home was ordered and clean. The empty island bench shone under the single light Grace switched on; the chairs were straight under the table, and the wine glasses stood in neat rows on their shelf. When she had walked in here for the first time, Grace had wondered whether she could ever survive in a relationship with someone who lived her life in such a regimented way.

She pulled her laptop from her bag and sat on a stool at the island bench. Louise had warned her against looking at the news sites, distracting her with food and wine before encouraging her to bed. All the while, Grace had felt her eyes slipping to her bag, the laptop, and the world of pain she knew she would find when she opened it. She could explain it away as morbid curiosity, but really, she wanted to feel something – to push back the numbness, even if it meant replacing it with anger.

The ABC was her go-to news outlet, so she started there. The first two headlines were about the accident. 'FEARS HELD FOR MISSING STUDENTS ON SCHOOL CAMP', the first read, followed by, 'SCHOOL IN SHOCK AFTER STUDENTS DROWN ON SCHOOL CAMP'.

Grace stared at the headlines for a full minute, transfixed by the way Jake, Roberto and Harry had become the fodder of national, probably even international, news. Their deaths, and her role in them, were public property now, to be read, interpreted and judged by millions of strangers.

She clicked on a third, more recent headline: MORE DETAILS EMERGE ABOUT SCHOOL CAMP DEATHS. It was an updated version of the earlier articles: measured, factual, almost restrained in its reporting of the tragedy and its impact. There was a repeat of the statement from Jim and a more detailed one from Pez about the recovery of the bodies. She was relieved to read she was still being referred to as *the teacher in charge*, rather than by her name.

Grace continued to scroll. There was mention of the helicopter footage and the filming of her running away in Colac. The way the article moved seamlessly from talking about the *teachers* to focusing on her caused her to draw breath. Why were Gerard and Tom being consigned to the edges of the story while she was skewered front and centre?

Grace closed the ABC tab and brought up the Channel Seven news website. The story led the page. Again, she wasn't named, but referred to as the teacher in charge. The video from the helicopter was grainy, and she didn't think anyone would be able to tell it was her. If she hadn't been there, she could almost convince herself it was someone else. But the sound of beating rotors that accompanied the footage, the harshness of the spotlight – they brought it all back: the panic, the instinct to run. She wished she had stood still, maybe crossed her arms and planted her feet firmly in the sand – a pose that said, *yes, I'm here. I haven't deserted my boys.*

Grace had no social media accounts to go to, since she'd deleted them on the way back from Colac, but it was an easy process to set up a new Twitter account under a different name. She linked it to an old Gmail address she hadn't used in two years, and within ten minutes, she was in.

She knew Twitter would be bad, but she told herself it'd be better to know what was being said.

#threeboysdrowned was trending. Grace clicked on it and scanned the tweets. She ignored the usernames and read comments at random. There were still expressions of shock, and prayers for the parents, but it didn't take long to slip into darker territory.

@stumpy1078 I know Juliet, fished there heaps of times. No way should kids have been swimming there. It's wild and dangerous.

@davos5792 Can't believe no one tried to help those boys. Hope the parents get their day in court.

@gin4tonic4gin That teacher couldn't be a mother or she'd have gone in after them. Any parent would. I'd die for my kids. Barren bitch. This is her.

Below the tweet was a picture of Grace, a frame from the video at the petrol station. She was bent forwards, picking herself up off the ground after she'd fallen out of the car. Her face was distorted, her lip curled into a snarl. She looked like a harried witch. Her hair was a wild nest, and you could see down her shirt to the top of her bra.

Grace stared at the picture for a minute, trying to see herself in it, trying to place herself back in the frenzy of the moment. This time, the memory was all but lost to her. She sniffed her hands for the lingering smell of petrol, but it had long been washed away.

Despite herself, she continued to scroll. She knew what she was looking for, and she found it without too much effort.

@sixxpacksix3231 Grace Disher, that's her name. The teacher in charge, the one that let the boys drown.

Grace slammed the laptop shut and rested her forehead on the cold metal of the lid. She could try to defend herself, but whatever she said would only be lost in the tsunami of outrage. She knew how it worked when a tragedy occurred, especially one involving kids. Years ago, she'd seen a doco on Madeleine McCann's disappearance. Relentless, vile shit was directed at her parents. No one was interested in allowing the police to do their work. They wanted a quick trial and execution so they could move on to the next outrage.

'What are you doing?' Louise had walked into the kitchen without Grace realising. She wore a white dressing gown tied with a cord that didn't match.

'I don't know,' Grace answered truthfully.

'How bad is it?' Louise asked, filling the electric jug with water.

'It's awful.'

'So don't look at it.'

'They've named me. Not Gerard or Tom, just me.'

'What?' Louise was aghast. 'Who's named you?'

'On Twitter.'

'They've got no right!'

'Rights don't come into it. You want to know what else they're saying?' She didn't wait for a response. 'That if I was a mother, I would have tried to save the boys.'

Louise came around the bench and stood behind Grace. She wrapped her arms around her and rested her chin on her shoulder. 'I'm so sorry you have to go through this.'

'Why is everything about me and not the boys? That's the tragedy here. There are three empty beds tonight, and Jake and Robbie and Harry are never coming home.'

'People need someone to blame.'

'I can't believe it's happening to me. This stuff happens to other people. You see it on the news all the time.'

Louise let go of Grace when the kettle boiled and poured two cups of tea. 'Did you hold your dinner down?' she asked.

'Just,' she said.

'I've got some tablets to help you sleep, if you want them.'

Grace leaned backwards, gathered her hair in her hands and tied it in a loose bun. 'I'm going to tell Jim tomorrow I don't want the forms backdated,' she said.

Louise pushed the cup of tea across the bench towards Grace.

'You're making a big thing out of this,' she said. 'It doesn't matter when they were uploaded, Grace, they were done.

You'd finished them. It was just an oversight that you hadn't put them on the server.'

'If it's just an oversight, then why lie about it?'

'We're not lying unless someone asks when the documents were uploaded. And why would they?' Louise couldn't keep the frustration from her voice. 'Everything about your trip will be examined in forensic detail —'

'*My trip*,' Grace interrupted. 'When did it become my trip? It was a school excursion.'

'Sorry. I meant *the* trip. But you were the teacher in charge.'

'What happened to the school wrapping its arms around me, Lou? That dropped away pretty quickly.'

'Jesus, Grace, you need to get out of the way of us trying to help you.' Louise stood opposite her, leaning her forearms on the kitchen bench. Her dressing gown had fallen open and she readjusted it, pulling it tight around her body. 'You've got to trust us,' she continued. 'We've never dealt with anything this big. Never. Jim's under huge pressure.'

'Oh, okay, yeah. *Jim's* under pressure.' Grace was on her feet, pacing the floor.

'You don't see it, do you?' Louise said. 'You don't see what we're doing for you. We're helping you shoulder the responsibility, protecting you.'

'By lying!'

Louise walked around the bench and stood in front of Grace, blocking her from pacing. 'Stop!' she said, grabbing Grace's wrists. She was holding her too hard, and Grace pushed her hands off.

'I'm sorry,' Louise said.

They had never been physically forceful with each other. The few times they'd argued words, then silence, were their weapons of choice.

'So,' Grace said, 'are you on Jim's side, or mine? Because I need to know if I'm safe here.'

'You will always be safe here,' Louise replied, ignoring the question about whose side she was on. She took Grace's hand and held it against her own cheek.

Not for the first time in the last couple of days, Grace was lost. Too many parts of her world were colliding, parts she had always managed to keep separate.

'I don't know what to think anymore,' Grace said.

'It's one in the morning,' Louise replied. 'You don't need to think about anything right now.' She laced her fingers into Grace's and led her to the bedroom.

The sheets were still warm when Grace slid back between them. Louise climbed into the bed and lay next to her. Grace rolled onto her side and Louise spooned her, softly kissing the back of her neck.

'It's going to be okay,' Louise whispered. 'It's going to be okay.'

Grace desperately wanted to believe her. She lay awake for a while until, finally, she allowed the weight of the day, which felt like the weight of an entire lifetime, to drain into the pillow – and she slept.

20

They usually listened to the radio when they shared a lift to school, but not today. Louise drove while Grace peered out the side window at the waking city. Joggers slogged their way around the Edinburgh Gardens, and two men sat outside a Greek milk bar on St Georges Road, sipping coffee from tiny cups. Cyclists flashed by. The morning sun reflected off shop windows and pedestrians walked briskly, earbuds in, eyes forwards.

Grace had done her best to dress professionally for the day. She wore a white top and dark jacket, matching them with yesterday's black jeans. The top could have done with an iron, but the jacket hid the creases.

It could have been any other school day, until they pulled up at a set of traffic lights. Outside a newsagent on the corner, the wired-caged headlines from the *Morning Star* shouted, 'THREE BOYS DROWN IN SCHOOL CAMP TRAGEDY'.

Grace closed her eyes, but the headlines were still there, burned into her retinas. When she opened them again, a pedestrian was passing in front of the car, a middle-aged man walking a small dog. He turned to look at her for just a moment too long. She averted her eyes and brought her hands to her face, wondering if this is how things would be now, having to hide herself from the world.

Following Fiona's advice, they avoided the school's main entrance on Grant Street and drove around the block to the back gate on Fitzgerald Road. It was only seven thirty, too early for students to be arriving. A female security guard sat by the gate nursing a steaming cup, a thermos on the ground next to her chair. She raised her hand, and Louise slid her window down and flashed her staff card.

The woman nodded at Grace. 'And you, Miss?' she said.

Grace pulled the lanyard from her bag and held it up for her to check.

'Grace,' the woman mouthed, unintentionally. She corrected herself, straightened her shoulders and waved them through.

'Even the security guards know,' Grace said.

'Of course they do,' Louise replied. 'That's their job.'

They drove around the football ovals and parked by the sports pavilion. Three of the college buses – including the one Grace had driven on the trip – were lined up in the middle bays, but otherwise the car park was empty. Just as Grace got out of the car, a dark BMW slid into the space next to theirs. The tinted windows hid the driver from view, but Louise gave a little wave. The door opened, and Jim stepped out, a metre from where Grace stood. There was a moment when neither of them knew quite what to do, but then Jim leaned in and gave her a hug. Grace's hands were full with her laptop bag, and she held herself more rigidly than she intended, but she was nonetheless reassured.

'How are you doing?' Jim asked after he'd let her go. They were caught in the tight space between the cars.

Grace tried to match the Jim she'd spoken to on the phone yesterday with the Jim who'd just hugged her. 'Okay, I guess.'

'It's going to be a tough day,' he said. 'For all of us. Did you sleep last night?'

'A bit.'

Jim's eyes turned to Louise, as though any talk of Grace sleeping now involved her as well. Louise walked around the car and stood close to him. 'I'm so sorry for your loss, Jim,' she said.

'Oh my God,' Grace said, remembering herself. 'I'm so sorry, too. He was such a . . .' Her voice trailed off, and Jim finished the sentence for her.

'He was,' he said. 'A great kid.'

Jim broke the awkward silence that followed by opening the back door of his car and taking out his briefcase.

'Fiona rang me after she'd been to see you last night,' he said, turning back to Grace. 'I'm sorry about the media harassment. We had a gutful of it here yesterday, but going to your home is next level. I'll talk to the police and see what they can do. And the social media stuff – I hope you're not looking at it.'

'I'm trying not to,' Grace said. She wished it was as easy as not looking, that she could close herself off and it would go away. Jim was old enough that he probably wasn't even on socials. He'd struggle to understand how much of her life she had given away online – how, even after she'd deleted her accounts, her footprint remained forever.

They began their walk together. St Finbar's was built on the side of a hill. The ovals spread across the flats of a small valley, with a series of concrete stairs and ramps leading to the buildings on the terraces above.

'We'll go straight to the admin wing,' Jim said over his shoulder. Grace noticed how easily Jim climbed. He looked fit. For most of her short time at the school, he'd been a presence on the stage at assemblies, a leader at staff meetings, a gospel reader at school masses, a delegator. Now they had been drawn more closely into each other's orbit, Grace was uncertain of their relationship, especially as his family had lost a child, too. It hadn't started well, with the phone calls at Juliet, but maybe it would be different now they were back on familiar territory. She hoped they were on the same side, but the issue of the backdated report would need to be dealt with. She guessed Louise had broken a confidence by telling her.

They entered the admin wing via the rear door. Jim swiped his card on the reader, stepped through and disarmed the alarms at the keypad on the wall. He ushered Grace and Louise along the passageway, flicking lights on as he went. They passed his office and opened the door to the boardroom, which looked out onto the top car park and student drop-off area. It was still quiet out the front, but they could see the huddle of media around the main gate.

'They must have been there all night,' Jim said. 'Louise, can you go up and check on security? I don't want parents or students harassed when they arrive.'

Louise shot a glance at Grace. They had planned to get through the morning together, but Jim was already separating them.

Grace nodded to say she'd be okay. Louise unlocked the sliding door and strode towards the car park gate.

'Good morning.' Erin bustled into the room holding a tray of takeaway coffees and a large brown paper bag that smelled of fresh pastries. When she saw Grace, she put the coffees and pastries on a side table and went straight to her. She took Grace by the arms and gently rubbed, like she was trying to warm her up. 'Hello, love' she said. 'I'm so sorry this has happened. How are you coping?'

Erin was another person at the school Grace hardly knew.

'Oh, you know . . .' she replied.

'Well, let's get some coffee into you, shall we? Have you had breakfast? I've got fresh croissants. I'll get some butter and jam organised.'

Erin was all business. Grace guessed that was a PA's brief.

'Thanks,' Grace said.

'How do you take your coffee?' Erin asked. She had already handed a cup to Jim, obviously a familiar ritual.

'With caffeine,' Grace said.

Jim sat down and opened his laptop. He reached into his briefcase and pulled out a folder, opened it and spread papers on the table in front of him. He looked at his watch. 'I've asked a few people to join us this morning,' he said to Grace.

She took a sip of her coffee. The smell of the croissants reminded her she'd had nothing more than a few spoonfuls of muesli before Louise had hustled her out the door and into the car.

'Gerard and Tom are coming,' Jim continued. 'Fiona and Luke, of course. And Minh Tran. He's our legal counsel.'

Erin had found butter and jam in the kitchenette, along with some plates. 'I want to see you eat,' she said to Grace. 'No nibbling around the edges, proper eating. You look thin.'

Grace forced a smile. 'What do we need to do?' she asked Jim. She was trying not to feel overwhelmed by the number of people she'd be dealing with.

'First, we'll bring you up to speed. Gerard and Tom, too. At some stage this morning, you'll need to give a full statement to the police. We'll have counsellors here again today and as much support as you feel you need.' He paused and looked squarely at Grace. His voice softened, as though he realised how impersonal he must sound. 'Like I said, it's going to be a tough day, Grace. The loss of Jacob, Roberto and Harry is affecting us all. The whole school community is mourning – and of course there's them,' he said, pointing to the media at the front gate. 'And parents aren't helping, spreading half-baked theories on Facebook. Honestly, I wish Mark Zuckerberg had died at birth.'

Grace forced another smile.

Everyone seemed to arrive in a rush, then, led by Fiona in power suit and heels. Gerard and Tom came in together. It was the first time she'd seen them since they'd left her at Juliet on Tuesday night. They were followed by Luke and a man Grace assumed to be Minh Tran.

Grace stood up, and Gerard enveloped her in a hug warm enough to make her want to weep. Tom made no move towards her.

'Hey, Tom,' she said.

'Hi, Grace,' he said, and sat down on the other side of the table.

Grace didn't miss the unshaven face and the darkness around his eyes. He looked like he hadn't slept since the accident. Her fingers felt for the bruises on her arms where he had gripped her on the beach.

Gerard moved around and sat with Tom. He gave him a reassuring pat on the shoulder.

'Let's get started,' Jim said.

Grace peered through the window, hoping to see Louise returning from the front gate. She didn't know how many allies she had around the table.

No one else had reached for a croissant. Grace didn't want to be the first. There'd be crumbs and flakes going everywhere. But Gerard saved her, grabbing one in his big hands and pulling it apart. Grace followed suit, earning her a reassuring nod from Erin.

'Firstly,' Jim continued, 'thank you to Grace, Tom and

Gerard for coming in this morning. We've been dealing with this tragedy at a distance here at school, but we know you three have been through a terrible ordeal. Obviously, all your teaching duties will be covered for as long as you need. We don't want you going back into the classroom before you are ready.'

Grace noticed the way Jim's eyes kept moving to Tom, who fidgeted with a pen and stared at the table. Up to this point, Grace had thought everyone's attention would be on her, but Tom's state was distracting them.

As if on cue, Tom pushed his chair back, sending it falling to the floor. He stood for a second, looking bewildered. 'Excuse me,' he said, then walked quickly out of the room.

Gerard got up to follow him, but Fiona stopped him. 'I'll go,' she said. 'You need to be here.'

Gerard nodded and sat down, throwing a worried glance at Grace.

The meeting continued for an hour. Neither Tom nor Fiona returned. Outside, a steady stream of Audis, Range Rovers and Mercedes slid into the drop-off zone of the car park, heralding the arrival of students. Grace listened as carefully as she could to what was being said – not just the information about the police, the boys' parents, the planned funerals and the media frenzy, but the way in which the whole situation was being discussed. She wanted reassurance.

The police would interview her, Tom and Gerard separately. Grace doubted Tom would be in a fit state to respond to any questions. She was quietly relieved to see someone coping worse than herself. If she could just hold strong for the day, keep herself upright, give the appearance of being in control, she was sure she would be treated differently; her story would carry more weight.

Minh was the last to speak. 'I'll sit in on each of your meetings with the police,' he said.

Grace noted his use of the word *meetings*, rather than *interviews*.

'I encourage you to be open and honest in your answers,' he continued. 'But also cautious. Stick to the known facts. Don't presume anything, don't speculate about on why the boys did what they did. Just state what you know, what you saw.'

'Can I just ask,' Gerard interrupted. 'Why do we need a lawyer here at all?'

Minh was quick to reply. 'That's a fair question, Gerard,' he said. 'This is a terrible situation we are dealing with. Three families have lost their boys. The CSD wants to make sure the school – and you, Grace and Tom – are given every support. We're not trying to hide anything. We just want to ensure the police, parents, staff and the media are dealing with the facts, not supposition.'

'Fine,' said Gerard. If he was unsatisfied with the answer, he didn't show it. 'Is it okay if Grace and I talk before the interviews?' he asked.

'I don't see why not,' Minh replied.

Jim checked his watch. 'Right,' he said. 'If there's nothing else for now . . .?'

No one spoke. Grace wanted to raise the risk management report, but it didn't seem like the right time.

21

The others departed quickly, leaving Grace and Gerard alone in the boardroom. They sat opposite each other at the wide table.

'So,' Gerard said. 'How are you really doing?'

Grace looked towards the closed door, unable to stop the tears welling in her eyes. She had been tensing again, bracing against the world, but Gerard's question floored her.

'Yeah, me too,' he said before she could respond.

'It's all so shit,' Grace said. 'Those boys . . .'

Gerard's big hands were shaking. He brought them together, intertwining his fingers. 'Still,' he said, 'the croissants are good.'

Grace half laughed, half cried.

'Have you been able to sleep?' he asked.

'Not much. You?'

'Same.'

'You've got family, yeah?' Grace realised how little she knew of Gerard's life outside school.

He nodded. 'They've been great. The kids are a bit young to understand, but Jodie – that's my wife – she hasn't let me out of her sight since I got home. And Mum and Dad came over last night.'

Grace yearned for the support of family. Her dad would be worried sick. She needed her phone back.

'I'm so sorry, Grace,' Gerard said. 'I feel terrible.'

Grace was torn. She desperately wanted to know how the boys had gotten so far ahead of the group, but she couldn't help thinking Gerard was already on edge. Unable to look at her, he blinked away tears.

'What happened?' she asked as gently as she could, reaching across the table to touch his arm. 'After I left you at Crayfish Bay . . .'

'We thought we'd done everything right,' Gerard said. 'We had your designated wait points marked on the boys' maps.'

'But the boys got separated?' Again, she kept her voice low, encouraging.

'The last break we had was three kilometres from the beach. When we did a head count, Jake and Roberto weren't there. They hadn't stopped. They were still walking.'

'Jake and Roberto. Not Harry?'

He shook his head and looked at the table.

'What?' Grace asked.

'Tom came up with the idea of Harry going after the other two. I didn't agree, but I didn't want to argue with him in front of the boys.'

'But . . .'

'I know, I should have spoken up. But Tom, he said it would be alright, and he's an experienced bushwalker. He sounded so confident.'

'Yeah, but surely . . .' Grace was careful not to let her anger show. This was the crux of everything that had happened: the inability of two grown men to see the obvious.

Gerard sensed her frustration. He leaned back in his seat. 'Harry being Harry, he was up for it. Said he'd catch them in no time and get them to stop and wait.'

Grace's mind was racing. You never send a student on their own. *Never.* Always with a staff member.

'So, I agreed,' Gerard continued. 'Reluctantly.'

Grace knew what she would have done: sent a staff member out to catch up to the bolters, turn them around and bring them back to the group. Maintain supervision at all times. They had already allowed two boys to become separated from the group, but then they exacerbated the situation by sending a third one after them.

'Okay,' Grace said, trying to keep the judgement from her voice. 'What did you do after Harry left?'

'We moved off as a group, but Tim Simpson had twisted his ankle and he was really slow. It didn't look that bad, hardly swollen at all, but he held us back.'

Simmo, Grace thought. *Jake's mate.*

'But Tom could have gone ahead with the faster boys,' she said. 'Why didn't you think of that?'

Gerard shrugged. 'I'm sorry, Grace. I really am. But we'd already lost sight of three boys, and the rain had hit us by then. We thought it was best to keep everyone else together.'

Grace looked away, took a deep breath and tried to view it from Gerard's perspective. She had only given Tom and him verbal instructions and the same trip handbook the boys received. They would have tossed it in their packs and not given it another thought.

'So,' Grace asked, 'then what?'

'The last section was three k's, like I said. We should have been able to cover that in forty-five minutes, an hour max. But Tim was whingeing like you wouldn't believe. Stopping every five minutes to complain about his ankle. The other boys were getting sick of it, but we still stuck together.'

Grace thought about Tim. He had been Jake's tent partner. And he would do anything to impress him. 'Did you see him sprain his ankle?' she asked.

Gerard shook his head. 'You think he faked it?'

'It's possible, isn't it? That they were in it together.'

'I dunno, Grace. He's a bloody good actor if he was faking.'

They sat in silence for a minute, both considering the possibility they had been set up.

'I don't remember him limping on the way back to the car park,' Grace said. 'He was in the front group with you, wasn't he?'

'He was, yeah. But I was caught up with looking after Danny. I wasn't watching Tim.'

Grace tried to recall if she'd noticed anything odd about Tim's behaviour at the car park, but all the small details were crowded out by the memory of the darkness closing in, the boys keeping warm on the bus, the arrival of the police and SES.

'So,' Grace said, returning her focus to the accident, 'over those last three k's there was no sign of Jake, Roberto or Harry?'

'No. We didn't see them again.' He stopped abruptly, understanding the implication of what he'd said.

'Just to be clear,' Grace said, 'do you think the boys planned to run ahead and swim at the beach?'

Gerard took his time to answer. 'It wouldn't surprise me if Jake and Roberto had planned it – or even that Tim was in on it with his sprained ankle. But Harry? He was such a sensible kid.'

Grace understood her failures in planning. She had thought she had covered all her bases, but there had been omissions, every one of which would be questioned. Most importantly, she hadn't instructed her staff on what to do if they lost sight of any of the boys. There was no requirement in the guidelines on trips like this for separate staff information folders, but even so, she should have briefed them more thoroughly. She tried to remember the discussion at Crayfish Bay on Monday night. She knew she would have given clear instructions to the boys about sticking together, not running ahead, taking regular breaks, and definitely not going anywhere near the water when they arrived at Juliet. But had Tom and Gerard been listening, too?

'What are you going to tell the police?' Grace asked.

'The truth, Grace. I'm not going to put you in the shit. We're all responsible, all three of us.'

'But I was in charge,' Grace said. She felt defeated. Even if the boys had set it up, she should have planned for the possibility.

'That doesn't mean you bear all the responsibility,' Gerard said. 'It was Tom and I who didn't think on our feet. We didn't see what was coming. You can't carry the can for that.'

Grace thought of what Gerard had said about his family, his kids. He had more to lose than her. And in her mind, what he had told her made Tom more culpable.

'What about Tom?' she asked. 'What's his take?'

'Honestly, I've got no idea. He hasn't been in contact with you?'

'No. Just the call in the car with you yesterday. But I haven't had my phone. He could have rung, and I wouldn't have known.' She explained what had happened in Colac.

'You saw him today,' Gerard said. 'He's not travelling well. He hardly spoke the whole time we were in Wheelers Bay. I tried to give him stuff to do, tried to distract him, but he was almost affected worse than the boys. And when I gave him a lift home from St Jude's, he barely said a word.'

There was a question Grace wanted to ask Gerard, but she wasn't sure how to frame it. She took a breath. 'Would you have . . .'

'What?' Gerard asked.

'You saw the conditions at Juliet, how dangerous it was . . .'

'Would I have gone in after the boys? Tried to rescue them?'

Gerard took his time to answer. 'Honestly, I don't know, Grace. All I can say is I wasn't there, so I never had to make that choice. And I'm so sorry you had to.'

'But do you think I did the right thing? I would have drowned.'

'Yes, I do. You dying wouldn't have changed anything. It'd only have made things worse.'

Grace wanted to hug him again. Her anger had abated, and nothing she had heard in the last two days, no reassurance of support, meant as much to her as Gerard's words. He had been there. He understood in a way no one else could.

They were interrupted by a knock at the door. A policewoman entered. She was tall, maybe early forties, and her uniform had sharp creases ironed into the arms and legs. A pair of reading glasses hung from a thin chain around her neck. She towered above them as they sat at the table.

'Morning,' she said. 'You must be Grace and Gerard.'

Grace thought she was trying to sound friendly, but it wasn't coming naturally.

'I'm Leading Senior Constable Petkovic. Call me Debbie. I'm based at Moreland, and I'm here with two of my colleagues to gather information about the accident. We've been briefed by Sergeant Heaney from Wheelers Bay – you both met him at Juliet Beach.'

Grace nodded, thinking about the not-so-subtle interrogation on Tuesday night.

'And we've also spoken to Senior Sergeant Pezzementi, from Search and Rescue,' Debbie continued.

Grace was pleased to hear Pez's name. She wished he were here now.

'What do you need from us this morning?' Gerard asked.

'We'd like to interview you separately, to begin with,' Debbie said. 'But just so you are aware, this is a more formal process than the conversations you have had with my colleagues up until now. We will be recording them.'

'So, they could be used as evidence?' Grace asked.

'No. We are just gathering information. There is no indication this is anything other than a tragic accident. But three boys have died, and the coroner is investigating the circumstances of the deaths. And, of course, the parents of the boys deserve to know what happened.'

'So, you're looking at who's to blame?' Gerard said.

'Absolutely not,' Debbie replied. A matronly tone found its way into her voice. 'This is not about apportioning blame. We're simply piecing the facts together to give everyone a clear picture.'

'To what end?' Gerard asked.

'To create a report for the coroner,' Debbie said. 'It's the coroner's role to determine the cause and circumstances of a death.'

'But they can press charges?' Gerard asked.

'No,' Debbie said. 'The coroner can only make findings. It would be up to the police to lay charges, but honestly, in circumstances like this, an accident on a school camp, that's incredibly rare.'

Grace knew there were worse things than being charged – like living with the knowledge everyone held you responsible for three young lives being cut short.

'What mostly comes out of coroner's findings are changes to procedures, to stop accidents like this happening in the future,' Debbie added.

Grace thought of the cases she had studied in her outdoor ed course – the drownings, rock-climbing falls and accidents that had claimed the lives of students or teachers. They always mentioned coroner's findings. She wondered whether Jake, Roberto and Harry would now be added to those units of study. The boys from St Finbar's College, plus Gerard Kruger, Tom Winter and the teacher in charge, Grace Disher; their names would become part of outdoor ed folklore, their every movement on that day analysed and judged by people who weren't there, who didn't know them, who didn't see how huge the seas were and who would most likely never have to face the sort of decision Grace had.

Throughout the morning, Grace was shunted from one room to another: meetings with the CSD people, a brief session with the counsellors to set up a longer one that afternoon, then the one she most dreaded – the police. She did her best to hold herself straight, to force her eyes to engage with whoever was asking the questions. She referred to her scribbled notes, mostly when she needed to concentrate, recentre herself or force a pause to regain her strength.

Minh Tran sat in on the police interview. Grace was grateful for his quiet presence. He only interrupted once, advising her that she shouldn't answer a question one of the interviewers asked about why she thought the boys had run ahead of the main group.

'Grace wasn't with them,' Minh had said. 'She couldn't possibly know why the boys did what they did.'

The interview wasn't what Grace expected. She thought Debbie would be asking the questions. Instead, there were two other uniforms: Collins, a man in his mid-forties with a neat moustache and a slight New Zealand accent, and a woman, Chol – older, but not by much – whose voice rose and fell as she spoke like she was reading a bedtime story.

They began by shaking hands with Grace and offering their sympathies. There was nothing hard-edged about either of them, which immediately put Grace on guard. She had prepared for similar tactics to Heaney's, but she guessed this was all about disarming her, getting her to relax before teasing out the detail of what had happened. She was especially wary when they left long silences for her to fill.

Grace's notes didn't list the sequence of events at Juliet, but rather what she had told people already – Heaney, Pez, Sarah, Fiona, Jim. She wanted consistency in her statements. She watched for any signals between Collins and Chol – a raised eyebrow, a murmured comment, a shared look at one of their notebooks. But she saw none of that. They were a well-rehearsed double act.

Grace had anticipated most of their questions. They asked her about her distance from the boys when they ran into the water, and they seemed to accept – as best Grace could tell by their muted responses – that she was close enough for them to see her and hear her, if not for the wind and pounding surf.

But then.

'We understand from your earlier statements that you made a decision not to attempt to rescue the three boys,' Collins began.

Grace nodded. 'First rule of rescue,' she said, trying to sound emphatic. 'Don't create another casualty.'

Collins leaned back in his chair and kept his eyes fixed on Grace. His face gave nothing away.

'You have a lifesaving qualification, don't you?' he asked.

They had done their homework. 'A Community Surf Bronze,' Grace said. 'It's different.'

'How so?'

'It's a qualification specifically designed for teachers who work with kids in the outdoors.'

'Doing what sort of activities?' Collins asked, leaning forwards again to jot something down.

'Surfing, canoeing, swimming, that sort of stuff,' Grace replied. 'All low level. Flat water canoeing. Swimming and surfing at low-risk beaches.'

'Low risk? Who judges that?' Collins' interest had been piqued.

'Most beaches in the state are rated.'

'And Juliet Beach?'

'High risk,' Grace replied.

'But you had your students there.' Collins said. 'On a day when the weather outlook was particularly bad.'

'Yes, I had them there. To *walk*.' She emphasised the word, struggling to keep the frustration from her voice. 'We were well equipped for the conditions, and the weather was forecast to ease that night.'

'Back to your qualification, then,' Collins said, seemingly satisfied about Juliet's risk status. 'Was it current?'

'Yes. I requalified in February.'

Chol had been tapping away at her laptop. Now she turned it to Collins, who took a minute to read whatever was on the screen.

'The Community Surf Certificate involves a run–swim–run component,' he said. 'How did you go in that part of the course? In February.'

Grace's hands were under the table. She gripped the sides of her chair and tried to remain calm. 'I passed,' she said.

'Tell us about the run-swim-run, Grace?' It was Chol who asked this time, her voice less interrogating than Collins'.

'Run two hundred, swim two hundred, run two hundred. All in eight minutes,' Grace said, recalling how she'd used the runs to make up time. She was a reasonably confident flat-water swimmer, but the time pressure of the test always made her lose her stroke, gasp for air, panic a little.

'And what was your time?' Chol asked.

'I can't remember exactly. Seven minutes something.'

Collins nodded. 'That would be recorded somewhere?' he said.

'By the examiner, yes. I was inside the required time,' Grace said, a little more forcefully than she'd intended. 'And look,' she added. 'They do the test at Port Melbourne. In the Bay. In flat water. Like I said, it's not a qualification designed for a beach like Juliet.'

'So, your training told you not to attempt to rescue the boys,' Collins continued.

'That's right,' Grace said. 'It would have been futile. And I'm pretty sure I would have drowned, too.'

'Pretty sure?' Collins asked. 'Or certain?'

'As certain as I can be.' Grace felt Collins was probing at an exposed nerve, searching for a response she was determined not to give.

Chol took up the questioning again. 'Just to be clear, Grace . . .' Her voice was quiet, deliberate, like she was thinking through every word. 'There were no other students on the beach at the time. Apart from the three boys who had run into the water.'

Grace shook her head. 'That's right.'

'So, no one witnessed what you are telling us happened.'

Grace pushed back in her chair. She tried to control herself, but her anger must have shown. 'No. No one,' she replied. There was a short silence.

'What I mean is,' Chol continued, 'you didn't owe a duty of care to anyone else at the time? Just the boys in the water. There weren't any other students there you had to look after?'

'No,' Grace replied. 'Just the boys in the water, who I couldn't save.'

When Erin brought in biscuits and more coffee, Grace took the opportunity to excuse herself and use the toilet. She needed to piss, but she also needed to compose herself. She splashed water onto her face and rolled her neck to relieve the tension that had built up there.

The toilet flushed in the cubicle behind her, and a woman opened the door. Grace didn't recognise her, but there had been so many people coming and going that morning, she wasn't surprised. The woman was in her fifties, slightly over-weight, wearing jeans and a dark blouse. She paused when she saw Grace's reflection in the mirror, then came to the sink next to her. She didn't break eye contact.

'Miss Disher,' the woman said.

Grace turned to look at her directly. Her eyes were rimmed with red, and she was bracing herself against the sink, as though struggling to stay upright.

'Are you alright?' Grace asked.

The woman's bottom lip trembled.

'Can I get something for you?' Grace asked.

The woman shook her head, steadied herself. 'You don't remember me, do you?' she said.

'No, I'm sorry, I don't.' Grace held her breath.

'We met briefly at the information night,' she said. 'I'm Felicity Edwards. Harry's mother.'

Grace reeled back, her hand lifting to her mouth.

The two women stood a metre apart, the silence thick between them. Then Felicity drew herself up and inhaled deeply. Tears ran down her cheeks as she held her arms out to Grace. 'You poor thing,' she said. 'I am so sorry this happened to you.'

Grace couldn't breathe. Felicity's words broke whatever resistance she had left in her.

Harry's mother opened her arms, and Grace fell into them without hesitation. She wanted to be held by someone who understood, whose loss was even greater than hers.

'I'm sorry, I'm so sorry,' Grace said, her body convulsing with grief and loss and guilt. 'I couldn't save them.'

'I know, I know,' Felicity said. 'Jim told me everything. It was an accident, Grace. They were boys. Stupid, silly, beautiful boys. Who knows what they were thinking?'

'Not just boys. Your boy. Harry.'

Felicity gently stepped back and held Grace by the arms. She moved one hand to Grace's face and lifted her chin to look at her. 'I will miss my son every day of my life,' she said. A strength Grace couldn't begin to understand had found its way into Felicity's voice. 'I've got four boys. Harry was my youngest. I've seen all of them do stupid things, dangerous things, without thinking. We can't be there all the time to protect them from themselves. I don't know why Harry ran into the water, or Jacob or Roberto. And I never will.'

Grace could hardly hear the words Felicity was saying. She was deafened by the kindness of this woman who had lost an entire part of her life.

'Now,' Felicity said, brushing her hands down the arms of Grace's jacket, 'we've both got more important things to do than stand around crying in the bathroom.'

Grace nodded, gathering herself.

Felicity took a card from her pocket and handed it to Grace.

'This is my number. Call me anytime, if you need to talk.'

With that, she picked up her bag and walked to the door.

'How can you do this?' Grace said to her back.

Felicity turned to her. 'Forgive?'

'Yes, forgive.'

'My husband, Harry's father, was a paramedic. He took his own life five years ago. We have to look after the living, Grace. Always remember that.'

Felicity opened the door and disappeared.

22

Back in the interview, Grace couldn't recall any more details she hadn't already told Collins and Chol. Distance from the events hadn't gifted her greater clarity, and the encounter with Felicity seemed to erase everything that had come before it.

Thankfully, they hadn't asked any questions about the risk management plan, so Grace didn't have to decide whether or not to lie. She was also aware that Collins did most of the talking, while Chol watched her intently. Grace was sure she was looking for tell-tale tics or pauses that indicated she may not be saying everything she knew. The intensity of it wore Grace down until, just after the two-hour mark, Minh stepped in again, saying he thought they should take a break. Chol and Collins looked at each other and agreed they had all the information they needed for the time being. They thanked Grace, offered their sympathies again, and encouraged her to get in touch if there was anything she remembered that she hadn't already told them.

After the police interview and before the session with the counsellors, Grace went back to the boardroom. Gerard wasn't there, and she wondered how he had fared. Erin told her Tom had been allowed to go home and would be interviewed later.

Grace found herself mercifully alone. Jim had discouraged other staff from coming to speak with her, as all their energies needed to be focused on the students. And Grace had no intention of visiting the staffroom or wandering into the yard, where no one would know how to approach her or what to say. She was sure those that knew her number would have tried to call. Not for the first time in the last twenty-four hours, she wished she had kept a better eye on her phone in Colac. At least she would get it back as some stage today.

Grace moved to a corner of the room and sat sideways on a low couch, pulling her knees up to support her laptop. She hadn't looked at any media since last night.

The ABC was still leading with the story, though now the focus had moved to the grieving families. She clicked on a video of Roberto and Daniel's family. It was filmed in front of a neat brick-veneer house that had an ornamental grape vine in autumnal reds and yellows framing a concrete porch. A dozen men and women, young and old, formed a half-circle around a family spokesperson as he read a statement. The caption identified him as Sam Lombardi, an uncle of the boys.

Behind him, Grace recognised Bruno, Roberto's father, who she'd met at the information night. She couldn't see Daniel.

In a halting voice, Sam read the prepared statement.

'Our family is devastated by the loss of Robbie, our gorgeous, smiling boy. He was so full of life, always telling jokes and messing around. He loved his family, he loved his football, and he and Danny were as close as brothers could be.'

Bruno's head dropped to his chest. He covered his eyes with his hand.

'We don't know how this terrible accident happened, but we know two other families are grieving, and our thoughts and prayers are with them. Robbie was taken from us far too young. He had his whole life ahead of him. We will never get to see him . . .' His voice broke, then he gathered himself. 'To see him grow into the beautiful man we know he would have become.

'This is as much as we can say right now, but we ask that you please respect our family's privacy. We will announce funeral details when they are available.'

When the video finished, Grace stared at the last frozen frame. It caught Bruno peering into the camera, like he knew she was watching. *I see you*, his eyes said.

Grace turned away from the screen, took five deep breaths to compose herself, then logged into her new Twitter account.

#threeboysdrowned was still trending. She clicked on it and scrolled. She hadn't seen any photos of the boys on the mainstream news sites, but all three were pictured here – even Jake, whose body had yet to be found. In the Twitterverse, you could always find information the traditional media was

too wary of defamation suits to publish. The video of the Lombardi family was posted multiple times, with thousands of likes and retweets. Grace scrolled through the comments. Most offered condolences to the family and questioned how the accident could have happened without directly apportioning blame. But at the bottom was the option to view comments that may contain offensive material. Grace hesitated, clicked on it and immediately wished she hadn't. There was more of what she'd read the night before, but the viciousness had been dialled up to eleven.

@tractorboy99 Someone has to pay. Fuck those useless teachers that let this happen.

@pinprick55 My cousin is a cop. He reckons this whole thing stinks. Gutless fuckin teachers watched the kids drown.

Grace closed her eyes, but her fingers continued to scroll. When she opened them again, her heart leapt into her mouth. There was a picture of her and Louise, taken on the beach at Elwood towards the end of summer. They'd met up with friends after a swelteringly hot day. They were standing in their bikinis, their skin golden in the light. She remembered they'd asked Jaz, an old school mate of Louise's, to take the photo. They were onto their second bottle of wine and a little drunk. Louise had looked directly at the camera, trying not to laugh, but Grace's face was turned to her, her tongue in Louise's ear. Her arm was looped around Louise's back, and the fingers of her right hand cupped her breast.

There were more than a hundred comments below the picture. Grace only got as far as the second one.

@davos5792 The bitch on the right she's the one the fuckin dyke that let the boys drown I'd fuckin drown her if got hold of her.

Grace's jaw clamped shut and her hands clenched into fists. The laptop slipped onto the couch cushions, and she wrapped her arms around her knees to hold herself tight. Her heartbeat thumped in her ears.

'Are you okay, babe?'

It was Louise. She moved quickly across the room and kneeled beside the couch. 'What?' she asked. 'What's happened?'

'I've gotta get out of here,' Grace said suddenly. She slid away from Louise's grasp to the end of the couch, grabbed the laptop and sprang to her feet.

'Wait,' Louise said. 'Talk to me. What's wrong?' She was still on her knees, looking up at Grace.

Grace felt dizzy. She propelled herself across the room to the kitchenette, clipping a chair and knocking it over. She vomited into the sink, barely aware of Louise's hands rubbing her back.

When she thought she had nothing left inside her, Grace splashed her burning face with cold water and straightened. 'Can you help me?' she asked.

'Of course. But what's happened? Was it the police? What did they say?'

Grace turned to look at Louise. The kitchenette was tiny, and they were so close to each other. 'Can I take your car?' she asked.

'Sure,' Louise said. She searched Grace's face. 'But don't you have the counsellors this afternoon?'

'I can't. I just can't,' Grace managed to say, her breath

coming in short bursts, unable to get enough air into her lungs. 'They let Tom go home,' she added.

'Tom's not well,' Louise said. 'You saw him this morning.'

Grace widened her eyes and turned her hands palms up. 'And me? I'm coping just fine, am I? Good old Grace, she's the tough one. She'll be okay.'

'That's not what I meant,' Louise said defensively. 'You're doing so well, you really are.'

'No, I'm *not*, Lou! I'm not coping at all. Inside, I'm on fire. I keep seeing the boys. I keep hearing them calling to me.'

Louise tried to pull her into an embrace, but Grace resisted, keeping her arms tight by her side. 'That's not the help I need,' she said, holding eye contact with Louise. 'I need your car keys.'

Louise let go and retreated to lean against the bench on the opposite side. Grace knew she was hurting her, but everything was closing in and she needed to run.

'I don't think you should be driving,' Louise said. 'Not in this state.'

Grace pushed past her. 'Fine,' she said. 'I'll walk.' She strode back across the room, picked up her laptop where she had dropped it earlier and pushed it into her bag. When she turned, Louise was blocking the doorway.

'Don't do this,' Louise said. 'Talk to me, Grace. Please. It's me.' She closed the door and stood in front of it.

Grace stopped in the middle of the room. Fumbling for her laptop, she opened it and turned the screen to Louise.

Louise stepped closer, leaning forwards to make sense of what she was seeing. 'Oh, fuck,' she said. 'No, no, no.'

'It must have been on my phone,' Grace said.

Louise stared at the photo. 'No,' she said, her voice slow and deliberate. 'I remember this photo. Jaz took it on *my* phone, and I never sent it to you.'

'Are you sure?'

'Positive.'

'But how, then . . .?'

'This is getting too weird. How are they getting hold of this stuff?'

Grace looked into Louise's eyes. Unable to contain herself any longer, she began to cry for the whole fucked up mess her life had become in the last three days. She cried for herself, and she cried for Lou, and she cried for Harry and Jake and Roberto.

The car was clean and smelled of air freshener. Louise had insisted an Uber was a better option than driving. The counsellors could wait. Louise would make the arrangements, then meet up with Grace later in the afternoon.

Grace knew exactly what she needed to do. She'd take the Uber to her place, pick up her car and some clean clothes, and then she'd go for a run. Thankfully, the driver wasn't the chatty type. He eyed Grace in the mirror once or twice but otherwise didn't seem interested in conversation. It wasn't until they exited the freeway and began to wind their way through the side streets of Flemington that he spoke.

'Terrible, what's happened at that school,' he said without

turning his head. He was middle-aged, greying at the temples but gym fit by the look of his arms straining his t-shirt.

'Hmm,' Grace replied, hoping her response would discourage him.

He waited a few seconds then said, 'I feel sorry for the parents. I mean, their boys go off on a school camp and they never see them again.'

'Just at the end of Grimshaw Avenue will be fine,' Grace said.

'Did you know them?' the driver persisted.

'No,' Grace said. 'I'm an IT consultant. First time I've been to St Finbar's.'

The man nodded. 'Shit's going to hit the fan,' he said. 'Someone's gonna have to pay. I mean, three boys –'

'This'll be fine. Stop here,' Grace interrupted. They were still a few blocks from her home. She'd walk.

The driver pulled over. 'You sure? Fare'll be the same if I take you all the way.'

'It's fine,' she said. 'Thanks.' She grabbed her bag, stepped out onto the footpath and shut the door.

The afternoon sun was unseasonably warm for May. The streets were quiet as Grace navigated her way towards home. After everything that had happened that morning, she wanted to feel something normal, like she was coming home from work early on a sunny afternoon. Maybe she'd had the day off and taken the opportunity to catch a train into the city to do some shopping. Or maybe she'd just come from a job interview and was already imagining herself in the new role.

But as she reached the end of Grimshaw Avenue, all the fantasies fell away, and she was gripped by the same panic that had taken up residence in her bones since Tuesday afternoon. Nothing was normal. Cars and vans were double-parked in the narrow street, and a dozen people congregated outside her place. Cameras sat on the pavement in an assortment of boxes and cases, and the reporters chatted casually with each other.

Grace turned towards the alleyway again. She walked past it first, to check whether the back entrance was being watched. She couldn't see anyone, so she turned in and ran for the gate, being careful not to slip on the uneven cobblestones.

1960 and the lock was open. She slid through and closed the gate behind her, being careful to lift it so it didn't scrape loudly on the concrete. This time she had her keys with her. She unlocked the back door and went straight to her bedroom, staying low so no movement could be detected through the stained-glass panel in the front door. She changed quickly into her running gear and packed a sports bag with a few days' worth of clothes – clean undies, socks and shoes – all the time plotting how she could get to her car without being spotted. Louise said she had parked it further down the street, closer to the station. She prayed she hadn't been blocked in by one of the double-parked media vans.

She was surprised at how clearly she was thinking now that she had another problem to deal with: staying hidden in a city where she was convinced everyone would recognise her.

She walked out to the yard, pulled the crate over from near

the gate and propped it against the side fence. She climbed up and called Vic's name.

'Grace. What's up?' Vic was on his knees weeding around the base of a lemon tree. He stood and pointed to the front of the house. 'It's a shitstorm out there. Want me to knock a few heads together?'

Grace almost smiled. 'Hi, Vic. I just need a distraction so I can get to my car.'

'Now?' Vic was a man of few words.

'Give me a minute. I'll go out the back way. But Vic . . .'

'Yeah, what?'

'Don't do anything stupid. I don't want you getting in trouble on my behalf.'

Vic laughed. 'I haven't thrown a punch in twenty years, Grace. Mind you, I reckon my left is still pretty solid.'

Grace could hear Mrs Spinoza in the background.

'Thel wants to know if you need anything. She's just made a mud cake and she says you could have some.'

'Maybe next time, Vic. But thank Thel for me, will you?'

'Stay safe, then,' Vic replied. 'And if you need help, anywhere, anytime, you call Vic, you hear?'

Grace bit her lip. Vic's brand of rough kindness touched her. 'Thanks, Vic. I'm on my way out the back now.'

Grace waited in the yard until she heard raised voices on the street. She didn't know what Vic was doing, but he clearly had the attention of the media crews. She broke into a jog once she locked the gate behind her. Past the turn onto the laneway, she slowed as she approached the intersection with the street.

Chancing a look around the corner, she saw everyone's attention directed at Vic, who was ranting about not being able to leave his own house and telling the assembled crews they should all fuck off before he called the police.

Grace took her opportunity and walked as casually as she could to her car. Thankfully, it wasn't blocked in. The motor of the ageing Subaru sprang to life, and she turned out onto the street with only the briefest glance in the side mirror. Her peripheral vision picked up the van just as it swerved to miss her. She heard the screech of brakes and looked up to see a delivery driver gesticulating. The media crews were only fifty metres away, and she knew they would be looking. She accelerated quickly, narrowly missing the van. At the end of the street, she nearly stalled at the stop sign but floored the accelerator and drove off, wondering when she would be able to return to Grimshaw Avenue.

The circuit of Princes Park was just over three kilometres, and Grace could usually complete ten k's in fifty-five minutes. After finding a park in a side street at the back of the cemetery, she did her stretches on the low railing fence that bordered the ovals and started her run at a fast pace. Running had always been her go-to de-stressor. She'd run the four hundred competitively at school, but the older she got, the more she liked the challenge of longer distances. Now she fell into the beat of her regular running playlist, coming via the ancient iPod mini she kept in the glove box.

Before leaving her car, she'd tied her hair in a low ponytail and pulled a tight peaked cap down over her forehead, then added a pair of wraparound sunglasses. It gave her the confidence to head out into a public place, certain no one would recognise her.

It was mid-afternoon, too early for the office workers from the CBD to have hit the track. There was a sprinkling of men and women, maybe shift workers or students from the uni, large, thin and everything in between, all chasing the same endorphins.

She steadied her pace, finding her flow and enjoying the soft give of the gravel under her feet. No one looked at her. There was no rule about which direction you ran in, but she had always chosen anti-clockwise on this circuit. She liked the long straight stretch along Royal Parade and the way the path followed the gentle curve of Bowen Crescent.

Grace had reached a shaded part of the track close to the Carlton football ground on her second lap when it happened. She'd been keeping good pace, wiping at the sweat sliding down the side of her face and feeling the release from the weight of the last few days. There was a break of about twenty metres between her and the person in front. Had she not had her earbuds in, she may have heard the runner coming from behind.

He took her totally by surprise. A firm hand met her squarely on the back – a hit more than a push – and she was propelled forwards. Her feet went from under her, and she sprawled onto the gravel, barely getting her hands out to break her fall. She turned her head sideways and her temple met the path with a sickening thud. She skidded more than rolled, tearing the skin on her knees, elbows and palms.

The knock to the head disorientated her as she tried to

sit up. Struggling to focus, she looked to see who had hit her, but all she could make out was the receding shape of a man wearing jeans and a hoodie. He veered off the track and crossed the street, disappearing behind a row of parked cars.

A woman approached and stopped to help.

'Are you okay?' she asked, crouching beside Grace, who was sitting on the grass.

'Did you see him?' Grace gasped. 'The man. He pushed me over. Deliberately.'

The woman looked at her sympathetically. 'Sorry, I didn't see anyone. Are you sure you didn't just fall?'

'He pushed me!' Grace said firmly.

'Okay,' the woman said, backing off a little.

Grace examined her hands, roughly brushing away the loose gravel to reveal the torn skin underneath. Blood ran down her forearm from her left elbow, and there was a deeper cut on her knee. Her sunglasses had been knocked off and lay broken by the path, snapped at one hinge.

'You should report him,' the woman said, picking up the glasses for her.

She was young, Grace saw. Long-limbed and clear-skinned.

'I'll be fine,' Grace said, struggling to her feet.

'Can I call someone for you?' the girl asked.

'I'm okay,' Grace said. 'My car's just over there.' She pointed towards the cemetery.

'If you're sure,' the girl said, shrugging.

Grace nodded and moved away slowly. 'Thanks,' she said over her shoulder.

'Don't I know you?' the girl called after her. 'Are you at the uni?'

Grace didn't answer. She waved her hand in the air and limped towards her car. When she looked back, the girl had resumed her run.

Blood trickled down her shin from the cut on her knee. She stopped and examined it more closely, hoping it wasn't as deep as it appeared. It might need stitches. Her whole body was sore. She imagined the bruises already beginning to bloom on her thighs and bum where she'd landed heavily.

As she turned into the side street where she'd parked, she slowed to look for anyone loitering near her car. She was usually wary, watching for men who looked longer than they needed to, crossed the street as they came towards her, observed her through tinted windscreens – the normal precautions a woman had to take – but now there was a more direct threat. She had become a person of interest, someone recognisable, thanks to the trolls and keyboard warriors. It heightened her senses so that she could no longer go about her life without second-guessing strangers' motives.

She walked on the opposite side of the street to where she'd parked until she drew level with her car. She surveyed the scene but saw only a mother walking with two small children in school uniforms. One of the kids was pulling her ahead, in a rush to get home. Grace crossed the narrow street, unlocked the car and quickly slid behind the wheel. Her heart sank when she saw the parking ticket stuck under the windscreen wipers. She was sure she'd checked the signs and that she was in a two-hour zone. There was no way she'd been away from the car for that long. Opening the door, she reached around and grabbed the slip of paper. Immediately, she noticed it wasn't attached with a piece of tape, like tickets usually were.

But it wasn't a parking ticket. It was a folded piece of paper torn from a lined notebook. Grace pulled the door closed and locked it before unfolding the sheet with shaking hands.

Scrawled in vivid red were two words: *GUTLESS DYKE*.

23

Louise was exhausted by the time she walked into the meeting at five o'clock. The day had been an endless stream of demands.

The photo on Twitter had rocked her. Up to that point, there had been a chance she could ride out the storm, supporting Grace and staying out of the spotlight. But the photo had changed all that. Her image had been plastered across the internet without her consent. Not the image of a professional administrator either, and not the grave face of a senior teacher at a school dealing with the loss of three of its students. No, the Louise Chan the public was seeing was squinting into the summer sun on a crowded beach, her mouth turned up in a wide smile as Grace's tongue licked her ear and Grace's hand cupped her breast.

They were seeing her body, the freckled shoulders giving way to a summer tan, the flesh dented by the colourful straps of her bikini and the tops of her breasts visible. To Louise, the photo had been somehow symbolic of everything Grace had brought to her life, the way she had opened her up to the world, allowing her to view it in a different way – inch-by-inch pushing aside the conservatism of her Catholic upbringing, giving her permission to express everything she used to hold back.

Now, she shuddered at the thought of her parents seeing the photo when it hit the mainstream media. Their daughter on display to the world. It would vindicate everything they had warned her about when she had finally come out and introduced Grace to them. They'd been supportive, of course, telling Louise they loved her 'no matter what' and welcoming Grace. But behind their eyes, Louise had seen the disappointment. Tread carefully, her mother had told her, warning her about living her life *too openly*. Those words had stayed with Louise, and now her mother had been proven right. She had been living her life too openly, choosing to believe the world was an accepting place. And now she was paying a price for her negligence.

What she still didn't understand was how someone had accessed the picture. After Grace had left that afternoon, Louise had opened her phone and scrolled though her photos, but it wasn't there. Her photos were synched to her laptop, so she checked there, too. Nothing.

The meeting was in the boardroom. It was becoming Louise's second home – the centre of crisis management as the school struggled to keep up with the onslaught of the tragedy and its aftermath. She wished Grace hadn't left in such a hurry. It had been all Louise could do to get her to use an Uber instead of driving herself. Louise had ordered it, setting the pick-up at the Fitzgerald Road gate, ensuring Grace could make a discreet exit.

Jim Sheridan looked tired. His face was drawn, and his usually healthy complexion had a washed-out greyness that wasn't there earlier in the day. There were bags under his eyes, and Louise saw how he struggled not to let his shoulders drop when he sat down. He was dealing with the double blows of being a principal and a grieving uncle.

Fiona Knowles somehow managed to appear as though she had spent the day at a spa retreat. Her hair was tied in an immaculate bun, her makeup had recently been reapplied and she sat ramrod-straight in her chair. Not bad for a woman who had been sleeping on the couch in her office. Also sitting around the table were Erin, Luke Thomas, Minh Tran, Sergeant Collins and Joseph Spender, from the Catholic Schools Directorate.

Louise rubbed her temples with her index fingers and tried to focus.

Jim took his time, checking notes and talking quietly to Erin, who stood up and disappeared into the kitchenette.

'Thanks, everyone, for being here,' Jim began. 'I know it's been a difficult day and you all want to get home, but I thought it was a good idea to bring you up to speed with where we stand.'

He looked at the faces around the table, pausing a little longer at Louise, holding her gaze as though it triggered something he'd forgotten.

'You all know Sergeant Collins?'

'Brian, please,' Collins replied.

'Brian is working with Debbie Petkovic,' Jim continued, nodding. 'They are gathering information for the coroner and keeping us updated on what's happening at the search site.'

Collins was sitting opposite Louise, and she studied him as he began to speak. There was a practised neutrality in his voice that portrayed sincerity without giving away his own thoughts.

'I've spoken to my colleagues at Juliet this afternoon and they are scaling back the search. As you know, the bodies of Harry Edwards and Roberto Lombardi were recovered yesterday morning, but it is now highly unlikely the third body will be found.'

'What exactly does scaling back mean?' Luke asked.

'We'll maintain a police presence for another day, mostly land-based along the coast to the east and west of Juliet, but the SES are withdrawing their units. This isn't unusual. If a body hasn't been found after forty-eight hours, experience tells us it won't be recovered. The continued presence is just to reassure the families and the public. And, unfortunately' – his voice lowered as though there may be someone listening at the door – 'there have been sharks sighted in the area.'

He stopped to let that sink in.

'Jesus,' Luke said, under his breath.

Collins continued after a short pause. 'Back here, we have concluded our interviews with Grace Disher and Gerard Kruger, but we haven't been able to speak to Tom Winter yet. We understand that may take a while to organise, but we don't need to rush this part of the investigation.'

'Thanks, Brian,' Jim said. 'Anything else?'

'Just this.' Collins reached into the bag at his feet and pulled out a clear plastic bag with a phone in it.

Louise recognised it immediately as Grace's. There was a sticker on the back, the feminist fist in black and white.

Collins handed the bag to Jim, who didn't seem to know what to do with it. Eventually, without saying anything, he slid it along the table to Louise.

She tried not to react. 'Thanks,' she said. 'I'll pass it on to Grace. When I see her.' She wasn't sure why she added that last sentence.

'There are a few other matters we need to deal with,' Jim said, but Fiona interrupted him by raising her hand.

'Fiona?' Jim said.

'I'm sorry,' Fiona began, 'but I think we need to address the elephant in the room.' Louise looked at her and saw that Fiona was waiting for her to speak. When she didn't, Fiona continued. 'I'm not sure how appropriate it is that Louise remains in this group when it is clear she has a conflict of interest.'

The room fell silent. Luke twirled a pencil in his fingers and Minh looked studiously at the tabletop.

Louise had thought this would be raised at some point, but she hadn't expected it to come from Fiona. So much for the sisterhood. But she couldn't ignore it, especially now that she had seen the photo on Twitter.

Erin bustled back in from the kitchenette with a jug of water and glasses on a tray. She slowed as she neared the table, picking up on the tension that seemed to be crackling around the room.

'Okay,' Louise said. 'I'm willing to step aside if you think that's what's best for the school.'

Erin set the glasses on the table and poured. Everyone waited.

Joseph Spender, who had been quiet up to this point, cleared his throat. He spoke slowly, drawing out his words as though he was navigating a minefield.

'It is unfortunate that this situation has come to light at such a difficult time,' he said. 'We are attempting to deal with the loss of Jacob, Roberto and Harry, but this issue with Grace is proving a distraction. We need to reassure our community by seizing back the narrative.'

Louise struggled to understand exactly what Spender was saying. She waited for him to explain, but he was looking at her, obviously expecting a response.

She tried to quell the anger in her voice but failed. 'Sorry, but when in the last three days did our concern for the boys' families and for Grace, Gerard and Tom turn into "seizing the narrative"?'

Louise didn't miss the slight twitch at the side of Spender's mouth.

'Of course, we have the utmost concern for the welfare of our employees,' he said. 'But –'

'Just not the gay ones?' Louise interrupted.

No one said anything, waiting to see how Spender would respond. Jim was suddenly sitting straighter in his chair and Fiona's eyes widened. Erin stopped pouring, the jug hovering over the last glass.

Collins looked distinctly uncomfortable. He stood up. 'I think I'm done here,' he said, gathering his things. 'Jim, you have my card. Don't hesitate to call.' He looked relieved when no one argued with him.

'I might remind you, Miss Chan,' Spender continued after they had watched Collins close the door behind him, 'of the contracts you and Miss Disher both signed when the school employed you. While everyone has the right to their privacy outside of school, the Directorate has made it clear that staff are expected to abide by the teachings of the Catholic church.'

Spender's words were designed to remind everyone in the room of his authority. Louise had the impression of a sharp blade moving towards her throat.

'I have always upheld those values at work,' she said, looking around the table for support. Only Jim nodded.

'Yes, but now your private relationship with Miss Disher has impinged on your professional life,' Spender replied, 'in a way that reflects poorly on the school and on the diocese.'

'My private life has nothing to do with how I operate at school,' she said firmly. 'Can anyone here give a single example of me not acting with complete professionalism during my time at St Finbar's?' She knew she was on solid ground here. She had been diligent in building her reputation as a hard worker, always organised and prepared, always willing to put in the extra hours.

'That's not what's at issue here,' Spender said. 'You have been in a same-sex relationship with a junior member of staff and you have kept that relationship from your employer.'

Louise was stunned. *A junior member of staff!* Was that how they were going to play it? She was not just a secret lesbian, then, but one who had exploited a vulnerable young teacher. *Jesus.* That blade was inching closer.

'Can we just –' Jim began, laying his hands on the table and spreading his fingers. 'Can we just bring the discussion back to the most important matters at hand? The impact of this tragedy on the families and our students. I think that is where we should be focusing.'

Louise looked down the table to Jim and understood immediately what he had done. The Directorate was his employer, too, and Spender was its representative. She gave him the slightest nod of appreciation.

But Spender wasn't finished. 'Thanks, Jim,' he said, pointedly. 'You are right, of course, but you have to understand this from the archbishop's point of view.'

Fuck, Louise thought, *now it's the archbishop, not just the school and the Directorate.*

'It's times like this,' Spender continued, 'when our whole system comes under scrutiny. Most people who call themselves Catholics don't go to mass, but they send their children to Catholic schools. So, our schools are the public face of our faith, and we need to be seen to be upholding the spiritual values of the church. That's our mission.'

'So, what are you suggesting, Joe?' Jim asked.

'The archbishop believes Miss Disher should be offered paid leave for the remainder of the term. We think it would be the best way for the school and the CSD to redirect attention to supporting the families and demonstrating our compassion for their loss.'

'And what about Gerard and Tom?' Louise asked, each word hard and sharp, accusatory. 'Will they be shoved off out of sight as well?'

Spender exhaled sharply. 'Miss Disher has been more traumatised by what happened – by the decision she made.'

'The decision she made?'

'Choosing not to rescue the boys.'

No one at the table moved. Outside, a car horn sounded.

Louise's mouth fell open. 'Are you blaming her?'

'Of course not,' Spender said. He took his time to consider his next words. 'But I do think of John 15:13.'

Louise was bewildered.

Spender closed his eyes. 'Greater love has no one but this, that he lay down his life for his friends.'

'Seriously?' Louise said. 'You are quoting the Bible at me now?'

'I'm simply explaining why Miss Disher should be placed on leave,' Spender said. 'The trauma of the ordeal aside, Mr Winter and Mr Kruger haven't allowed themselves to be compromised in the way she has. I don't see any need for them to go on extended leave.'

'Just Grace, then?' Louise asked. 'What about me? If this is all about who's compromised themselves?'

'You didn't lose three students,' Spender replied sharply.

Louise could smell bridges burning behind her.

'So,' she said, 'you are going to hang Grace out to dry. All your Catholic compassion doesn't allow you to protect a young woman who's been through a terrible trauma, seeing three of her students drown in front of her. And why won't you support her? Other than the fact your Bible tells you she should have drowned as well? Because in her private life — which is none of your business — she doesn't live up to *your* values. Well, I'm sorry, that's just pathetic.' She could hear the rise in her voice and knew how overly dramatic it sounded.

Spender stared at her. Keeping his movements slow, he opened his laptop, tapped at the keyboard, scrolled, and then turned the screen so everyone could see.

Louise's stomach turned.

It was the photo.

There was an audible intake of breath around the table.

Spender turned his attention back to Louise. 'How do you propose we deal with *that*, Miss Chan?

THE MELBOURNE STAR
THURSDAY 25 MAY
QUESTIONS ASKED OF TEACHER AT CENTRE OF SCHOOL CAMP TRAGEDY
A ROSE COTTER EXCLUSIVE

Following the drownings of two boys – with a third missing, presumed dead – at Juliet Beach, in the state's south-west on Tuesday, the *Melbourne Star* can reveal more details about Grace Disher, one of the teachers on the school bushwalking trip.

Miss Disher, who has only been a member of staff at St Finbar's College for four months, was the teacher in charge of the camp, even though two more senior male teachers, Gerard Kruger and Thomas Winter, accompanied the group of year ten students.

When contacted by *The Star*, James Sheridan, principal at St Finbar's, defended the school's decision to put Miss Disher in charge of the excursion. 'Grace Disher was the most qualified bushwalker on the trip, and she followed all the school's risk management guidelines,' he said.

However, a teacher at St Finbar's who spoke to *The Star* on condition of anonymity said concerns had been raised within the school about the planning for the trip.

'Naturally, the school community is doing everything to support Grace, Gerard and Tom but some of us are questioning whether the trip should have gone ahead at all,' the teacher said. 'The school's senior outdoor ed teacher wasn't able to go, the weather forecast was terrible and that stretch of beach is notorious, so it really has to be asked: why were they there in the first place?'

Life Saving Victoria has issued a statement saying that while they couldn't comment on cases being investigated by the coroner, the first priority of rescue was not to create another casualty. The statement also said that there were multiple drownings on Victorian beaches last summer that involved rescuers dying in their attempts to help others.

It is believed, however, that Miss Disher was a qualified lifesaver.

The Star can also reveal Miss Disher left her previous position at a Perth high school following alleged inappropriate conduct with a male student. A parent at East Perth Consolidated School, Greta Munez, has told *The Star* her son had complained to the school's principal about Miss Disher's conduct but the allegations were 'swept under the carpet'. *The Star* has been unable to contact the school's principal for comment.

It is also alleged by a parent whose son attends St Finbar's that Miss Disher had a poor relationship with some of the students on the excursion, and had argued with them the night before the drownings.

Meanwhile, Miss Disher's current whereabouts and movements are a mystery. A Victoria Police spokesperson, Leading Senior Constable Deborah Petkovic, confirmed investigators have spoken with Miss Disher and that she is cooperating fully with their enquiries.

24

When Grace got back to Louise's place, she ran a hot shower and felt the burn of the water against the abrasions on her hands, elbows and knees. There was a small graze on her temple, and bruises were already visible on her hips and thighs. She cleaned her injuries. The pain was not unwelcome.

She had taken a circuitous route to Louise's, checking and rechecking her rear-view mirror. She tried to figure out how anyone had known she would be running in the park. Had they followed her from school? From home? Were they still tracking her movements? And who were *they*?

As Grace stood in front of the mirror, drying herself, she thought about what to do next. Only one plan made sense to her: she had to get away. Not far, but far enough to be out of the spotlight. But how? And where? Jim had said she could take as much time as she liked, but she was pretty sure that meant staying in Melbourne, being available to the police, the counsellors and the school. And the funerals, they would be happening soon.

She did her best to dress the cuts, using steri-strips to pull the edges of the wound on her knee together. Once she had cleaned it, she saw it probably needed stitches, but she wasn't about to try to find a clinic when she had so much else going on. Dressed in a pair of jeans, a t-shirt and runners, she began to pack. She wished she had taken more time at her place to think about clothes, but a quick rummage through Louise's wardrobe yielded enough to see her through at least a week. They were a size too big, but she could buy anything else she needed along the way. But along the way to where? If the media were onto her, and her picture was splashed across the internet, chances were she'd be recognised wherever she went. Her dad was down on the Peninsula, but if they'd found her place, they could find his, too. Besides, she hadn't heard back from him yet. She knew he didn't have Louise's number, but he may have tried to contact her via the school. She kicked herself for not having checked at the office before she left.

Grace carried the sports bag through to the kitchen, moving carefully to protect her injuries. She'd tied her hair back again, wedged the cap onto her head and experimented with using a scarf to hide more of her face.

Formulating a plan was a useful distraction. Her gut was still knotted, and she was nauseous every time she thought about food. And the voices in her head were growing louder: Rick Bolton's abuse, Fiona's patronising lectures, Jim's half-arsed support, Louise's attempts to calm her – even, eons ago, Jake's cheeky provocations at Crayfish Bay. All of them were shouting at her now, goading her to take the fall, to accept she had failed the boys, that she'd come up short when she was needed most. And swamping it all were cries for help from Roberto, Jake and Harry. She had no recollection of actually hearing them at the beach, with the wind screaming and the swell pounding the beach, but she heard them now.

Help, Miss. Help!

Her thoughts were interrupted by the sound of a key turning in the lock and the front door swinging open. Louise stopped for a second, silhouetted in the doorframe against the early evening glow of streetlights. Grace stood at the other end of the hallway and waited. Something had shifted between them in the last two days. It wasn't just the photo; it went deeper, making them question who they were together. Grace couldn't name it, and she was sure Louise couldn't either, but they both felt the change. They were usually so physical with each other, on their own if not in public – Grace in particular. But now there was a barrier between them, something neither one seemed to know how to push through. Maybe it was because their relationship had become common knowledge, public property to be judged and assessed by anyone with a phone and a need to be outraged.

'What the . . .?' Louise said, dropping her bag at the door and walking quickly towards Grace. 'What happened to you?'

Somehow, Grace hadn't prepared for this. She spoke quickly, not wanting a scene. 'Nothing,' she said, adjusting the cap on her head. 'I went for a run and fell over. That's all.'

Louise touched Grace gently under the chin and turned her face to the light. 'A run? Was that a good idea?' she said. She tried to keep her voice even, but Grace heard the exasperation.

'I just had to burn off some energy,' she said, shrugging. 'And it worked. I feel better.'

Louise wasn't convinced. 'How did you fall?' she asked.

'I wasn't looking. I bumped into someone. It's fine, really. A few scratches,' she said, holding up her palms for Louise to see. 'I was lucky. It could have been worse.'

Louise held her gaze for a few seconds then walked back up the hallway. 'I've got something for you,' she said. She brought her bag through to the kitchen and handed Grace her phone.

'Oh, thank Christ,' Grace said. She almost dropped the phone in her haste to plug it into the charger and turn it on. When she entered her passcode, notifications lit the screen up like a Christmas tree – the result of a full day's disconnection from the planet. She quickly scrolled through the messages and felt a swell in her heart. They came from all over: friends, colleagues, outdoor ed mates – and her dad. All of them asking if she was okay, if she wanted to ring them, if there was anything they could do. There were too many to deal with individually.

Tears welled in Grace's eyes, blurring the screen. She couldn't understand why this was somehow more consoling than having Louise right there next to her. Maybe it was the distance, the choice of who to talk to and when. Since Juliet, too many things had come at her too quickly, too immediately – blows delivered at lightning speed that, as much as she ducked and weaved, she couldn't evade.

Then Louise was behind her, her forehead resting on Grace's back, her arms looping around her waist. Grace tried not to flinch when she pressed against her sore hip, but Louise felt it.

'What is it?' Louise asked, her mouth shifting close to Grace's ear.

Grace took a deep breath. 'I didn't exactly fall,' she began, but she was interrupted by her phone ringing. It was Jim.

'Take it,' Louise said, seeing the name on the screen. 'You need to talk to him.' She moved away towards the fridge and pulled out a bottle of white wine before Grace could question her.

'Hi, Jim,' Grace said.

Louise held up two glasses and Grace nodded.

'Grace,' Jim said. 'You've got your phone back. That's good. How are you doing? You left school early today.'

'Sorry, it was all a bit much,' Grace replied, understating the fierce need she had felt to escape.

'That's fine, Grace. Really. It's best that you take it slowly.'

Jim left a long enough pause for her to begin to feel uncomfortable. Grace took the glass Louise offered and drank.

'Grace,' Jim continued, finally, 'there are few things I need to let you know about. Have you spoken to Louise this evening?'

'Only briefly,' Grace said, shooting a glance at Lou. Louise lifted her glass to her lips and sipped her wine.

'That's good,' Jim said. 'It's probably best you hear this from me. The executive thinks it would be wise for you go on paid leave until the end of term – come back fresh after the holidays, when all this will have settled down a bit.'

Grace sank slowly onto the stool at the island bench. *Come back fresh when all this will have settled down a bit!* Like there'd been some disagreement in the staffroom, tempers had flared and regrettable things had been said. That's the sort of situation that would *settle down*. How do you start *fresh* when three of your students have died?

'Of course,' Jim went on, 'we will still be here for you, but you need to take time away, Grace. The media are making things very difficult, I know, and we're feeling that pressure, too. There have been some unfortunate leaks: unauthorised statements from someone on staff and – well – I'm not sure if you have seen it yet, but a compromising photo of you and Louise has been posted online.'

'Someone stole that photo, Jim,' Grace said, anger rising in her voice. 'And not only that. Someone is stalking me. Not online. In real life. I was attacked this afternoon.'

Fuck! Louise mouthed. *Why didn't you say?*

Grace turned away from her.

'I'm sorry, Grace. What happened? Are you alright?' Jim said. 'Have you called the police?'

'I'm okay,' she said. 'A few bruises, nothing too bad. Someone knocked me over when I was out running.'

Grace had her back to Louise, but she could feel her bristling.

'And you think you were followed.'

'Yeah, I do,' Grace said. 'There was an abusive note left on the windscreen of my car.'

'You need to be careful,' Jim said, a paternal note in his voice. 'This is getting out of hand. Have you got someone there with you?'

'Louise,' Grace replied.

'Of course. Yes. Good.'

'Is that all, Jim?' Grace asked.

When he didn't respond immediately, Grace braced for the next blow.

'Actually, I just got off the phone with Bruno Lombardi, Roberto's father. They are going to have the funeral at St Catherine's on Tuesday.'

'Okay,' she said, relieved. 'Thanks for letting me know.'

'It's just' – Jim cleared his throat – 'the Lombardis have asked that you don't . . .'

'Don't what?'

'They just think it would be better if you didn't attend the funeral.' He rushed the words out.

'What?' Grace was incredulous. 'Why?'

'I'm just relaying the message from the family, Grace. I'm sure it's just that they don't want any undue media attention. Not on such a sad day for them.'

'You mean they don't want the teacher who couldn't save their son there?'

Jim exhaled deeply. 'They are grieving, Grace. They're not thinking clearly.'

Grace ended the call and slammed the phone onto the bench.

'What now? Louise asked. She put her glass down and reached over to touch Grace lightly on the hand.

'The Lombardis,' Grace replied, her voice breaking. 'They don't want me at the funeral.'

'Oh, babe. I'm sorry.' Louise hesitated. 'But it might be for the best.'

'What?'

'Listen to me –'

'You're supposed to be on my side,' Grace interrupted, before Louise could continue.

'I *am* on your side. You know I am. And I'm doing my best to help you.'

'How are you helping me, Lou? Tell me, how?' Grace pulled her hand away and crossed her arms defiantly.

'You're so buried under the weight of everything that's happened, you're not thinking straight. The Lombardis are grieving.'

'Why do you sound exactly like Jim?'

'Because Jim is trying to help you as well. We all are.'

Grace heaved a defeated sigh and slumped onto the bench.

Louise brought her hand to Grace's face and touched a finger to the graze on her temple.

Grace winced.

'What happened this afternoon?' Louise asked, her voice gentle now, encouraging.

Grace couldn't bring herself to look at Louise. 'I was going to tell you,' she said, knowing it sounded feeble. 'I just didn't want you to worry.'

'So . . .' Louise said.

Grace told her about the hit, the fall, the note.

'Did you see them before they ran off?' Louise asked. 'Could you identify them?'

'My vision was blurry. It was a man, solid. That's about it.'

'And you think they followed you to the park?'

'How else would they know it was my car when they left the note?'

'We need to tell the police, Grace. This is dangerous. Someone with knowledge of your movements, who knows your car, is stalking you.'

Grace considered making a call, maybe to Pez. But what could he do? Put a guard on Louise's place? As far as she could tell, no one knew this address, so they were safe for the time being. But the idea of getting away from Melbourne, was now fixed in her mind.

'They could have just randomly followed me from my place this afternoon,' Grace said. 'That wouldn't have been hard. Tailed me from a distance, watched where I parked.'

'Media, you mean? That's who would have been at your place. If it was, why didn't they take your picture or film you? That's what the media do. They don't attack you and leave messages on your windscreen.'

Grace drained the rest of her wine. 'You know,' she began, hesitantly. 'I've had this feeling for months, since I came back to Melbourne and started at St Finbar's.'

'What sort of feeling?'

'Like I'm being watched. Followed. Remember that bunch of roses left on the bonnet of my car at school?'

Louise looked sceptical. 'We talked about that. You said you thought it was just a student with a crush.'

'Yeah, but what if it wasn't?'

'You're overreacting, Grace. I doubt there's a link to what's happening now.'

Grace told Louise about the cut straps on her pack.

'You think it was one of the boys?' Louise asked.

'Yeah, I do. There was so much going on at the car park, it would have been easy to get at the pack.'

'They would have needed a sharp knife . . .'

'Honestly, Lou, I don't know. Everything is so confusing. I can't think straight. I just . . .' She shook her head.

'What?'

'I need to get away for a bit.'

'Come on, you know how that will play out.' She made air quotes with her fingers: '"Teacher at centre of tragedy disappears", "Where is Grace Disher?" It'll just feed the fire.'

'Why is the media fixated on me, like I was the only teacher on the trip?'

Louise leaned over the bench and ran her fingers along the back of Grace's hand. 'I don't know, babe. I really don't.'

'I do. It's because Gerard and Tom are men. Everyone assumes they would have tried to rescue the boys. They think Jake and Roberto and Harry died because it was a woman who saw it happen. The police, Jim, they all think the same. And now Roberto's parents don't want me to go to the funeral. Why do you reckon that is?'

'It doesn't matter what they think, Grace. They weren't there.

You were, and you made the right decision based on your training. That's what you've got to focus on.'

Grace ran her hands through her hair. 'Do you know the worst thing? I think if it *had* been Gerard or Tom, they *would* have tried to save the boys. It'd have been stupid and reckless, and they would probably have drowned, but they'd have tried. And they'd have been heroes.'

'You don't know that, babe. But if one of them had tried, there'd be four people dead instead of three. No one is ever going to say this out loud, but it was the boys' own fault they died. They made a stupid decision and they paid with their lives. When it comes down to it, you can't guard against teenage stupidity.'

'Can't we? Don't we do that every day at school? Isn't that why we patrol the yard at lunch and recess, to protect them from themselves? How many times have you stopped a boy from climbing onto the roof to get a ball? Or told them off for sliding down the rail on the outside stairs?'

'All reasonable care, Grace. That's what we provide. But accidents still happen. Kids still do dumb things. They break bones and smash windows and fight each other. There's only so much we can do.'

Grace was about to tell her about meeting Harry's mum when she heard a loud thump at the front door.

They froze.

'Are you expecting anyone?' Grace asked.

Louise held her index finger to her lips and shook her head.

They waited.

Silence.

Slowly, Louise tiptoed up the hallway, Grace behind her. They edged into the bedroom and Grace looked through the parted curtain. The porch was illuminated by the streetlights, but there was no one there. She turned back to Louise and shrugged.

In unspoken agreement, they moved back into the hallway.

'Hello?' Louise called. She reached for the lock, turned it and opened the door a few inches.

They were immediately hit by an animal smell. There was a chicken on the doormat, its throat cut, its feathers a crimson red. The door was splattered with blood.

'Jesus,' Grace exclaimed, pushing past Louise. She ran out onto the footpath and looked up and down the street, then stepped onto the road and screamed. 'What do you want from me, you gutless arseholes? What do you want?' She spun around with her arms outstretched. 'Here I am!'

A porch light switched on across the road and the front door opened cautiously.

'Keep it down, will ya?' A man's voice. 'We've got kids in here.'

Then Louise was beside Grace, pulling her back through the gate. She had kicked the chicken carcass into the garden, but blood stuck to the soles of her shoes. Grace struggled but eventually allowed herself to be dragged inside.

25

'I told you I had to get away from here.' Grace had returned to the kitchen and picked up her sports bag. She stood, ready to leave, with the bag hanging over her shoulder.

'We need to call the police,' Louise said. 'This is out of control, Grace. You were attacked this afternoon, and now they've got this address.'

'You can call the police. I'm out of here.'

'For fuck's sake, stop and think for a minute. They're following you. It's too dangerous to leave. We're safe here for now.'

'Safe? Someone killed a chicken and sprayed its blood all over your front door. How does that make you feel safe?'

Louise stood in front of Grace, not blocking her path but not allowing her to leave either. 'Okay,' she said, 'I think you

257

should leave, too. But not yet. Let's sit down and work out a plan. Together.'

Grace held her ground but didn't try to push past her. This was so like Louise. A *plan.* How could you plan against someone who seemed to know your every move?

'Remember what we agreed the other day, in that paddock outside Colac?' Louise continued. 'That we'd get through this together, no matter what.'

'Yeah, but we didn't know they'd come at us like this. The media's bad enough – and socials are completely feral – but now I've got some psycho stalking me, too.'

'I know, but we've just got to be smarter, more careful. And racing off now – to who knows where – will only make things worse.'

Louise reached for Grace's sports bag and slid it off her shoulder. Grace slowly loosened her grip and allowed her to take it.

'I need to make some calls,' Grace said, pulling her hand away. 'Dad, to start with.'

Louise nodded. 'Have you eaten?' she asked.

Grace honestly couldn't remember. 'I don't think so.' She knew preparing a meal would soothe Louise. She was always happy cooking, providing. 'Could you make pasta? I might be able to hold that down.'

'Not chicken soup?' she said.

Grace smiled despite herself. 'Nah, not tonight.'

Grace retreated to the bedroom and called her dad, but it went straight to voicemail. He wasn't the type to carry his phone with him; and he'd be out doing something, keeping busy. It wasn't just undivided love and attention she wanted from him. Grace's uncle, her dad's brother, owned a beach shack down on the west coast. It would be an ideal hideout: close enough to get back to Melbourne if she was needed, but far enough away to escape the shitstorm.

She waited for the beeps and composed herself. 'Hi Dad. It's Gracie. Again. Things are pretty messed up here. Love to talk to you. Give me a call as soon as you can. Love you.'

There were too many other messages to deal with right away. Grace didn't want to get caught up explaining the accident over and over, and she didn't want to hear the pity in her friends' voices. She wrote a generic message reassuring them she was okay and promising to get in touch soon, then cut and pasted it to her WhatsApp groups and into texts to her closest friends.

The smell of frying onions and garlic wafted in from the kitchen, and Grace's stomach rumbled. Just as she opened the bedroom door, her phone rang.

'Hi, Dad.' She felt a sudden tremble in her voice.

'Ah, sweet pea, are you alright? I've been trying to call you for two days.' His voice rose above the sound of a radio.

'Where are you?'

'At the boat shed. You told me not to come to Melbourne, so I've been trying to distract myself from seeing my daughter all over the papers.'

Grace could picture the scene, her dad's hands covered in fine dust from sanding the hull of the couta boat he'd been restoring for years. The place would smell of old paint and shellac.

'You're masked up while you're sanding, aren't you, Dad?'

'Course I am. My daughter would rip me a new one if I wasn't.'

'That's good.'

Her dad's voice never lost its blokey tenor, even when he was expressing fatherly concern. 'Tell me what's been happening, darlin'. The media's full of shit. I hate those bastards.'

'I'm okay, Dad. It's been awful, though.'

'Fuckers! They just want someone to blame.'

Grace knew she'd get what she needed from her dad: unconditional support. Louise was trying her best, but she was compromised by being on the executive. She had to have her feet in both camps. And right now, Grace wanted someone wholly on her side.

'Is Lou there?' he asked. 'Is she looking after you?'

'Yeah,' Grace said. 'She's here. She's been great.'

'I haven't got her number. I reckon it's time you sent it to me.'

'I will, I promise.'

'What about the school? I don't see them coming out guns blazing to back you.'

'It's complicated, Dad.'

'I rang them half a dozen times trying to find you.'

'I'm sorry. Long story, but I didn't have my phone. Dad, does Uncle Gav still have the house down at Browlea?' It was years since Grace had been there, but she remembered its isolation – a fibro shack buried deep in the tea trees, a back gate leading to the dunes and the beach minutes away.

'Yeah. I went over there last summer for a few days. That's about as long as I could put up with him. But the shack's still standing. Christ knows how, he doesn't look after the place.'

'I need somewhere to get away, Dad. The media aren't going to leave me alone if I stay in Melbourne. They're following me everywhere.'

'Come and stay with me. If they hassle you down here, I'll show them the thick end of a cricket bat.'

Grace pictured her dad on the news, waving a cricket bat at the cameras like a crazed loon.

'I need somewhere they can't find me, somewhere they don't know about.'

'How would they find you here?'

'I don't want to risk it. They've been tracking me since the accident happened. I dunno how.'

'You're not still doing that Facebook rubbish, are you?'

All social media was Facebook rubbish to her dad.

'No. I shut all that down straight away.'

'Good. It's dangerous, that stuff. You give away too much and it comes back to bite you on the bum.'

'Gav's house?' Grace reminded him. 'Do you reckon he'd let me use it for a few days?'

'Yeah, of course he would. I'll ring him. The spare key is in the outdoor dunny. Lift the lid off the cistern and it's hanging on a piece of wire.'

'Thanks, Dad. You're a gem.'

'Yeah, alright. But I want you to call me every day. And I'll come over on the ferry on the weekend, see how you're going.'

'That'd be great.'

'You remember how to find the place?'

'Course I do. That house was part of my growing up. I loved it there.'

'Yeah, your mum did, too.' He let out a little groan. Grace pictured him stepping down off the ladder.

'Your back still playing up?' she asked.

'Ah, you know. Could be worse.'

Grace smiled.

It occurred to Grace after she said goodbye that he hadn't asked anything about the accident – how it happened, who else was there, whether she could have saved the boys. His concern was entirely for her: how she was coping and what he could do to help. She knew they'd sit down on the weekend and talk through it in detail, but for now all that mattered to him was that she was okay. She loved him without reservation.

Now that she had a plan, Grace wanted to get moving. But there were logistics to work out – food, transport and setting herself up at the beach house. She wanted to go tonight if she could.

Louise had set two places at the small table in the corner of the kitchen. They rarely ate there, preferring the stools at the island bench, but Grace knew she was making an effort on her behalf. Sauce simmered in the pan, and the pasta was on the boil. Louise had loosened her hair and taken off her jacket. Grace watched her. Everything about the way she cooked was methodical. She cleaned up as she went, so by the time dinner was served, there were no dishes to wash, just the pasta bowls they ate from and the cutlery they used.

'Did you speak to Colin?' she asked, bringing food to the table.

Grace had toyed with the idea of not telling Louise where she was going, but she knew that would be cruel. And she would need her help to get away without being followed.

'Yeah. He sends his love.'

They sat down and Grace told her the plan.

Louise sprinkled parmesan over her meal. Her face gave nothing away, but she nodded as she listened. 'It could work,' she said, eventually. 'You'd have to stay away from the towns and shops, but we could organise food from here. We've got those emergency meals in the freezer.' She checked her watch. 'I can still get to the supermarket tonight to top up our supplies.'

Grace was relieved. She'd expected Louise to argue with her, to try to convince her she should come along. An unexpected wave of love swept through her.

The pasta was a Louise special, made with anchovies, capers and cherry tomatoes. As much as anything, the familiarity of it was comforting. Grace began forking it into her mouth like it was her last meal, suddenly ravenous now that she had a plan.

'What about the cops?' Louise asked. 'Should we call them?'

Grace didn't see the point. What could they do? But she knew Louise had been dragged into the mess she had created, and she didn't want her harassed any further.

'I've got Pez's number,' Grace said. 'I trust him. He won't overreact.'

'But isn't he search and rescue?' Louise asked. 'I'm not sure they do dead chicken call-outs.'

'Exactly,' Grace said. 'He'll know what to do, though, maybe give us a contact in Melbourne we can trust not to leak to the media.'

'Should we tell him about you leaving?' Louise asked.

Grace thought about this for a minute. Her bowl was almost empty, but she could hardly remember eating. 'We'll just tell him I've got somewhere safe to go for a while.'

Louise placed her knife and fork neatly on her plate and sat back in her chair. She shook her head. 'I've been trying to figure it out,' she said. 'Who could be behind the harassment? I mean, you're copping it from all angles, but it's not completely random.'

'And . . .?' Grace said.

'I think it could be someone associated with the school. Think about it. They know your car, and probably mine, too. They could have seen you come and go.'

'What about Rick Bolton? He was so angry at me yesterday.'

Louise wobbled her head. 'I don't know. They still haven't found his son's body. He'd be a mess, and this stuff is calculated. Smart.'

Grace wasn't convinced. She couldn't forget the fury in Bolton's eyes when the two of them had spoken in the tent. His disgust at her attempts to console him. The way he spat the word *cunt* at her.

'Jim said there'd been a leak from inside the school,' Louise said. 'A staff member? An older student, maybe. A brother of one of the boys in your class?'

'That doesn't explain the pictures.'

They looked at each other across the small table. Nothing made sense anymore, and they both feared what might come next.

After they cleared the dishes away, Grace brought the esky in from the back shed and started filling it from the fridge and freezer. Louise took stock of what else Grace might need and grabbed her car keys and a shopping bag.

'Maybe head out the back way,' Grace said.

Louise thought for a few seconds. 'You know what? Fuck them. I'm going out my front door, and if anyone tries to follow me, I'll give their car a Pajero enema.'

Grace had only seen glimpses of this Louise before, the gritty, determined one who called out other people's shit.

'I reckon if the best you can come up with is chucking a dead bird at my door, you're seriously wanting in the guts department,' Louise said, striding down the hallway. She opened the door wide and closed it loudly behind herself.

26

The Geelong freeway was quiet once Grace got past Werribee. Her dad had texted with the all-clear from Uncle Gav. Louise was certain no one had followed her to the supermarket, and she had returned with the Pajero stocked with enough food to feed a small family for a month.

Grace had had a long conversation with Pez. He was already aware of the media harassment and the Twitter storm, but he was much more concerned when she told him about the running incident and the chicken.

'Okay,' he'd said, 'I'll get onto some colleagues in Melbourne and have them check it out. I'm worried someone has both your addresses. Take extra care, Grace. Whoever it is – and it might be more than one person – they are escalating their actions.

That's never a good sign.'

'Thanks, Pez. I appreciate it.'

'There's another thing,' he said. 'Rick Bolton has disappeared off the radar. We haven't been able to contact him.' He paused. 'The attacker in the park. Could it have been him?'

'Honestly, I couldn't say. I was dazed and all I made out was a dark shape. It was a man, though. Definitely a man.'

'Okay. But if you see or hear from him, contact triple O immediately. In the meantime, we'll put out an alert.'

Louise had insisted Grace drive the Pajero. They had taken the precaution of driving both cars to the nearest petrol station. They'd dressed similarly, dark clothes and red peaked caps. They filled the two cars and went inside to pay. When they exited, they swapped cars, Grace taking the Pajero and Louise the Subaru. Then they headed off in opposite directions. Grace had driven around Carlton for fifteen minutes, edging the SUV into a series of tight alleyways and cruising slowly down Rathdowne Street before cutting across Royal Park to the freeway. By the time she got to the on-ramp, she was certain no one was tailing her. Still, she drove warily, over the West Gate Bridge, through the roadworks and finally onto the open freeway. Every set of headlights in the rear-view mirror felt like a threat. She changed lanes regularly, slowing to allow cars to pass if they'd been behind her too long, speeding up in the fast lane to leave others in her wake.

Now, as she travelled further into the night, Grace thought more about Rick Bolton. He knew her Subaru. He was a car dealer and she recalled him pushing his card into her hands at the information night in February, saying something about upgrading to a real four-wheel drive. He would be familiar with the area around the school, and he'd know where to wait if he wanted to follow her. She tried to remember the car he'd driven when he arrived at Juliet on Wednesday morning. It was a big SUV, but what colour?

Past Geelong, she exited for Torquay, following the highway through the sprawling subdivisions that crept towards the coast. Browlea was a remnant of an earlier time – a few dozen houses squeezed between the coast and the surrounding wetlands. Established in the fifties, it was a cluster of shacks away from the bustle of the larger towns, with no shop, no petrol station, nothing.

Grace turned off the highway and followed the winding road through farmland until it gave way to the coastal flood-plain. Most of Browlea was hidden in tea trees, tucked up hard against the back of the dunes. It was past midnight by the time Grace arrived, and most of the houses were dark. She guessed a lot of them would be either holiday properties or retirees' homes. Either way, not a lot of action on a Thursday night in May.

Eventually, having pulled over to allow a car behind her to pass, Grace turned into South Beach Road. It was little more than a dirt track winding its way through the overhanging trees. When she found the property, there was a chain across the gateway but no lock. As Grace stepped out of the car, the brisk southerly whipped the trees above her and cut through the thin jacket she was wearing. The driveway was steep, held together by heavy sleepers buried in the sand and gravel. Grace parked by the side of the shack and used the torch on her phone to locate the key in the old toilet attached to the back verandah. Then she had to find the fuse box and switch on the power, by which time the cold had seeped into her bones.

The front door was jammed so tightly she thought the key might not be working. It turned in the lock, but she couldn't budge the door. Eventually, she used her already bruised hip to push it open. Switching on the lights, she was hit by a flood of childhood memories with cousins and uncles and aunts: swimming and surfing and throwing themselves down the faces of sand dunes, returning to the house in the late afternoon, dancing around in the freezing outdoor shower, communal meals, games of cards and Monopoly, the kids sleeping in a big tent in the backyard while the adults talked and drank into the night – only to do it all again the next day.

The furnishings were a mishmash of op-shop chairs and couches. A threadbare rug, grainy with sand, struggled to cover the exposed floorboards. The house smelled of damp and Grace guessed no one had been here since January. She was too tired to do anything more than unload the frozen food, her toilet bag, clothes and doona from the car. She made the bed in the front room and collapsed onto it. As she drifted towards sleep, she felt safe for the first time in days. The house was close but remote, hidden in plain sight among the other holiday shacks, and the memories of summers past were a comfort, as though all those people were still there, closing their familial arms around her, watching over her.

She had no idea what she would do next, but those decisions could wait until morning. She texted Louise: *arrived safe, all good, love you xx*

For the first time since Juliet, Grace slept without dreaming of drowning. And for the first time, when she woke, she wanted to feel Louise next to her, wanted to feel her skin and the warmth of her breath. She knew Lou had reached out, tried to hold her close a dozen times over the past three days, but guilt and grief had somehow made her feel unworthy. Now, with a full night's sleep behind her, she thought maybe it was the exhaustion as well. With so much having happened so quickly, she hadn't coped at all, hadn't wanted anyone – not even Lou – to see how completely overwhelmed she was.

She lay in bed and rang Louise, knowing she'd be at work and that it'd go to her voicemail.

'Hey, it's me,' she said after the beeps. 'Just ringing to say hi. Hope you have a good day.' She paused. 'I know I've been hard work this week, and I am so grateful you've been there for me. I love you.'

There were more than thirty messages from friends and colleagues, all responding to her cut and paste texts of the night before. She scrolled through them and was warmed by the support. Still, she wished they were game enough to defend her on social media.

The last message in the long list seemed strange. It was from Tom Winter. She hadn't spoken to him since the meeting yesterday and even then, he'd barely responded. They weren't friends at school, though he'd filled in a couple of times on their mixed netball team. Grace had given him and Gerard her phone number at the beginning of the trip, as a safety protocol.

Hi Grace. Hope you are healing okay. Wondered if we could get together somewhere for a chat just to talk about what happened. I'm taking a few days off so could meet you wherever. Tom.

Grace reread the message. *Hope you are healing okay.* What did that mean? Did he know about her fall in the park? Was it common knowledge already, and if so, how did it get out? She'd only told three people: Pez, Jim and Louise. Which one of them would have told Tom? Or was she overreacting? Did he mean healing from the trauma of the accident?

Either way, Grace didn't want to meet with him. She was having a hard enough time on her own without worrying about his skewed take on what happened at Juliet. And she wasn't sure she'd be able to stop herself from asking why the fuck he had sent Harry out after Jake and Roberto.

Grace craved coffee, but most of the food and supplies were still in the car, so she took a fresh towel and her toilet bag and headed for the bathroom. There was a full-length mirror on the back of the door. She pulled off her T-shirt and pyjama pants and examined her wounds. The cut on her knee had bled through the bandage, which she carefully unwound. The steri-strips were still in place, but the gash was seeping. After showering in surprisingly hot water, she sat on the edge of the bath and cleaned the cut with cotton buds, then smeared her knee with antiseptic cream and bandaged it again. The other grazes were drying into scabs. Then there were the purple blooms on her hips and thighs. She'd always been a bruiser. Flashes of the fall came to her. The force of it, the intent, the suddenness that hadn't allowed her time to react. Why would someone do that? Why did men so readily default to violence?

By mid-morning, she had unpacked the car and settled herself on the front deck. It would never have passed a building permit. Grace was pretty sure her uncle and dad had knocked it up themselves – probably on a long weekend over a slab of Coopers Ale. Still, it had weathered the assaults of wind and rain and, even though it creaked under her every step, Grace loved the view it offered over the treetops to the wetlands. The late autumn sun lit the front of the house and a smattering of clouds scudded by in the light onshore breeze.

She was onto her second coffee when she heard a car turn off Dundas Road and make its way towards her. It was moving slowly, a diesel with a rumble to its exhaust. Grace slipped back inside and watched from behind the living room curtain. South Beach Road was a dead-end street, so it seemed strange that someone unfamiliar enough with the area to be crawling along would be here on a Friday morning. When the vehicle came into view, it was a dark-coloured four-wheel drive. Again, Grace tried to remember the colour of Rick Bolton's car. The four-wheel drive stopped so it blocked the driveway, and a man stepped out onto the road. Grace let her breath go when she saw it wasn't Bolton. This guy looked to be in his sixties, small but solidly built, with a shock of white hair. He looked up and down the road, then started the climb up the driveway towards the shack.

'Hello,' the man called from the bottom of the steps. 'Anyone home?'

Grace tried to assess his voice. It didn't have an aggressive tone, sounded more concerned. She stepped out onto the deck.

'Can I help you?' she said, trying to sound assertive.

The man pushed his sunglasses to the top of his head and looked up at her.

'G'day,' he said. 'Des Carton. Live at number seven. Keep an eye on the place for Gav.'

'Ah, okay,' Grace replied, careful not to introduce herself. 'Thanks. I'm just here for a few days.'

The man eyed her sceptically. He looked at the Pajero parked by the side of the house, as though he might find an explanation there. 'From Melbourne?' he asked, turning back to Grace.

'Yeah.'

'Right. Friend of Gav's, are ya?'

Grace nodded. Disher wasn't a common name, and he might link it to the woman on the news.

An uncomfortable silence fell. Grace tried to hold the man's gaze. She suddenly realised how quiet it was. She had come to the shack thinking the isolation would protect her, but now she felt vulnerable.

'Alright,' the man said, eventually. 'I'll leave ya to it. Give me a hoy if you need anything.'

He turned and walked, legs splayed a little for balance, back down the driveway. When he opened the door of the car, he looked up at Grace and gave a short wave. He stood there a little longer, as though deciding whether to say something more, then climbed in and turned the motor over. She followed the rumble of the engine as it edged further along the road, before it finally moved beyond her hearing.

Grace was unnerved. She'd come here to hide, and someone had found her on the first day. Des was probably harmless, but men his age, retirees with long days to fill between rounds of golf, could be snoopers, sticking their noses into other people's business under the guise of 'keeping an eye on things'. They were the mainstays of Neighbourhood Watch, taking it on themselves to know every movement on their street.

If Des recognised her from the papers or the six o'clock news, everyone at the bowls club, the golf club and the local supermarket would know that the teacher who watched her students drown was staying down on South Beach Road in Gav Disher's old place.

She went inside and poured another coffee, then opened her laptop and connected it to the hotspot on her phone. Her instinct for self-flagellation was kicking in again. And there was always the faint hope some new outrage had distracted the keyboard warriors. It took only few seconds to realise how futile that hope was.

Twitter still had *#threeboysdrowned* trending. *Fuck*, Grace thought. That was three days now. Three days of whack jobs pontificating and theorising, one bit of guesswork leading to another, each post more absurd than the one before, as though they were daring each other to go one step further. And now that her guilt had been established in the court of public opinion, the big mystery had become her whereabouts.

@hyperskye3131 The teacher, Disher, is in witness protection. Wonder what they're protecting her from.

The post was followed by an emoji of a noose.

@whipperskipper22 My bro seen her at Cairns airport yesterday morning he works security there.

@timkothegreat17 Why would they have a woman in charge of an all-boys trip. This whole thing stinks.

@davos5792 She's a dyke she needs a good fuck.

Grace tried to stay calm. She clicked on a couple of the posters but, of course, they had no profile pictures and hardly any followers. She was tempted again to use her own anonymous account to defend herself, but soon realised she had already been scrolling for twenty minutes and the day was wasting away before her. She was more resigned than angry. Nothing she did seemed to have any effect on the storm of vitriol and abuse. And the people who should be supporting her – the school, the police, the diocese – had no presence on social media.

She was scrolling so quickly she almost missed it: a slightly blurred photo looking along Juliet Beach, towards Moonlight Head. It was a screenshot from Instagram, of the picture she had uploaded from the viewing platform:

#bestjobintheworld #dreamjob #Juliet #loveyoumum

She only read the first comment before turning away.

@stubbsie222 She had time to take a photo but couldn't get there in time to save the kids. Fucking negligence.

27

Friday morning, three days after the tragedy at Juliet, and Tom Winter had hardly slept. He'd tried going into school yesterday but had only lasted an hour before needing to get away. Jim Sheridan had rung and left messages. So had Fiona Knowles and Luke Thomas. He didn't want to talk to any of them. Grace hadn't tried to contact him, and she'd ignored him at the meeting at school, cosying up to Gerard.

The house was cold. He lay in bed and listened to the steady hum of cars on the freeway, two blocks away. He could tell the time by the traffic noise: the morning rush was easing, meaning it was after nine. He drew the covers up to his chin and tried to forget everything that had happened. But the images of the beach – the screaming wind, the crying boys, the sheer hopelessness of searching there for hours – they all piled on top of him again and drove him deeper into his own head.

And always, every time, he came back to her. Grace Disher.

They'd only known each other a few months but, before Juliet Beach, he'd felt such a connection with her. The little buzz she set off in him whenever she entered the staffroom, the way she lit up end-of-week drinks at the Tilers Arms. The way she ran her fingers through her hair and pulled it into a ponytail. He wanted to stand behind her and hold her hair for himself, bunch it in his hands and take in her scent.

He'd been to her house after netball that one time. They'd drunk wine and talked, and he'd sat next to her. He'd excused himself and gone to the bathroom, just to touch her towels. Her underwear had been drying on a rack by the heater. So many pairs, she wouldn't miss one.

Then he'd found himself parking on her street and watching the house – just a couple of nights a week, after pistol training. At least, it started as a couple of nights. She had no idea he was protecting her, a guardian angel. She never saw him, but he was there for her, watching and waiting, always ready to step in.

Which made her betrayal all the harder to accept. Louise must have been ten years older. And she was on the executive at school. Surely, that was wrong. At first, he thought Grace was being misled, and he desperately wanted her to know he was there to help. But the closer he looked, the more he realised Grace was complicit in the relationship – the little smiles and nods they gave each other at school, buying each other drinks at the Tilers, always sitting together, touching under the table. He saw it all and couldn't believe how blind the rest of the teachers were.

Then the outdoor ed trip had come up – a long-awaited chance to speak to her away from school, away from Louise. He'd thought he'd be able to get closer to Grace, have a casual conversation while they were walking, careful not to let on how much he already knew about her: the school she'd gone to, the year backpacking through Asia, the outdoor ed course in Bendigo, her last school in Perth.

But the trip hadn't gone as planned, even before the accident. She'd bossed him around, telling him to mingle with the boys rather than talk to her. And that night at Crayfish Bay, when he'd tried to stay up and chat with her, she'd brushed him off, telling him they'd had a big day and she needed to sleep. He could have forgiven her that. She was tired, and the confrontation with Jake in the debrief had rattled her.

But then, the day at Juliet.

He walked to the kitchen and put the kettle on. His housemates had left for work and uni, and he had the place to himself. He looked out the kitchen window to the chicken coop at the end of the yard and remembered he hadn't collected the eggs since he'd left on Monday. The morning was cool as he crossed the patchwork of weeds and gravel, walking to the little structure he'd built when he'd moved into the share house at the beginning of the year.

Returning to the kitchen with three eggs, he made an omelet and forked it into his mouth. He checked his phone to see if Grace had replied to last night's message. Nothing. He went straight to Twitter and logged in. The pile-on was growing in strength, and with every like, every retweet, the attention was moving further away from him and onto her. Soon, no one would even remember he had been there.

Tom made a strong, black coffee and returned to his bedroom. He switched on the desk lamp and brought his screens to life. He liked this set-up, a central console with two additional screens in an arc. It was like sitting in a cockpit, when everything was lit up. The servers, the databases, the configurations that kept the school functioning were a complete mystery to most teachers and administrators. And principals were often the most ignorant; they had so much else on their plates. Tom and his team of three techies never had to explain anything they did. Everyone just wanted the system to run smoothly – they didn't particularly care or understand how.

He had access to everything. The school had a lease–buy arrangement with teachers for their laptops, so they all kept their personal lives – their private emails, photos, socials – alongside their professional work. When they needed an upgrade or new software installed, they dropped off their laptops at the tech desk, effectively handing their lives to Tom and his co-workers. That's how he'd gotten to know Grace. He wasn't interested in all the staff, just the single females. He liked to keep track of their movements, their clumsy attempts at hiding their web history. He stored everything on a hard drive he kept at home.

Now, as he logged into the school's servers, he saw an alert on a document in the database. That wasn't unusual. Teachers were always fucking stuff up, putting files in the wrong place, using compromised passwords, enquiring about problems a primary schooler could deal with. If he hadn't seen the name of the staff member attached to the flagged file, he would have dismissed the alert as nothing of consequence. But it was Grace Disher.

The file was titled *Risk Management Plan, Cape Nelson Bushwalk, 22–25 May*. But something wasn't right. Tom opened the document details and immediately saw the problem. The file had been edited. It was originally added to the database on the 19th of May, three days before the trip, which made sense. But with a little work, he was able to identify the original name on the file: *Staff Leave Requests*. The risk management plan had been cut and pasted into the leave request document, and the time stamps were there for anyone to see: the file had been changed on Wednesday 24 May. A new file titled *Staff Leave Requests* had been created the same day.

Tom shook his head and smiled.

'Oh my God,' he said aloud. 'You didn't log your risk plan until *after* the trip. After the boys were dead.'

Tom sat back in his chair and stared at his screens. He had to find her now. He was still pissed off at having fallen for the switch at the petrol station last night.

He went searching in the school's employment files, where they kept all the contracts, personal details, next of kin. There was no record of Disher's mother, but her father lived in Rye.

If she wanted to hide somewhere safe, where better than with family? He checked back through the media reports earlier in the week and found the name of the copper in charge. Then he brought up Grace's father's details and rang the number.

'Hello, is this Colin Disher?'

'Who's asking?' He sounded angry. Tom guessed this wasn't the first cold call he'd had about his daughter. He imagined the media would have found him by now.

'I'm sorry to disturb you, Colin,' Tom said, softening his voice. 'My name is Senior Sergeant Mario Pezzementi, Victoria Police.' He paused to allow Colin to grasp the official nature of the call. 'Your daughter, Grace, she may have spoken to you about me. I'm in charge of the investigation into the accident at Juliet Beach.'

'Is she okay? What's happened now?'

'Grace is fine, Colin, as far as we know.'

'As far as you know? What does that mean?'

'I'm just trying to ascertain Grace's whereabouts. She isn't at home, and I'm concerned for her welfare. There have been some unsavoury incidents since she returned to Melbourne, directed at her, you understand?'

'Unsavoury?'

'Nothing that's hurt her, but . . .'

'You said she was okay.'

'You've not spoken to her? She's not there with you?'

'No. But why don't you call her? You must have her number.'

'She's not answering our calls.'

'What about Louise, have you tried her?'

'The thing is, Colin, Grace hasn't exactly been receptive to our attempts to keep her safe, so I thought we might be able to just keep an eye on her discreetly.'

'Spy on her, you mean?'

Tom tried not to let frustration leak into his voice.

'Can I talk to you as a father, Colin?' Tom said, changing tack. 'When I spoke to Grace at Juliet, she seemed a very' – he paused to find the right word – 'headstrong young woman. Very independent. But right now, she needs as much help as she can get. If you know where she is, we can protect her without her even knowing she's being protected.'

'Like how?'

'I can get plain-clothed officers, in unmarked cars, to keep her under surveillance. Keep her safe.'

Colin didn't answer immediately. Tom didn't know how far he could push the deception.

Finally, Colin said, 'She's gone down to a shack my brother owns on the coast. The media are hounding her, and she wants to be left alone. She'll be safe enough there without police protection.'

Tom jotted on a notepad on his desk: *coast, uncle.*

'Fair enough,' Tom replied. 'But honestly, Colin, if it was my daughter, I'd want to take every precaution. We're concerned some of the harassment is escalating, and it'll only be a matter of time before they find her.'

Colin stayed quiet for so long Tom wasn't sure he was still on the line. 'Colin?'

'She wouldn't know she was being guarded?'

'She'd have no idea. We're very good at this sort of surveillance, Colin. We do it all the time.'

Another long pause. 'It's 11 South Beach Road, Browlea,' he said.

'Thank you, Colin. I promise we will do everything we can to keep her safe.'

28

By mid-afternoon, Grace was beginning to relax. She'd dismissed Des's visit as harmless. The sun shone brightly, taking the edge off the breeze. She'd sat out on the deck most of the morning, eating toast and drinking too much coffee. By this time of the year, summer was usually a distant memory, but today it was giving a last hurrah before surrendering to the approaching winter. Grace kicked herself for not having brought her swimmers. If it kept up like this, she could walk the half kilometre along the beach to the Mermaid's Pool. It was a grotto, accessible at low tide, where she and her cousins had spent hundreds of happy hours daring each other to jump from higher and higher ledges into the deep water below.

The north side of the deck was screened by greenery

and not visible from the road, so she spread a towel on the uneven boards, stripped to her underwear and lay on her back, shading her eyes with her forearm. She could feel herself burning almost immediately but she didn't care; she wanted to dry out the cuts and scratches on her limbs, and besides, a little sunburn would remind her she was alive. Beads of sweat trickled down the side of her face as she closed her eyes and tried to conjure up the mixture of excitement and safety she had felt at the shack as a kid.

Eventually, she dozed off.

She was startled awake by a man's voice.

'Grace, are you there?'

Someone was standing at the top of the driveway. She grabbed her phone and looked at the time. It was nearly five, and the deck was mostly in shade now.

Grace sat up and wrapped the towel around herself. If she stayed low, she couldn't be seen from the drive. She considered crawling towards the door, but she'd have to slide the screen across to get inside.

'Grace?' the man called again.

She didn't respond. Grace rolled onto her stomach and lifted her head enough to see through the gap at the bottom of the rail.

'Are you there? It's me, Tom.'

Tom Winter. Grace froze. *What the fuck?* How had he found her here? Then she remembered his text, the one she'd felt uncomfortable about. *Hope you are healing okay.*

'Come on, Grace. I know you're here. We need to talk.'

Grace pulled the towel tightly around her body and stood up, reaching for her clothes and bundling them under one arm.

Tom was at the bottom of the stairs now. He stopped abruptly when he saw her. 'Shit,' he said, smiling. 'You gave me a start.' His eyes drifted down her body to her bare legs.

Grace edged back towards the door and felt for the screen. 'Tom. What are you doing here?' she said, trying to breathe evenly.

'Did you get my message?' Tom asked, his foot on the first step. A daypack was slung over his shoulder.

'Yeah, sorry. I meant to reply, but you know what it's been like.' She reached behind her and pulled the screen aside.

Tom continued up the stairs until he was on the deck.

'Wait here, okay?' Grace said, sliding the screen closed between them. 'I'll just put some clothes on, and we'll have a cuppa.'

It made no sense at all, him being here. A creeping dread came over her. Only two people knew where she was, and neither of them would have told Tom.

'Sure,' Tom said. 'But hey, Grace, I think you'll want to hear what I've got to say.'

She thought he was trying hard to sound friendly, like he had just dropped in for a chat on his way to the beach. He must have parked his car out on the road.

'Okay, yep. Sure. I'll just . . .' She pointed towards the bedroom.

She closed the door behind her and sucked air into her lungs. She tried to figure out how Tom fitted into everything that had happened. He'd lost his shit on the beach after the accident, gripping her arms hard enough to leave bruises. She remembered the fever in his eyes. And even before the trip, she had often felt uneasy around him, the way he had tried to corner her at end-of-week drinks, the halting conversations at school she couldn't wait to escape.

She peered past the corner of the closed blind and saw Tom take a seat at the weathered pine table on the deck. He was looking away from the house, sitting casually with his legs crossed and checking his phone.

Maybe she was overreacting. Tom hadn't been coping, that's what everyone had said. He could just want to debrief. He was a bit awkward, that's all – and awkward could be misinterpreted as creepy.

She pulled on a pair of trackpants, a t-shirt and a sloppy hoodie, feeling the need to hide herself in her clothes, to make herself as unattractive as possible.

Then she quickly texted Louise: *Tom Winter here at house. Doesn't feel right*. She switched her phone to silent and tucked it into the pocket of her hoodie.

Grace walked through to the kitchen. 'How do you have your tea?' she called, trying to sound casual.

'You haven't got anything stronger, I suppose?' he replied.

'Sorry. Haven't had the chance to do any shopping yet.'

There was beer in the fridge, but she wasn't about to add alcohol to the mix of anxiety and discomfort she already felt.

Grace looked to the back door. She hadn't opened it since she arrived, and there was no key in the lock. If she had to get away quickly, it'd have to be off the front deck. She returned to the bedroom and slipped on a pair of runners.

'So,' she said, walking out onto the deck and carefully placing the cups of tea on the uneven tabletop. 'How did you find me here, Tom?'

He shook his head. 'Doesn't matter,' he said.

'It matters to me.'

'Seriously, we need to talk, Grace. About what's happening.'

'Did you follow me last night?'

He tried to hide a smirk before looking back to his phone.

Grace studied the side of his face, saw how pale he was, the way he kept blinking. He didn't look well. 'Okay,' she said, warily. 'How are you coping, Tom?'

He didn't answer, just picked up his cup and blew on the hot liquid before taking a cautious sip. He placed the cup back on the table and began to chip at the flaking paint with a fingernail.

'Ah, you know. Trying to keep it together. What about you?'

Grace approached the small talk cautiously. She was sure he hadn't come all this way to check how she was going. 'Same. It's all so awful, isn't it? The media, everybody wanting someone to blame.'

'I know, right? I can understand it, though.'

'You haven't been copping what I have. Threats. Disgusting stuff on Twitter.'

'You don't think you deserve it?'

Grace tried to hide her shock. She placed her cup carefully on the table and edged her seat back a little from his.

Tom's hands trembled. He squeezed them between his knees to still them. 'I mean . . .'

'You mean what, Tom? That I deserve to be to be told by anonymous men that I should be raped, or put in a chaff bag and drowned?'

'No, of course not. But . . .'

Grace stood up abruptly. 'I think you should go, Tom.' Her voice was higher than she intended, strained. 'I don't know how you found me here or what you want, but I've called the police and they're on their way.'

He looked up at her and smiled. Shook his head. 'I'll leave when I'm good and ready. You're in deep shit, Grace.' His voice was calm, malevolent.

Grace felt sweat at the back of her neck. She shivered. 'We're all in the shit, Tom. Gerard told me it was your idea to send Harry after the other two.'

'And he agreed!'

'Whatever. We all fucked up one way or another,' Grace said. 'Now, please, I'd like you to leave.' She took a step towards the stairs.

He turned in his seat, following her with his eyes. 'We're not all equally to blame, though, are we, Grace? Some of us acted in good faith.'

'What do you mean by that?' Grace's gut began to churn.

'I did some digging in the school servers this morning. That's my job, you know, to keep things running smoothly, to fix other people's mistakes.'

Grace felt for the rail.

'You know what I found?'

She shook her head, knowing what was coming.

'It was bad enough you stuffed up on the trip, Grace – not being at the rendezvous point on time, not even attempting to save the boys – but then you compounded your mistakes by lodging a false risk management plan. After the fact.'

'You think I did that? All this creeping around in other people's business, and you didn't realise it was Jim who changed the date on the plan?'

He showed his teeth, then pulled his lips into a tight smile. 'Bullshit!' He slammed his fist on the table, sending the cups flying, the hot tea splashing onto the deck. 'It was uploaded from *your* laptop, using *your* password. You're a liar, Grace. You're trying to blame anyone but yourself, and I'm not going to cop it.'

Grace felt for the first step with her foot. She wasn't sure she could outrun him, but she might make it to Des's place. What number was he again? She'd look for the four-wheel drive.

'I'm sorry,' Tom said. He was standing now, both hands up, palms out, placating. 'We can work this out together, Grace. I can help you, if you'll let me.'

Grace stayed where she was. She needed to calm him down, de-escalate the situation. 'Thanks, Tom, I appreciate that, I really do.' She stepped back onto the deck, trying desperately to make her movements seem natural. 'But I still think you should go.'

She moved aside to allow him to get to the stairs.

He picked up the daypack and unzipped it.

Good, Grace thought. He was putting his phone away, getting ready to leave. She felt a wave of relief. Almost pity.

'I'm sorry, Tom. I appreciate you coming all this way, but . . .'

When he straightened up again, he held a gun. A pistol.

'What the fuck!' she exclaimed. 'What are you doing?' She'd never seen a real gun before. She wondered if it was a fake.

'Shut up, Grace. Just shut up.'

He moved quickly to block her escape down the stairs, pushed the gun into her belly and shoved her back against the rail.

'Your phone,' he said, his mouth close to her ear. 'Give it to me.'

Grace felt the threatening proximity of his body, smelled his sweat. She carefully pulled her phone out from the pocket of her hoodie.

'Passcode,' he said, turning her around and twisting her arm behind her back until she had to rise onto her toes.

'170992.'

He laughed. 'Your birthday.'

'How do you know my birthday?'

He scrolled through her phone. 'Strange that I can't see that call to the police, just a message to Louise.'

'Come on, Tom. Let's –'

'Car keys,' he interrupted. 'Where are they?'

'Inside. On the kitchen bench. Take the car, it's fine. Just take it and go.'

He pushed her through the door and stayed close behind while she retrieved the keys.

Grace frantically tried to think. Was he going to take her somewhere? Leave her here without her car or phone? What was he planning?

'Let's go,' he said.

'Where?'

'For a drive.'

'What? No!' She grabbed hold of the kitchen bench like it might anchor her there, keep her from being swept away. 'Let's just sit back down and talk, huh? I mean, really talk. We can sort this out, just the two of us. There's some beer in the fridge.'

He laughed then. '*We can sort this out*,' he said, mimicking her voice. 'It's a different story now that you've been caught, isn't it? Now, the car.'

He followed her out onto the deck. She couldn't feel the gun at her back, but she knew it was there. She heard the door pull closed and his heavy steps on the stairs.

'You're driving,' he said, pushing her through the passenger door so she had to climb over the console to get to her seat. Her first thought was to open the other door and escape that way, but she was off balance, and he kept hold of the back of her trackpants.

'Where are we going?' she asked.

'Shut up. I'll direct you.'

Grace turned the engine over and carefully reversed down the steep driveway. She expected to see his car somewhere along the road, but it wasn't there.

'Left,' he said as they exited South Beach Road.

She was relieved. They were heading towards Torquay. Towards people and cars and shops. He held the gun low, so it couldn't be seen from outside, and kept it pointed at her belly. She glanced at it. It didn't seem like any gun she'd seen on TV or in the movies.

'It's a target pistol,' he said, seeing her look. 'At this range, it'll still kill you.'

She remembered an article in the school newsletter about him winning some big pistol shooting competition.

Grace turned her attention back to the road. How quickly the whole situation had slipped out of her control. Just a few days ago, this man had walked beside her, making small talk. And now he was abducting her at gunpoint. She realised she was breathing fast, sucking air into her lungs in short bursts. She tried to slow down. One thing she understood: this wasn't just about the risk management plan. He'd had the opportunity to call the police about it if he wanted to. But, was it that big a deal, anyway? It was unethical, but surely not criminal. And it didn't necessitate kidnapping her.

It was weird that he had been able to find her at the shack, and it didn't look as though he had driven there. She couldn't think of an explanation. Somehow, he had gotten to Louise or her dad. And how did he know so much about her?

When it hit Grace, she could have facepalmed her forehead: *her laptop.*

Twice in the last couple of months, he'd sought her out at school, telling her he needed to update her software or download new programs. She hadn't thought twice about it.

293

He was the IT guy. He did this for everyone, including Louise. And of course, *of course*, he knew their secrets. Photos, emails, browsing history, he had it all. And being at school, he'd know their cars. She shivered at the memory of him at her house after the netball game. Now, with the benefit of hindsight, she saw how odd it was that he'd volunteered to play when they were short. He hardly knew the rules, kept stepping. And he'd hung around until she'd invited him for drinks afterwards.

And then his text: *Hope you are healing okay.* Was it him who'd knocked her over in the park?

Evening was falling, and the setting sun shone directly into Grace's eyes. 'Why are you doing this, Tom?' she asked. 'What can you possibly gain from being so reckless? I thought you were a smart guy.'

'You're the reckless one, Grace.' He snorted. 'You and Louise, and your disgusting affair.'

Grace swivelled to look at him again. 'Affair? What sort of word is that?'

'You know what I mean.'

'Is that what this is about, Tom? Me and Louise? Did you think you had a chance with me?'

Now she laughed, knowing she was pushing him – but with her at the wheel, what could he do?

'Oh my God,' she said. 'It was you! You cut the straps on my pack.'

He ignored her. 'I could have given you . . .'

She shook her head. 'Given me what? You're not stable, Tom.

Everything that's happened in the last week, it's tipped you over the edge.' She slowed the car and tried to pull over to the side of the road, but he brought the gun up to her face.

'Just drive,' he yelled. 'And shut the fuck up. You ruined everything. Those poor boys you left to drown. And now you want to pin the blame on me and Gerard.'

Grace felt his saliva hit the side of her face. She needed to stop provoking him, to placate him instead. She veered back onto the road.

'Okay, okay,' she said. 'Can you at least tell me where we're going?'

He didn't answer but told her to cross the highway when they reached it. It was Friday evening, and cars streamed towards Torquay and the other towns along the Great Ocean Road for the weekend. Tom had Google Maps open on her phone. He directed her west, parallel to the coast following the inland route.

Grace forced her anxiety down so she could think. He was deliberately taking back roads. There were a few cars, but not many, and she started looking for farmhouses with signs of life. She considered crashing the car, maybe swerving suddenly off the road into a fence. Not a serious crash, but enough to disable the car and to attract attention.

'Whatever you're thinking,' he said quietly, 'don't.'

He'd been watching her eyes darting around the car, peering out the side window. He slid his hand over and undid her seatbelt. It triggered an alarm on the dash, but he ignored its beeping.

'If we crash, you'll die. And if you think I'll hesitate to shoot you, you're wrong. I don't give a shit anymore.'

Grace side-eyed him. He had turned in his seat and was watching her intently. 'Keep your speed up,' he said. 'And don't do anything stupid.'

He was silent then, scrolling through messages on her phone, replying to some, deleting others. His fingers darted across the screen.

By the time they reached the outskirts of Birregurra, a small town not far from Colac, the sun had dipped below the horizon. Before she could slow to sixty, Tom directed her to turn onto a side road. From there, he navigated until they began to climb into the ranges that separated the town from the coast.

With a clawing feeling in her gut, Grace realised where he was taking her. He'd deliberately avoided Colac, and now the winding roads through the hills were taking them south. To Juliet.

29

Nothing about the approach to Juliet looked familiar to Grace. It was completely dark now, and the forest canopy blocked the rising moon. They descended towards the coast before crossing the Great Ocean Road. Here, the bush gave way to farmland, and Grace tried to note the locations of houses and sheds with lights on. It was dairy country, and they might still be milking.

The road snaked through the gateway into the national park. Remnants of blue-and-white police tape were still attached to the fence. The gravel turned to sand, and they drove along the back of the dunes until they reached the first of three car parks. It was empty.

'Keep going,' Tom said. The dash lights were too dim for

Grace to see him clearly. He had pulled the hood of his jacket over his head, and his face was partially hidden in shadow.

They reached the second car park. Grace prayed for other cars to be there – a campervan full of rowdy backpackers, even a couple of grey nomads – but it was deserted, too.

Finally, they came to the last car park, the one where Grace had parked the bus on Tuesday afternoon, a lifetime ago. The last time she was here it was bustling with police, SES and media. There had been vans and trucks and cars. The Search and Rescue chopper had landed in the adjacent paddock. Grace's heart sank as she scanned the area illuminated by the car headlights. There was no one here, either. They were completely alone.

Tom reached for his daypack from the floor behind Grace's seat and pulled it into the front, all the while keeping the gun aimed at her. He opened his door and slid out, then beckoned her towards him.

'This side,' he demanded.

Grace climbed over the console again and stepped awkwardly out into the cold. The wind wasn't as fierce as it had been on Tuesday, but it was still strong, sweeping in from the south. It bit at her exposed skin, and she wrapped her arms around her chest.

She had been desperately thinking of what to say when they arrived, how she could talk him down. He was angry – and crazy obsessed, she knew that for certain – but there must be a way to deter him from whatever he had in mind.

'What is this, Tom?' she asked. 'Some sort of attempt at catharsis? You think it will change anything, coming back here?'

He looked warm in his jacket and jeans. 'Nothing can bring Harry and Jake and Robbie back, Grace. But someone has to be punished for allowing them to die.'

'Punished?' Grace said sharply. 'What the fuck? You think I'm not being punished? My life is ruined, Tom. You do get that, don't you?'

'It's not enough!' he yelled above the wind. 'Why should you live when they died?'

'I lived because I followed my training. It was the right decision.'

'Bullshit! You didn't do enough, and you should have to pay for it.'

'Pay? It's not your job to make me pay, Tom. That's for the police to decide, not you.'

'The police have swallowed your lies!'

She turned from him, towards the car. This whole situation was too surreal. It couldn't be happening.

Then his arm was around her throat, dragging her backwards. Her heels dug into the dirt. She didn't know where the gun was.

'Fucking shut up,' he seethed.

She heard the car's locks beep.

Grace was gagging, struggling for air. 'Please, Tom,' she managed to say, before his hand came up to cover her mouth. She flung herself sideways and bit his hand as hard as she could, until she tasted blood.

Something hard hit her. Then, nothing.

When she regained consciousness, Grace was on the beach.

There was sand in her mouth and a throbbing pain at the back of her head. She cautiously moved her hand and felt her hair matted with blood. Pushing herself up onto her elbows, she saw Tom looming above her.

He leaned over and brought his face close. 'Stand up!' he barked.

Grace tried to get up, but dizziness overwhelmed her, and she fell back onto the sand. She tried again and this time managed to get to her feet. Everything was out of focus.

She reached out to him, trying to grab hold of his jacket. 'Stop, Tom, please,' she said. 'We can talk. I can help you. You're not well.'

He pushed her away, and she fell to her knees. Then he squatted in front of her. 'I'm not the one who needs help, Grace,' he said. 'But you do. You're going for a swim.'

'What? I'm not going in the fucking water, Tom. No way.' Grace looked over to the ocean, which growled and fumed behind him. Waves swept up the beach, almost to where she kneeled.

He brought the gun up to her face. 'Suit yourself,' he said. 'This would probably be quicker, anyway.'

There was something in his voice now, something she hadn't heard before. He truly didn't care. And that scared her more than anything. Up to that point, she hadn't truly believed he'd use the gun. She'd thought she'd be able to talk him down – to use reason and logic – because this was Tom, the IT guy from school, not some stranger who'd abducted her in a dark alleyway. She knew him!

'Wait! Wait,' she said. 'What do you want me to do?'

'Like I said, I want you to swim,' he said.

'What? Where to? What do you mean?'

He pointed. 'Out there,' he said. 'As far as you can go.'

'But why?'

'Because that's what you should have done on Tuesday. You should have gone into the water and rescued those boys.'

Grace looked at the sea, a grey, seething mass of waves and whitewater. It wasn't as furious and violent as on Tuesday, but it sounded the same, and she couldn't see further than about twenty metres.

Her mind was fizzing from the knock to her head, but she tried to think. *How long could I last? How cold is the water?*

'You want me to drown, don't you?'

'Now you're getting it. You won't last ten minutes out there. Someone will find your car, then your neatly folded clothes with your phone and keys. It'll all be so believable. The grief-stricken teacher goes back to the beach where it all happened and walks into the sea.'

'They won't believe it. Louise won't.'

'That's why I'm going to send her a text message. She'll believe it, then.'

'But you'll need the car to get back.'

He pointed at his daypack. 'I'm walking out to Wheelers Bay. I'll be in Melbourne before the alarm is even raised.'

Grace was still on her knees. She looked up and down the beach. The wind whipped her hair, and a fine spray clung to her face. She wondered if she could outrun him. But she wasn't even certain she could get to her feet. Her head throbbed, and she was feeling nauseous.

'Stand up,' he demanded again.

Grace put her hands underneath her body and tried to push up in the soft sand. She made it to her feet, but her head was still spinning. Bracing herself as best she could, she flung herself at Tom, hitting him with all her weight. He staggered a little but stayed on his feet. She flailed at him with clenched fists, hitting him again and again, but the blows seemed to glance off him. He was laughing.

When she had exhausted herself, he took her by the shoulders and started to push her down the steep beach, towards the water. She could feel the metal of the gun against her neck.

He was really going to do this!

Tom stopped pushing. Grace was close enough for the waves to wash around her ankles. He pulled her back up the beach a little and let go of her shoulders. 'Your clothes,' he said. 'Take them off.'

Grace leaned down and fumbled with the laces on her runners. Slowly, trying to give herself time to think, she removed them.

She stood up and turned towards Tom. 'This is what you really want, isn't it?' She pulled the hoodie over her head then peeled the t-shirt off. She wobbled a little as she dropped her trackpants and stepped out of them. Tom had taken two paces back, and his eyes washed over her body. She reached around and unfastened her bra. For the first time since arriving at the beach, he looked uncertain. It was perilously cold, but she put her hands on her hips and stared him down.

She kept her voice soft, coaxing him. 'Why don't we walk back to the car, eh?' she said. 'It'll be warm in there.'

She took an unsteady step and reached out to him.

'Come here,' she said.

He allowed her to take his hand. She placed it on her stomach, then guided it up to her breasts.

Suddenly Tom moved, hitting her with the full force of his body then lifting her over his shoulder. He carried her into the water and threw her at the waves. Grace was winded, gasping at the bone-deep cold and lashing out at Tom with all the strength she could muster. A wave hit them, and then he was on top of her, pushing down, holding her head under. She tried to find the surface but took in a mouthful of water. Her feet touched the bottom and she pushed against Tom's weight. When her head was above the water, she caught a quick breath before he thrust her under again. Animal panic coursed through her, and when she fought to the surface the next time, she turned her body and freed her arms. She aimed between his legs and landed a blow that caused him to relax his grip for an instant, and she took her chance to stumble away into deeper water. She couldn't fight him – he was too strong – and she couldn't outrun him. Against all her instincts, she dived under an oncoming wave and began to stroke away from him, certain he wouldn't follow her out.

The moon shed enough light for her to see the shape of the approaching waves, so she could anticipate when she needed to take a breath and kick under. But now the adrenaline that had allowed her to tolerate the frigid water was giving way to exhaustion and fatigue. She treaded water between waves, peering back at the beach to see where Tom was, but all she could make out were shifting shadows. She was certain of one thing – she couldn't last much longer. The cold was inside her, already slowing her movements, turning her legs to lead. And compounding it all was the ache in her head where he had hit her. In a lull between sets, she tried to float to conserve energy.

When she looked up again to take her bearings, Tom was strafing the waves with a high-powered torch, searching for her. It gave Grace a point of reference in the dark, and she realised she was being pushed parallel to the beach in a strong side current. It was carrying her away from the torchlight, towards the rocks underneath the platform near the car park. Gathering the last of her strength, she swam with the current. She didn't want to be dashed on the rocks, but if Tom was walking the other way, towards Wheelers Bay, every stroke took her further from him. Side waves hit her again and again, but she kept her arms rolling over until she was spent.

She stopped stroking and concentrated on keeping her head above water, but each new wave seemed to hold her down longer, pressing her towards the bottom. Time and again, she swam to the surface, only to be hit by the next surge of whitewater.

This is it, she thought. *This is where it ends.* Just like it had for Jake and Roberto and Harry. Another wave broke over her, washing her hair into her face. She held her breath for as long as she could, but when she came to the surface, she could no longer get air into her lungs. Water filled her mouth and nose. Her body had nothing left to give.

When the next wave came, Grace didn't fight it. She surrendered and allowed it to take her. Lifted first, then driven below the surface, she felt her consciousness, her connection with everything she knew and loved, begin to fade.

30

The force of hitting the rocks jolted Grace back to consciousness. The dark shadows of the point loomed above her. She was sucked back as each wave receded, only to be thrown towards the rocks again with the next surge. Every time, tiny shells with razor edges tore at her skin, shredding her hands as she tried to cling on against the current. When a large wave flung her further up, she was able to jam her arm into a tight crevice. The force of the ocean pulled at her, but she held strong. Her skin ripped and bled. When the surge receded, she managed to get her feet underneath herself, scrambling until she was beyond the reach of the waves. Her body was slick with blood and she shook uncontrollably, but she kept moving higher. Once she could make out the beach to her right, she cautiously started to descend, slipping and falling, picking herself back up each time.

When she reached the last rock before the sand, she sat with her back against it for cover. Her body shuddered with every attempt at movement, but she pulled herself to her feet and looked along the beach. Where was Tom? She was too far away to make him out, but she could see the torchlight. He was walking away from the water, back up towards the dunes. The light died for a full minute, then came back on. She guessed that's where her clothes would be. Then he swept the beam in a wide arc, up the beach towards Moonlight Head, then slowly through the shallows and around to the rocks where she was hiding. Grace threw herself back into the shadows. The beam seemed to hover above her head, then move slightly up and down. He was walking towards her!

Grace scrambled further into the darkness until she felt a bed of kelp caught in a fissure in the rocks. The light was getting closer, probing the gaps, flicking and flashing. She crawled into the kelp, burying herself in its slimy arms.

Tom was close enough that she could hear the scrape of his boots on the rocks. Grace closed her eyes and tried to make herself small.

Help me, Mum.

She had no idea how long she lay there, but when she dared look, the light was gone. Slowly, cautiously, she pulled the kelp from her body and crawled out. When she was able to stand and gain a view of the beach, the light was bobbing away from her. He was leaving. She knew he couldn't wait too long if he was to get across the river and make it out to Wheelers Bay.

Grace staggered out onto the sand and fell to her hands and knees. She vomited sea water then collapsed and pulled herself into the fetal position, hugging herself tight. The last of her energy had kept her body functioning to that point, but now she was dangerously cold.

Move, Grace! You have to move.

Her head spun as she stood and tried to get her bearings. She was below the platform, only a short walk from the car, but she knew it was locked. And warmth was her first priority: she was shuddering, and her breath came in short gasps. Her legs wobbled and buckled when she tried to walk, but she managed a drunken stagger that got her up onto the high, dry sand. Staying close to the dune at the top of the beach, she placed one foot in front of the other, all the while watching for the light of Tom's torch. She didn't see it, but even in her fogged state of mind, she knew he wouldn't want to risk being seen, so he would have turned it off as he walked away.

Grace felt like a puppet, her limbs jerked by unseen hands, but slowly, she made progress towards the promised warmth of her clothes. She fell repeatedly, but finally she saw the neat pile in the sand. Her clothes had been folded and her phone placed on top. Struggling to control her hands, Grace pulled on her t-shirt and hoodie, then her trackpants. The sand grated against her wounds. She managed to get her socks on but knew her runners would be a bridge too far.

The clothes only gave temporary relief. She needed to keep

moving, but the temptation to lie down and curl into a ball was all-consuming. She wanted desperately to close her eyes, to bury herself in the sand and sleep.

But when she thrust her hands into her hoodie pockets, she felt the plastic and metal of the car keys, and it was enough to kindle new hope – the car, the heater.

She sat on the sand and rubbed her legs as vigorously as she could, then her arms. There was a trade-off between the small amount of warmth it generated and the pain it caused. She knew all the signs of hypothermia – and the treatment. The patient had to be warmed slowly, and rubbing didn't help. But it felt good anyway.

She put her phone in her pocket and stood up. The wound at the back of her head felt like it allowed the cold to go directly inside her skull. She pulled her hood up and drew the strings tight to keep the wind out. The walk back to the car took an eternity. She lost count of how often she fell, but each time, she drove herself to stand and push on. The final climb up the dune to the track forced her to crawl. She hauled herself up until she felt gravel under her hands, then stood and grabbed hold of the fence for support. The stones tore at her socked feet, forcing her to hobble.

The further she went, the more protected the track was from the wind. Finally, it opened into the car park – and the Pajero. Grace fumbled for the keys, pressed the keyless entry. She pulled herself up into the driver's seat, closed the door on the wind and cold, and locked herself in. Using both hands, she jammed the key into the ignition. She didn't think she could drive, but she turned the motor over and switched the heating up to high.

As the air inside the car began to warm, she lost all track of time. Her attempts at movement were slow and awkward, like her body was crumpled and needed to be stretched back into position to work properly. Hoping to steady her hands enough to use the phone, she held them up close to the vent. They tingled and burned.

Slowly, Grace. Slowly.

When she finally gained enough control over her fingers, she wiped them clean of blood, then pulled her phone from her pocket and touched the screen: *10.42pm.*

Opening her messages, she read the last one sent. It was to Louise at 9.08: *I'm so sorry. This is the only way. I love you.*

There were ten missed calls from Louise.

'Fuck you, Tom Winter,' Grace said aloud.

She pressed Louise's number and waited for the call to connect.

'Hey, it's me,' she said.

ONE YEAR LATER . . .

ABC ONLINE
THURSDAY 3 OCTOBER
**CORONER FINDS DEATH BY MISADVENTURE IN
ST FINBAR'S CASE**

A Victorian coronial inquest has found a Melbourne boys' school could not be held responsible for the deaths of three students on an outdoor education excursion in May of last year.

Coroner Isabelle Jenkins this morning handed down her findings into the deaths of Jacob Bolton, Roberto Lombardi and Harry Edwards, who died at Juliet Beach in the state's south-west.

Ms Jenkins told a packed Coroners Court in Melbourne that the three boys from St Finbar's Catholic College drowned when they became separated from their bushwalking group and entered the ocean against the instructions of their teachers.

She said that while the body of Jacob Bolton had never been found, unlike those of the other two students, it was reasonable to conclude that he had also drowned.

In her findings, Coroner Jenkins stated that while there were some irregularities in the school's preparation and conduct of the excursion, she did not believe they were significant enough to have altered the outcome of the tragedy.

A breakdown in communication between the supervising teachers, Grace Disher, Gerard Kruger and Thomas Winter*, led to the boys becoming separated from the group. Ms Jenkins noted that it was an accumulation of small ill-fated decisions that led to the boys arriving at the beach before the arranged rendezvous time. The coroner accepted Ms Disher's account of events, stating that she was satisfied the teacher did everything reasonably possible to stop the boys entering the water.

The conditions at Juliet Beach on 23 May were unsuitable for swimming, Ms Jenkins said, with a large swell, strong winds and rain. In light of Grace Disher's evidence – and evidence presented by Life Saving Victoria – the coroner found Ms Disher made a decision consistent with her training in not attempting to rescue the students.

Coroner Jenkins said that while all three boys were strong swimmers, the conditions at Juliet Beach that day were beyond their abilities. She said there would probably never be an answer as to why the boys chose to swim in such a treacherous area. She concluded that the boys were not responsible for their own deaths but that they miscalculated the conditions and overestimated their abilities.

Ms Jenkins also noted in her findings that the refusal by the parents of a boy who survived the bushwalking trip to allow their son to appear before the inquest was regrettable and hindered her ability to fully investigate the timeline of events on the day of the tragedy.

Ms Jenkins recorded three deaths by misadventure.

Speaking outside the Coroners Court after the hearing, Richard Bolton, the father of Jacob Bolton, said he was disappointed by the findings of misadventure. 'This does nothing to answer the questions we still have,' he said. 'We are being told to accept that our boys have died but that no one is at fault. Parents should be able to send their kids off on a school camp confident they will be kept safe by the teachers in charge. This didn't happen for us.'

THREE BOYS GONE

Felicity Edwards, the mother of Harry Edwards, also spoke outside the court. She said she accepted the coroner's findings and thanked her for the detailed investigation into what was ultimately a tragic accident. 'I hope everyone can get on with their lives now and cherish every minute as a way of celebrating the memories of Harry, Jacob and Roberto.'

Members of the Lombardi family were also present but declined to speak to the media.

Neither Grace Disher nor Gerard Kruger attended the final day of the inquest. A spokesperson for St Finbar's College, Acting Principal Fiona Knowles, said both teachers were still working at the college and the inquest findings were a relief for the whole school. 'We have sought to move on from the tragedy and to offer the best possible education and spiritual guidance for our students. The families who lost their boys will always be part of the St Finbar's community.'

*Thomas Winter remains in police custody after being charged with the abduction and attempted murder of Grace Disher, three days after the drownings.

ACKNOWLEDGEMENTS

*T*hree *Boys Gone* was written on the unceded land of the Wadawurrung people and I pay my respects to their elders – past, present and emerging.

This book draws on my thirty years' experience in outdoor education. I am indebted to my mentors in this field who deeply influenced my approach to taking students into the wild (and often the not-so-wild) – Peter Martin, Pete Dingle and Tom Burrows, to name just three. They encultured a love of remote places, of wild rivers and isolated coastlines. While the events depicted in *Three Boys Gone* are fictitious, I know outdoor educators will relate to the what-ifs, the near misses and the fine line we walk between allowing our students to engage freely with wild places and keeping them safe – often from themselves.

Three Boys Gone was a gamble from the start – writing in a different genre, searching out an agent who believed in the manuscript and finding a new publisher to bring it to fruition. It wouldn't have found its way into readers' hands without the proverbial village getting behind it. I am indebted to my first readers: Nicole Maher from Great Escape Books in Aireys Inlet, Lynne Batson, Irene Haas and Belinda Sharrock. Each of you freely gave of your time and expertise to help wrangle those early drafts into the book you see here.

Similarly, thanks to Tony Paatsch and Kerrie Moroney, who provided insights into the inner workings of schools and the police. Your feedback was invaluable, and if there are any mistakes relating to those two areas, they are entirely my own. Sarah Bailey has used the term 'feasibility with stretch', and I've adopted it here, particularly in relation to the police investigation and the reactions of the school's hierarchy.

Thanks to Miranda Luby for her counsel and insights into how a woman in Grace's position would be treated.

A huge shout out to Laurie Steed. This manuscript was destined for the bottom drawer before I reached out to him and asked his advice. It is a rare person who can be simultaneously critical, constructive and supportive in their assessment of a manuscript. Laurie, you gave new life to *Three Boys Gone* and I am in awe of your skills in identifying its myriad problems and gently steering me towards the final drafts.

Heartfelt thanks also to the three writers who backed this manuscript before it was pitched to publishers: Jane Harper, Sarah Bailey and Michael Brissenden. Thank you for your time and for your considered and thoughtful endorsements. Thanks also to Mark Brandi and J.P. Pomare for your generous support.

Thank you to my publisher, Alex Lloyd, for his unwavering support of *Three Boys Gone*, to Belinda Huang, for her detailed and intuitive editing, and to the entire Pan Macmillan team who have helped bring this book to readers. Everything felt right about this book finding its home at Pan Mac, from the first conversations through to the editing, design, cover and marketing. It has been a privilege to work with you all.

To my agent, Daniel Pilkington, a huge thank you for championing this book and guiding me through the twists and turns of the pitching and publishing labyrinth. It has been a pleasure to have you in my corner. Let's climb back into the ring again soon.

My mum, June, passed away while I was writing this book, but I discussed it with her at length and I know she would be chuffed to see it on the shelves. Thank you for your love and I'm sorry for the sweary bits.

Writers need a huge support network, a network from which we go missing for long periods while we do what writers do. My love and thanks to Lynne, who tolerates those long absences and who still rocks up to events to listen to me tell the same stories over and over. And, finally, to Oliver, Bella, George, Daisy, Maddy, Harley and Celeste, who continue to inspire me and keep me grounded by refusing to make a fuss over having an author for a father, father-in-law and grandfather. Long may it be so!